# TOOLS OF PROPHECY

## M.A. ROTHMAN

Primordial Press

Copyright © 2020 Michael A. Rothman

Cover Art by Allen Morris

This is a work of fiction. All of the characters and scenarios portrayed in this novel are either the imaginings of the author or are used fictitiously.

All rights reserved.

ISBN: 978-0-9976793-6-6

# ALSO BY M.A. ROTHMAN

**Technothrillers:** (Thrillers with science / Hard-Science Fiction)

- Primordial Threat
- Freedom's Last Gasp
- Darwin's Cipher

**Levi Yoder Thrillers:**

- Perimeter
- The Inside Man
- Never Again

**Epic Fantasy / Dystopian:**

- Dispocalypse

- Agent of Prophecy
- Heirs of Prophecy
- Tools of Prophecy
- Lords of Prophecy

## CONTENTS

| | |
|---|---:|
| Prologue | 1 |
| Becoming a King | 7 |
| Coronation | 20 |
| Damantite | 30 |
| Visions and Dreams | 38 |
| Assassins | 48 |
| Eluanethra | 57 |
| The Training Begins | 64 |
| A Different Kind of School | 82 |
| Training | 95 |
| Leaving Eluanethra | 113 |
| A Return Home | 119 |
| Interrogation | 130 |
| School Starts | 141 |
| Dominic Strikes | 151 |
| The Hunt | 162 |
| Practicing Skills | 176 |
| A New Castle | 186 |
| Swamp Cats | 195 |
| The Contest | 208 |
| Awards Ceremony | 224 |
| The First Protector | 231 |
| Revenge | 249 |
| The Seed | 265 |
| Destruction | 279 |
| | |
| Preview – Lords of Prophecy | 289 |
| Author's Note | 305 |
| About the Author | 311 |

*This page purposefully left blank.*

# PROLOGUE

Malphas breathed in the aroma of scorched flesh and sulfur as he awaited instruction from Sammael, the Lord of the Dark Host. Demonkind weren't known for their forgiving nature, but despite Malphas's past failures, Malphas felt secure in the belief that his lord would have a role for him in the coming offensive. After all, he'd come so close to victory during the last assault.

Though it had occurred over five centuries ago, Malphas could still clearly recall the moment he broke through the entrance into the world above. The taste of the air, the feel of the sun, the smell of the burning cities, and the combined might of the human, elf, and dwarf armies falling beneath the blades of his forces… just the thought of it still set his heart racing. Yet even with his early victories, Malphas had ultimately tasted defeat. All thanks to the wrath of a single human—an Archmage of devastating power.

Prior to the Archmage's intervention, the war had gone just as Lord Sammael had foreseen. Towns were pillaged, fields laid to waste, bodies burned in great pyres. Then the Archmage constructed his barrier, his magical wall. It wiped half of Malphas's army from existence in the blink of an eye, and sent the remainder of his forces scattered back into the Abyss from whence they'd come.

And so things had remained... until now.

Lord Sammael had recently begun assembling his troops for a second surge. After five centuries of trying to find a way through the barrier—and failing—Sammael's frustration had reached a boiling point.

Having been called, Malphas now knelt before his master, the black scales of his knees pressed against the stone floor. At twenty feet tall, General Malphas usually towered over his minions, but here, kneeling before the high and immense throne of blackest stone, he felt utterly insignificant.

The Demon Lord didn't even acknowledge his presence, he merely stared into the distance. In this region of the Abyss, the temperatures always bordered on freezing, yet singeing waves of heat emanated from Sammael's skin.

Finally, after a very long wait, Sammael turned his attention to his general. *"I have learned that a new wizard has entered Trimoria."* He said the words without speaking. His voice, inky and coarse, erupted as if from within Malphas's head. *"You will find out how such a thing was possible. If one can enter, others can as well."*

"But, my lord," Malphas said in his gravelly voice, "how can that be? I thought you arranged for the purging of those who followed Seder."

The Demon Lord's rage bubbled to the surface. *"Don't ever mention my brother's name again. I will not hear it spoken by the likes of you."*

Malphas bowed low, touching his forehead to the stone floor, before looking up into the harrowing heat of his master once again.

Sammael calmed as quickly as he'd become enraged. Closing his eyes, the heat he spewed changed to light, his very skin projecting a series of holographic images into the air between them.

The first showed a human wizard standing at the base of the throne's imposing dais. Malphas had seen this human's image before; this was the wizard over whom Sammael held control. In the hologram, the wizard stood before a group of humans, and bowed slightly in a show of greeting.

*"Greetings,"* the wizard said. *"My name is Azazel. I fear that I have intruded on your happy home, so I will impose upon your time with only a few simple questions."*

A large soldier stepped forward. *"I am Throll Lancaster,"* he replied. *"Protector-general of Trimoria. How can I help you, Lord Azazel?"*

The feigned pleasantries continued, but not for long. Soon the encounter turned to battle. Sammael's wizard sent blasts of energy at his foes, scattering them like leaves in a storm. Malphas saw that they were no match for the wizard's powers.

But then, to the general's surprise, an adolescent human stepped forward, his robed garb rustling in the wind, and met Azazel's assault with a powerful magical attack of his own.

Malphas gave a grunt of surprise. A rogue wizard in the Trimorian Valley? How was it possible?

Azazel quickly met this new foe and demonstrated his mastery over the young wizard. But just as he prepared to finish him off, a second gray-robed wizard appeared in the distance and struck Azazel with a powerful blast to the chest.

Yet the master's wizard seemed pleased. *"Two wizards?"* he said with a smile. *"Oh, I will savor this for years to come."*

A fury of light and heat ensued. Pulsing streams of sizzling energy flew between the competing wizards, a sparking collision of tremendous powers.

Finally, one of the gray-robed wizards faltered, leaving only the human adolescent standing to face Azazel. Malphas felt his excitement rise. The demon forces would win the day.

And then, with a single harrowing blast, the adolescent sent the dark wizard flying backwards, impaling him on the wooden handle of a cart. For a moment, he coughed up blood... and then he disappeared in a crackling ball of black and red plasma.

Malphas couldn't believe what he was seeing.

Azazel had lost.

Defeated by a *child*.

The scene shifted. Azazel lay helplessly on a forest floor,

wheezing, choking back death, his eyes struggling to remain open. Three humans approached—the large soldier from the first vision accompanied by the pair of rogue wizards. Azazel lifted his hand, and the aura around him solidified into a dense cloud of darkness.

And with that, the vision came to an end.

Malphas's menacing jaw hung open, but he quickly snapped it shut and directed his eyes to the gray stone floor when his master rose and descended from his dais. He saw only the long black shadows cast by his master, but Sammael's grating voice echoed within his head.

*"Not only are there two rogue wizards, but there is another Archmage walking in Trimoria. It seems as if Ellisandrea's plan to kill wizards in avoidance of the prophecy has failed. The time of prophecy approaches."*

Still kneeling, Malphas dared to look up at the Demon Lord. "I never trusted that elven witch's dreams. What can we do? The barrier remains around the valley. We cannot enter."

Sammael smiled. *"I can still project my influence into anyone who stands near the Seed. My brother remains ignorant of my abilities. The same is true of his Archmage puppet. They ignore the Seed at their peril."*

The Demon Lord then waved his hand over the general's horned head, and a mist formed all around him. Nervously, Malphas breathed it in. And then his tension fell away. This… this was *his power*. The power he'd been missing for centuries. His master was restoring what had long ago been stripped from him.

*I am whole once again.*

"Yes, Malphas. I am returning your powers. You could not have foreseen your failure five hundred and sixty-three years ago. The first Archmage was a variable I had not considered. But you have done your penance, my dear disciple, and I have plans for you."

The general smiled. *"Thank you, Lord,"* he said in thought. With his power restored, he could now communicate telepathically again. *"I look forward to hearing your plan."*

Sammael's form shifted, settling into its true, amorphous shape. "And you will. For now, rest assured that you will get your war... and we will have our victory. For I have taken control of a new human champion within the barrier."

## BECOMING A KING

*Gathered in a field is a vast army that includes all manner of soldiers—humans, dwarves, even elven races. Through their midst rides a young general on horseback, barking directions to the various platoon leaders. He is handsome, with defined cheekbones and sparkling blue eyes, and his armor and sword glow with a fiery-red glint.*

*The general unsheathes his sword, waves it above his head, and points to the ridge just ahead. Beyond that ridge a black cloud has formed, radiating despair, and beneath that cloud is another army—this one borne of nightmare.*

*The armies begin to advance on one another.*

The scene flashed white.

. . .

*A giant ogre walks a natural stone bridge across a chasm, whipped by wind that threatens to pull him into the abyss below. The ogre is equipped in plate armor that glows a pristine white and emits sparks with every movement. His sword, sheathed at his side, is a tremendous greatsword with a pommel of red.*

*Following behind the ogre is a blue-eyed wizard, a look of concern on his bearded face. In one hand he carries a sparking metal staff, and in the other, a brilliant diamond the size of a melon. It pulses with radiant power.*

*Crossing the bridge from the opposite side of the chasm is a fiend of blackness and fire, reeking of brimstone and emanating waves of heat. The fiend matches the ogre in size, and it, too, wields a giant sword.*

*As the two great beasts, ogre and fiend, meet at the middle of the bridge, another presence is felt. Behind the fiend, at the edge of the chasm, stands a deeper, darker presence, palpably evil, so enormous that it dwarfs both fiend and ogre.*

*The ogre clashes with the fiend, and the wizard raises the diamond above his head.*

---

Ryan Riverton startled awake, groaning. *Every night, the same dream.*

He yawned and stretched, and tried to ignore the soft snoring of his brother, Aaron, in the next bed. And then he smiled with excitement when he remembered what today was.

It wasn't every day that people you lived with were crowned king and queen.

In fact, that would have been an impossible thought just two short years ago. But then again, almost everything they'd encountered since that fateful day when they first set foot in Trimoria was impossible. Magic. Bearded dwarven warriors. Elves. Evil wizards. Demons. All these things would have been seen as nothing but fiction straight out of an epic fantasy to the Ryan Riverton who lived with his family in the state of Washington. Back in those days, he and his brother were normal, everyday students. His mother was a teacher, and his father was an engineer who dabbled with a forge he'd built near the garage. Their life was ordinary. Good, but ordinary.

And then, two years ago, they took a vacation to Arizona… and found themselves stuck in a cave in the middle of an earthquake. And when the earthquake was over… they were in Trimoria.

They still had no rational explanation for that. Trimoria was a land that defied rational explanation.

In this world, Ryan was a wizard. An actual, real-life wizard—which even in Trimoria was incredibly rare. His father was a wizard too, though a reluctant one; Jared Riverton had far more enthusiasm for his newfound career as a blacksmith. His mother, Aubrey, had discovered that she was a magical healer, and his brother, Aaron—at seventeen, two years Ryan's junior—had the gift of extraordinary strength that he had parlayed, through obsessive training, into incredible combat ability.

And these were the least of the changes to Ryan's life. For there were prophecies, received in the form of dreams that every resident of Trimoria had every night, that foretold fateful roles for both Ryan and Aaron.

Aaron was the general leading the army.

Ryan was the wizard on the bridge.

It was quite a responsibility for two ordinary teen boys from Washington.

A pounding on the door made Ryan jump, and Aaron woke with a start, launching from his bed as if someone had lit his underwear on fire.

"Wake up, boys!" came Dad's booming voice. "It's time to get ready for the coronation. Get dressed properly and meet me in the living room in ten minutes."

Aaron groaned. "I hate wearing my formals."

Ryan laughed. "You don't hear me whining about it."

"That's because all you need to do is slip a nicer robe over your head. It's the same clothes you always wear. I have to wear full armor—*and* it needs to be buffed."

"It doesn't have to be buffed," Ryan said.

"It does if I don't want Throll to have a fit. It was bad enough having regular old Throll yelling at me. Now I'm going to have Throll, the Crowned King of Trimoria yelling at me."

That was, Ryan knew, the downside of Aaron being Throll's protégé. Throll could be demanding and impatient, and Aaron was on the receiving end of that attitude more often than anyone.

"Fine," Ryan said. "I'll help you put it on." He added with a smirk, "As soon as I put on the same clothes I always wear."

Despite his snark, Ryan had set aside his best robe for the occasion. He wanted to look his best for his betrothed, Arabelle, in the event she managed to make it back to town in time for the ceremony. He quickly dressed, then went to help his brother.

Every piece of armor Aaron wore had been expertly pounded into shape by their father, then imbued with magic by Ryan. That magic made the metal glow a bluish-white, the only outward indication that it could withstand far more damage than an ordinary suit of armor. Ryan helped with the chest plate, pulling the straps tight behind Aaron's back, but for the rest of it, Aaron did everything himself, insisting it needed to be just so. Ryan gave him a full inspection, buffing out any spots that needed it, and then together they headed downstairs.

But in the hall, they bumped into Sloane, Throll's sixteen-year-old daughter—and Aaron's betrothed. She was normally tomboyish, but today she wore a dress of fine blue satin that was absolutely stunning, and her long blonde hair, normally in a single braid, now hung in gracious tresses down to the middle of her back. Even Ryan did a double-take.

It was weird being betrothed. In fact, it was weird even using the *word* "betrothed." But in Trimoria, it was the custom to marry young and to get betrothed even younger. And the boys didn't mind. Aaron clearly adored Sloane, and Ryan had fallen head over heels for Arabelle. As attractive as

Sloane was looking right now, Arabelle's beauty was incomparable.

"You boys better watch out," Sloane said, twisting anxiously in her dress. "My father is in a sour mood. If you value your skin, don't make any jokes about 'Your Highness' or anything. He isn't taking this king thing well."

"But isn't that the proper way to address a king?" Ryan asked. "With a 'Your Highness'?"

Sloane sighed. "Try it and see. Within this house, His Highness doesn't want to be called anything other than 'Dad' or 'Throll.'" She pointed to Aaron. "And when I say 'try it and see,' I mean don't. Especially you, Mr. Troublemaker."

Ryan chuckled. Aaron did have a tendency to tease people. And he might even be stupid enough to tease the protector-general and future king of Trimoria.

Aaron gave Sloane a lopsided grin. "Sorry, did you say something?"

Sloane glared.

"He's just too stunned by your beauty to listen," Ryan said, playing peacemaker. "You really do look great, Sloane."

Sloane smiled coquettishly, batted her eyes at Aaron, and twirled on her toes to show off her dress. She could go from playful and alluring to serious and intimidating in an instant. And as far as Ryan figured it, it was exactly the kind of attributes she needed to be able to handle his brother, whose stubbornness rivaled that of even the most ornery of mules.

"Is that true, Aaron?" Sloane said coyly. "Do you like what you see?"

Aaron blushed. "You know I do."

Sloane sniffed and turned up her nose. "Well, you don't tell me that often enough."

"That's not fair," Aaron argued. "I barely even get to see you other than at meals, surrounded by family. Any other time I look for you, your mother seems to make sure you're out of reach."

Sloane's expression brightened. "You look for me?"

"Well, I—"

Ryan came to his brother's rescue. "He looks for you constantly because you're the most beautiful woman in the world and he can't stand to be apart from you—or so he tells me. Now let's get going before we get in trouble for being late."

---

As they entered the living room, Throll was arguing with a small man with a ledger. Throll's wife, Gwen, was watching with amusement from the table, and seated with her were Ryan's parents. His mother was holding Rebecca, Ryan's baby sister, who slept contentedly despite the noise.

"I didn't ask for any of this!" the seven-foot-tall ranger yelled. "Why in the world should I be expected to worry about the tax rates on farmers or whether the price of wool is going up because some merchant has run a monopoly on all the ewes in Trimoria?"

"Your Highness," the small man whined, "I know this is

all new to you, but you *must* establish your own rules for trade and laws for proper behavior. At a minimum, you must study the laws established by your ancestors and evaluate them. You must agree with them if you're going to have them enforced, wouldn't you say?"

Throll stepped closer to the little man. "What is your name again?"

The little man looked up at the soon-to-be king towering over him. "M-my name is Grendel, Your Highness. Grendel Hawthorne. I was the head accountant for the city of Cammoria. Mine was the unfortunate responsibility to report annually to Azazel on the financial state of the town and its surrounding properties. But in truth, Your Highness, I'm also a historian. I have a keen interest in the times before the demon invasion."

Throll took a deep breath and laid his massive hand on Grendel's shoulder. "I appreciate what you're trying to do, Grendel. And I don't mean to be ill-tempered. But as you said, this is all new to me. I'll need to assemble a council to help me review and establish the laws and—"

Grendel interrupted with excitement. "Oh, yes! Much like the ruling council established for the races in year 4953. It was recorded as part of the Tribunal of Tashkent and—" He stopped himself, as if suddenly realizing he'd just interrupted his king. "Your Highness, I'm so sorry. I tend to get carried away. It's just that your thoughts mirror the wisdom of your ancestors. It shouldn't be surprising; it stands to reason that their wisdom courses through your veins." He bowed humbly. "I beg your forgiveness, Highness."

Throll roared with laughter and stomped his foot on the ground. He laughed so hard his face turned red.

"Grendel," he said, wiping a tear from his eye, "I think you've just ensured your position as one of the members of my council. I need someone with a good head on his shoulders and enough spunk to use it. We'll talk more about this later."

"Uh… yes, Your Highness." With a confused expression he bowed deeply and took his leave. And at almost the same moment, Arabelle walked in.

As often happened, the sight of her nearly made Ryan's heart stop. She was beautiful. Shapely, with raven hair framing a comely face. Today she wore a form-fitting crimson dress that glided over the floor, propelled onward by her long, elegant strides.

"Arabelle!" he breathed. "You're here!"

He ran to her and swept her off her feet, pulling her into a hug that made her laugh like a little girl.

When he set her on her feet again, he gave her a quick kiss on the lips. "I didn't know if you'd make it. Where's your father?"

"Right here," came a voice from the entryway. Arabelle's father, Honfrion—the merchant king of the caravan—stepped inside and grinned. "Far be it for a humble merchant and his daughter to miss such a grand coronation."

Zenethar, Sloane's two-year-old brother, darted in from the kitchen and leapt into Arabelle's outstretched arms. "Belle!" he cried, then giggled as she tickled his belly. "Wanna play with Silver?"

Silver was the Rivertons' cat, who upon arrival in Trimoria had transformed into a giant swamp cat. He was currently curled up in the corner of the room, sleeping as usual.

Arabelle laughed. "Not just yet. For now I'll just play with you." She tickled Zenethar again, much to his shrieking delight.

Arabelle's father stepped up to Throll and cleared his throat. "I appreciate being invited to your house, Your Highness—"

Throll growled and raised a hand. "Stop right there, Honfrion. Your daughter and mine are both betrothed to the Riverton brothers—and in my book, that makes us relatives. I might have to tolerate this 'Your Highness' nonsense from the rest of the people out there, I won't allow such honorifics within my family and between these walls. I will be called 'Throll,' if you don't mind."

Honfrion smiled and winked. "Of course, Your Highness."

Throll's lips twitched as he held back a smile. "That was the last time, my friend. My name is Throll, and I guarantee you that it will still be Throll tomorrow."

"I told you he'd be grumpy about the 'Your Highness' thing," Sloane whispered.

Throll turned to his daughter. "I'm not..." He paused, shook his head, and laughed. "All right. Maybe I *am* a little on edge. Sorry, folks. Honestly, I can't wait to just get this coronation over with."

"Me too," said Aaron. "But first we're going to eat, right?"

"Yeah," Ryan added. "I'm starving."

Sloane and Arabelle exchanged a look.

"Predictable, aren't they?" Sloane said, and they both laughed.

---

Dominic had spent the past two days hiding in the shadows. From the gloom, he'd observed the Riverton brothers preparing for the upcoming coronation. And every moment he watched, he felt his anger grow stronger. *Those bastards won't be celebrating for long*, he thought.

As he stumbled into his windowless room, his head throbbed. He told himself that the headache was due to the constant skulking around, and not to all the liquor he'd been drinking. The price on his head necessitated that he maintain a low profile, and through the help of a few of his seedier contacts stationed in Aubgherle, he'd managed to gain access to a boarding room with no questions asked—one above a tavern that often served the very same kinds of people Dominic sought to hire. But on this day, he'd been unsuccessful in finding the men he needed, and so instead had turned to strong drink.

Though he needn't have bothered. Ever since the day he'd encountered Sammael at the abandoned shrine in the woods, things had changed—including drinking. Drinking no longer brought Dominic any pleasure; it only brought him headaches. The sound that rumbled through the floor from the revelry below didn't help.

He'd just plopped down on his rickety cot when the door to his room opened and a dirt-encrusted, middle-aged man stumbled in. He clutched a large mug of ale, its contents slopping onto the floor with its owner's wobbling steps.

*Great,* Dominic thought. *A drunk who doesn't realize he's stumbled into the wrong room.*

The man looked down at Dominic. "I heard you were looking for an ass... er..." He burped. "Assass... uhh..."

Dominic couldn't help but feel a touch of amusement "Assassin?"

The man's glassy-eyed stare brightened. "Yeah! I heard you were looking for one. Well..." He kicked his arms to either side as he bowed, spilling most of his drink at the foot of the bed. "Here I am."

Dominic sighed. "Had you been listening carefully, you would have heard that I was looking for a *pair* of assassins. If you have a friend, and you are talented, maybe I can use you both. When you are less drunk."

The man leveled his stare, and the hair prickled on the back of Dominic's neck.

"If you have the money to hire two of us," the man said darkly, and with sudden lucidity, "I can collect the fee and we can be done with the transaction now."

Dominic was taken aback, but he shook his head. "No. Bring your friend. I need to make sure you're the right men for the job."

The man looked around the room, squinting in the dim

light, then shut the door behind him. His drunkenness had utterly disappeared; clearly it had all been a ruse.

He faced Dominic, pulled a dagger from his belt, and expertly flipped it. "You might reconsider that decision," he said with a sneer. "No one would hear a thing."

Dominic actually laughed aloud. "You make a good point, my friend. As a matter of fact, I'm reconsidering my decision right now."

His newly acquired powers surged through him. Weaving invisible threads of energy, he draped them around his guest and within the blink of an eye, cinched them tight. The would-be assassin gasped as he was lifted off the ground, his mug and dagger clattering to the floorboards. Dominic then flicked his wrists—and slammed his captive against the wall, splintering the wood.

Dominic stood and stepped closer. "It's just as you said: no one will hear a thing."

He clenched his fist, and his web tightened around his captive. Bones cracked like twigs. A stench permeated the room as the would-be assassin involuntarily emptied his bowels. Dominic savored the moment as he felt the life drain from his victim.

This… this was his potent drink.

This was what now brought him pleasure.

## CORONATION

As Ryan stepped out of the farmhouse with the others, an armored ogre of gigantic proportions stepped forward to greet them. Zenethar wriggled out of Arabelle's arms and ran toward the ogre.

"O'buk up!" he yelled. "O'buk up!"

The ogre smiled down at the boy, then looked questioningly at Throll and Gwen.

"Of course, its fine, Ohaobbok," Gwen said. "You know he just likes to ride on people's shoulders. The higher the better, and there's none who lift him higher than you."

"All right, little prince," Ohaobbok said softly, putting Zenethar on his shoulders. "But remember to hold on. I don't want to have to catch you because you decided to fall asleep."

Zenethar grabbed hold of Ohaobbok's collar and bounced up and down. "Go!" he yelled. "Go, horsie!"

Throll shook his head. "My two-year-old is riding a twelve-foot-tall ogre like a horse on the way to my coronation. I would never have predicted any of this a couple years ago."

As they walked, Rebecca began to fuss in her mother's arms.

"Can I hold her?" Arabelle asked.

"Of course." Ryan's mom handed Rebecca over to Arabelle, and within a minute, the baby was giggling and gurgling contentedly.

"I think we have a good candidate for babysitting," Gwen said.

Arabelle kissed Rebecca on the top of her head. "I would love to babysit any time I'm around. I can't wait until I'm a mother."

Ryan blushed at the thought. He and Arabelle were nineteen, old enough to marry, but had agreed to wait until the prophecy had run its course first. But children… that thought was terrifying. Him, a father?

Still, the thought seemed more plausible when he watched Arabelle playing with his little sister. *She'll make a great mother. And I'll figure it out eventually.*

On the way to the center of town, a dozen lightly armored soldiers joined them, a formal escort for their future king. Swords were belted to their waists, and several had crossbows strapped to their backs. To Ryan, it seemed excessive, but it did mean they didn't have to push their way through the crowds that had gathered along the main street to watch the guests of honor arrive.

He heard many of the onlookers whispering, almost in reverence.

"The royal family," one said.

"The wizards who killed Azazel," said another.

"Isn't he gorgeous?"

"That really is a tamed ogre!"

"I hope they aren't like Azazel."

An elevated stage had been constructed in the square, with rows of benches on top. As Throll led the procession onto the stage, he waved to the crowd, and the people erupted with cheers. The population of Aubgherle had swelled substantially; people must have traveled from all corners of Trimoria to witness the first coronation of a king in generations.

And it was not just humans in attendance. A pocket of dwarves had gathered up front, holding up mugs of ale and slapping each other's backs with laughter. And in the back, at the very edge of the square, stood a group of elves. As always, they were doing an exceptional job of blending into their surroundings, and Ryan's eyes almost passed right over them.

The soldiers escorted the royal procession to the benches —all except Throll, who remained standing—and then took their places on the edges of the platform. Throll nodded at Ryan and his father, and just as they had practiced, the two wizards counted down from three before simultaneously sending a fiery display of magic into the air, hundreds of feet above the crowd. Wide eyes followed the awe-inspiring explosions, then turned with even greater awe to the men who'd created it. Ryan forced himself not to fidget under the heat of their stares.

Grendel, the day's master of ceremonies, stepped onto the platform and marched to Throll with a sealed wooden box in his outstretched hands. The little man cleared his throat and projected a surprisingly loud voice.

"Welcome, everyone, to this momentous occasion," he boomed. "Traditional wisdom has it that the last descendant of the kings of Trimoria perished over eighty years ago. But that is not the case. The last of the line of kings decided to hide one of his offspring from the tyranny of Azazel, thus preserving the line of succession. Before us today stands the grandson of that first hidden prince of Trimoria. I present to you Throll Lancaster, the oldest direct descendant of our last monarch, King Harold Thariginian."

The crowd exploded with cheers and whistles and cries of "Long live the king!"

Throll humbly bowed his head, then waved to the crowd. Ryan could tell he was uncomfortable being the object of adulation, but he understood his role.

Grendel removed a whistle from his pocket and blew it sharply. When the assembly had quieted again, he continued. "Now we have reached the moment we have all come to witness: the formal crowning of our new king."

Due to the height difference between Grendel and Throll, a guard had to slide out a set of stairs for the little bureaucrat to climb. When he reached the top, Grendel opened the box he carried.

"The original crown of Trimoria was lost with King Harold," he announced. "So with the help of Aubgherle's preeminent blacksmith"—Grendel extended a hand to Ryan's father—"a new crown was made."

Throll turned to Dad, his eyes wide in surprise. Dad just smiled and winked.

As Grendel lifted the crown from the box, the onlookers gasped. It *was* extraordinary. A circle of gold served as its base, with tiny metal swords rising from it. And from what Ryan could tell at this distance, those swords had been sculpted from the legendary dwarven metal known as damantite. The crown was adorned with scrolls, shields, and laurels, along with finely wrought script flowing between them.

And the whole thing glowed, Ryan noted proudly, for he'd been the one to create that glow, when he imbued the crown with potent magical energy. He hadn't previously seen the results of his work, because Dad had made him close his eyes while imbuing the crown. That had seemed a silly demand at the time, but now Ryan understood his father probably wanted him to enjoy the crown's reveal along with everyone else.

Throll kneeled, and Grendel carefully placed the crown on the large man's head. When Throll stood upright once more, now officially king, the crowd roared.

Throll waited long moments before motioning for silence, giving his people time to share their jubilation. Then he spoke.

"Thank you, citizens of Trimoria. I swear to you that while I execute the responsibilities of my position as king, I'll be fair and open with all of my decisions. In the next few weeks, I'll be implementing a variety of changes and clarifications to the laws, to ensure that everyone is treated fairly and our society prospers."

Many heads in the crowd nodded in agreement.

"We must also prepare for what is to come. You all know of what I speak—the battle with the demon horde—because you have all seen the same visions, the same prophecy. To be ready for this, we must raise an army. We must put aside our differences and break down the walls of isolation that we have constructed over the years. The many peoples of Trimoria must be united in combat against the demon threat." He gestured to the dwarves next to the stage. "In that spirit, I would like to warmly welcome the dwarven emissaries I see among you. I hope your trip from the mountains was safe and uneventful."

The dwarves, clearly surprised that they'd been noticed at all, shouted their excitement.

"Huzzah! Throll, King of Trimoria!"

Another dwarf quickly added, "And huzzah for the alemaker of Aubgherle! We be needin' to trade recipes!"

The crowd burst into laughter.

Throll chuckled. "Yes, the ale here is quite good." With a twinkle in his eye, he pointed to the group of elves. "I also want to thank the emissaries from Eluanethra for attending. So few of my people have even seen elves, that I'm ashamed to say many believed your kind to be mere myth and legend. Welcome, my friends."

The crowd stirred, whispers skipped through them like a stone on water.

"We are a nation of three major races," Throll continued. "We should look upon each other as brothers in arms, since that is exactly what we shall soon be."

The crowd murmured approval, and one of the humans nearest the elves tentatively passed a mug of ale to them. The nearest elf bowed, quickly drained the mug, and let out a gigantic burp.

"Dat be a respectable belch for an elf," shouted the dwarf who had commented on the ale.

The crowd again broke into laughter.

Throll raised his voice above the din. "Before the celebrations begin, let me announce my first three orders. It's been discovered that all of the First Protector's fountains bear a corruption of the original message they were supposed to carry. Starting tomorrow, all fountains will be re-inscribed with the original Protector's message."

The king cleared his throat. *"Bring to me your children for testing as they are newly born,"* he recited. *"For the waters declare them Wizard, and our hope abides with them. A weekly bath will inoculate the wizard from the sway of evil."*

Throll paused to let the message settle in. Then he continued.

"My ancestor who first inscribed that phrase on the fountains had good reason. I'm confident that following those instructions will make the difference between victory and defeat in our upcoming battle with the demon forces.

"Which brings me to my second order. Every citizen of Trimoria, not just the newborns but people of all ages, even the dwarves who are in the mountains and the elves in the forests, will bathe once more in the fountains. We need to find any mages that escaped Azazel's persecution, because we are rebuilding an army not only of warriors, but of wizards. And if we do find mages among us, we will not banish them, but cherish them as honored citizens. We'll never again tolerate the persecution or denigration of our wizard citizens. In fact, our visions show us that wizards will be destined to fight where no regular soldier can bear to go—into the reaches of the Abyss."

Ryan considered the embarrassment of a weekly public bathing. But if it inoculated him from evil…

Throll turned to the benches and gestured for Ryan's parents to join him. The looks on their faces made clear that neither of them had expected this. But they obediently rose and walked over to him, and he stepped between them and put his arms around their shoulders.

"Many centuries ago, there was an academy of learning for wizards, which was long ago destroyed. Along with the training grounds we have already established for mustering troops, my third order will be the reconstruction of an academy for these wizards to learn their craft. That academy will be led by two teachers who are not only among my dearest friends, but who are soon to be part of the royal family.

"I am delighted to introduce you to Jared and Aubrey Riverton," Throll said.

The crowd cheered and applauded. Mom and Dad looked uncomfortable, but exchanged a small grin.

Throll continued. "Along with his two sons and our cherished ogre friend, Jared was not only instrumental in destroying Azazel's enforcers, but in destroying Azazel himself. And Aubrey has tremendous magical abilities in the healing arts. She has proven capable of bringing people back from death's door. Together, Jared and Aubrey will be responsible for organizing and running what I will officially be naming the Riverton Academy of Magic."

Now Mom and Dad were dumbstruck. But when Mom drew a breath as if to protest, Throll merely smiled and shouted to the audience.

"Our reluctant headmaster and headmistress need some encouragement, folks! What do you think of them leading this new academy?"

The crowd cheered and whistled and stomped their feet.

"All hail the king!"

"All hail the Rivertons!"

"Huzzah the ale!"

Throll waved for the rest of those assembled on the benches to come forward. When Ryan reached the lip of the platform, he looked back to see that Ohaobbok alone had not moved from his spot. Throll whispered something to Zenethar, and the boy toddled over to the ogre, yanked on his knee, and pulled Ohaobbok forward to stand with the others.

Throll held his arms wide, a gesture meant to encompass them all, as he faced the assembled crowd. "I and my family want to thank you all for the trust you have placed in me."

Another cheer.

Then Throll placed his hands on Ryan's and Aaron's shoulders. "But now, I suspect that some among my party have been wondering when they might eat. Let it not be said that I kept anyone unduly from their breakfast. I know we all smell the wonderful food, so let's move this ceremony to the feasting. Again, thank you all for being here. Now let's eat!"

As Ryan stepped down from the stage, he glimpsed a robed man standing at the edge of the square. Two flaming eyes crackled and blinked from beneath his darkened cowl. But before Ryan could get a closer look, the man vanished into the crowd.

## DAMANTITE

Ryan's stomach grumbled in protest as he strolled through the marketplace, holding Arabelle's hand. *I hope I don't get sick. I hope I don't get sick.*

Aaron and Sloane walked beside them, arm in arm. "Ryan," said Aaron, his face showing a greenish tint, "I don't know about you, but I don't think I want another chicken wing ever again. I can barely move."

"Forget chicken wings—if I even *see* one more fried doughnut, I'm going to literally be sick," Ryan replied.

Sloane laughed. "I'd say you two earned everything you're feeling."

"Hey!" Ryan complained. "I was eating in honor of your father's coronation."

Sloane laughed. "Ha. You boys are just gluttons."

Arabelle squeezed Ryan's arm. "But they're *our* gluttons. I wouldn't trade them for anything in the world."

Sloane sighed and said to Arabelle in a stage whisper, "Arabelle, that isn't how the game is played. Mother says we're supposed to look like we're upset with them. Then the boys will spend extra effort trying to make us happy again."

"And how are we supposed to know if you're really angry or just playing?" Aaron demanded.

"I'll tell you when we're definitely *not* playing," Sloane said. "Those girls today? What was *that* all about?"

"Wha—? Are you upset with me? It's not my fault that some random girl handed me a flower."

Sloane sniffed. "I don't care about the girl with the flower. She was, what, eight years old? It was kind of sweet. But those two sisters who asked you two over for dinner, while Arabelle and I were standing right there… that was *rude*. And you just grinned like an idiot."

"That was weird," Ryan said. "They don't even know us."

Arabelle laughed. "Oh, my poor naïve betrothed. You don't know what some girls can be like." She turned to Sloane. "Do keep an eye out for those vultures when I'm not around. Our boys evidently don't realize that from now on they'll be targets for all of the town's harlots."

"Fame is strange," Ryan said. "I'm just an apprentice blacksmith with a few magical powers. If those girls only knew my days are filled with getting singed by hot metal or accidentally burning myself with one of my magical experiments."

"At least you have some sparks you can show off," Aaron said. "I can see girls thinking that's kind of interesting. Between Throll and Ohaobbok, I spend all my time gathering bruises."

Sloane shook her head. "You boys are both clueless. Keep this up, and you'll convince me and Arabelle that we could do better."

"Hey!" said Aaron. "No backing out now. And anyway, you said you *like* my bruises."

"And," said Ryan, turning to face Arabelle, "you know I only have eyes for you."

She wrapped her arms around his neck and pulled him in for a long kiss. One of the soldiers in the escort chuckled and whistled.

When Arabelle broke off the kiss, Ryan had to catch his breath. "What was *that* for?" he asked.

Arabelle smiled sweetly, then grabbed his arm to continue walking. "That was for you to remember what you're missing when I'm not around."

"Do you really have to leave so soon?" Ryan asked. "I was hoping you could stay for a while."

Arabelle shook her head. "You know my father. It isn't right for him to be too far from the caravan. And until I get married, I must live in the tent of my father. Only after marriage can I share a tent with someone else."

"I hope you don't mind that my tent looks more like a house with a wooden roof," Ryan joked.

Arabelle squeezed his arm. "I wouldn't care if the roof of your tent was the evening sky, as long as I could be with you."

Aaron made retching sounds.

Sloane smacked him on the arm. "Oh, grow up."

---

The people gave Jared a wide berth as he wandered through the market. He understood why. They had grown up fearing magic, which meant they feared him. He may have been well known as a law-abiding citizen and an unassuming man, but he was also a powerful wizard, and it was going to take some time for them to get past that.

It didn't help that Jared was currently glowing with a white nimbus of energy, the result of his difficulty in tracking down his intended target. So many people crowded the market square that the dwarves he sought could have been standing a cart's length away and he wouldn't have seen them.

He closed his eyes in frustration, concentrating on the vision of Silas Redbeard, leader of the Redbeard clan, whom Jared had met during their trip to confront the wizard Azazel. Jared had seen him in the crowd at the coronation, but hadn't been able to find him afterward.

But now, as he concentrated, he had a sense of which direction to go. With the dwarf fixed in his mind, he increased his pace.

Silas Redbeard lounged in a tavern called the Bloated Buzzard. A waitress deposited another mug in front of him.

"Me good lady," he said, "dis ale be quite excellent. Are ye da brew mistress?"

The brown-haired girl, barely of age, put her hands on her hips. "Do I look like a lady to you? I just serve the drinks. My father made the ale." She hitched her thumb toward the round-bellied barkeep, then left for another table.

Apparently having overheard, the portly proprietor walked over.

Silas raised his mug. "Me good man, I must be sayin' dat dis be quite adequate ale. It's not be nuttin' like da swill in the marketplace. Dis has a fine quality to it dat reminds me of home."

"Why thank you, good sir." The barkeep leaned in conspiratorially. "I used to the brew master for the caravan owner, Honfrion. He had very particular tastes. But now that the cursed wizard Azazel has died, I was able to break away from the caravan and settle down. I'm a family man, after all. Sadly, most of my customers just want to get a buzz in their head. They don't much care whether the ale tastes like horse piss."

"Well, know ye dat I appreciate your efforts, barkeep. And for Silas Redbeard to say dat, it be sumtin'. I'll be lettin' my fellow clansmen know about yer establishment, don'tcha worry."

At that moment, Silas's vision blurred, and he was overwhelmed with a mental picture of the elder wizard, Jared Riverton.

"Tanks again," he said distractedly to the barkeep, plopping a silver coin in the man's hand. "I'll be back, ye can be sure of it. Time fer me to find someone."

"Can I help you find them?" the proprietor asked. "I know most people in Aubgherle. I could point you in the right direction."

Silas shook his head. "No need. I be feelin' it won't be necessary."

*In fact I suspect* he's *going to find* me.

---

As Jared approached the alehouse that bordered the market square, its door banged open and out stomped Silas Redbeard, his flaming red beard swinging left and right as he scanned the crowd.

When the dwarf's eyes met Jared's, he called out. "I swear, wizard, ye need to git yerself outta my head!"

Jared shook Silas's hand. "What do you mean, get out of your head?"

"May my beard fall out if I be lyin'," the dwarf said, craning his neck to address Jared, "but only moments ago, I was mindin' my own business and havin' me first decent drink in days, and yer ugly face flashed into my head. Da surprise almost soured a perfectly good mug of ale. I suddenly felt compelled to find ye."

Jared scratched his chin. "How very unusual..." He narrowed his eyes, thinking what this might mean.

"Well?" said the dwarf. "Ye got me attention now. I assume ye want ta be speakin' to me, wizard?"

"Yes. I was seeking you out to continue a discussion we had… well, nearly two years ago now, in the caves near Cammoria."

Silas smiled and pulled a rock from his pocket. He tossed it to Jared. "You want to talk about dat?"

Jared raised a brow. "Is this damantite ore?"

Silas looked from side to side as if to make sure no one was listening. "Lord Wizard, I be thinkin' da glow yer givin' off is attractin' a bit of attention. P'raps we should continue our discussion inside, o'er a mug of the proprietor's fine ale."

Jared suddenly noticed the crowd that had gathered to stare at them. "Yes. Perhaps you're right."

As they headed into the bar, someone in the gathered crowd grumbled, "Bah, I thought he was going to zap the dwarf."

"Shut up, Phineas, before he zaps you!" said another man.

Silas laughed and held the door for Jared. "After ye, my Lord Zapper."

"Very funny," Jared replied dryly. "Keep it up and people will start calling you Silas Sizzlebeard."

As they took a table against the wall of the smoke-filled tavern Silas said, "I was jes' teasin', Lord Sensitive."

Jared rolled his eyes. "I know you were, you fuzzy-faced, ale-soaked anvil-banger."

The dwarf roared with laughter. "Ha! I tink I'm gonna like you."

"I hope so, because I'd like to talk about a trading agreement. For damantite."

Silas nodded. "Dat's what I figgered. But ye do remember dis stuff be cursed and revered by our smiths. It's terrible to work wit, nearly impossible to melt or refine."

Jared smiled. "And you'll recall that I'm able to generate rather a lot of heat." He held up his hand, sending arcing filaments of sparking energy bouncing from one finger to another.

"I do. How could I forget? If I'm bein' honest, if ye can work dat demon's metal as easily as ye think, ye'll likely be findin' lots of dwarven smiths volunteerin' to help. Almost makes me want to be a smith meself." He frowned. "I could have several wagonloads of dis stuff on its way to yer smithy before da week's out. But let's talk terms."

Jared smiled. "Yes. Let's."

## VISIONS AND DREAMS

*S* *teaming relics of burnt siege engines dot a battlefield covered with the dead and the dying, a blanket of misery. And yet to the west, the battle still rages.*

*On one side are human soldiers fighting desperately. Among the humans are short bearded warriors that chant in unison as they swing their giant sledgehammers.*

*On the other side... are demons.*

*The demons are a motley horde. Some are mottled brown, others bright red, still others black as midnight. The smallest are like children; the largest are giant monstrosities, towering well over ten feet tall. But all are dangerous, all meant for battle. They slash with vicious, dagger-like claws, bite with protruding fangs. Even the bony ridges along their joints are sharp enough to slice open any soldier who has the misfortune of brushing against them.*

*The defenders are falling back, moving eastward, unable to hold the onslaught. Soon they have converged at a hill, their last redoubt. Midway up the hill, a circle of lithe fighters draw their longbows again and again, raining a thick stream of arrows down on the enemy. And at the top of the hill, protected by an encircling low stone wall, stands a robed man holding an orb in his hand.*

*The man is a sharp contrast to the battlefield. Though all around him is ruin, and all who fight are bloodied and stooped, this man's white robe is immaculate, and he is calm. Contemplative.*

*All his concentration is focused on the orb.*

*The demon horde presses up the hill, breaking the ranks of the soldiers. For a moment, it appears that all is lost.*

*And then the robed man lifts the orb high over his head. It blazes so brightly that the sun would seem dim by comparison. The orb's light expands, slowly, spreading away from the man, rolling down the hill, continuing across the fields beyond.*

*Every enemy it touches is rendered aflame and then reduced to ash.*

*The light expands more rapidly now, drinking up the earth until it stretches from horizon to horizon. What was night has turned to day. What was certain defeat has turned to victory.*

Jared rolled over in bed, only half-awakening. The dream—the prophecy—was beyond familiar; it came to him practically every night, as it did to everyone who inhabited Trimoria.

*Ohaobbok crosses a natural stone bridge across a deep chasm. He is equipped in plate armor that glows a pristine white and emits sparks with every movement. At his side is the largest great sword Jared has ever seen. Its blade is sheathed, but its pommel is red.*

*Following him is Ryan, his face bearded. In one hand he holds a sparking metal staff; in the other, a brilliant diamond the size of a melon, pulsing with radiant power.*

*Crossing the bridge from the opposite side of the chasm is a fiend of blackness and fire. It matches Ohaobbok in size and wields an equally giant sword, this one branded with flame.*

*As Ohaobbok meets the fiend at the middle of the bridge, a dark presence of palpable evil appears on the far side. It's enormous, dwarfing both fiend and ogre.*

*Ryan raises the diamond above his head.*

This dream, too, was part of the prophecy. The prophecy that proclaimed his family's central role in the future of Trimoria.

But tonight, the dream differed. Jared was experiencing it while still half-awake. His eyes were closed… or were they? He couldn't feel anything. Was he dreaming, or was he… actually there?

He felt a strange calm come over him as a field of white engulfed all he could see.

And then a voice spoke.

*"Greetings, Jared Riverton."*

Jared looked around. He saw nothing but white. "Hello? Who are you? What's happening?"

*"My true name would be incomprehensible to you. You may know me by the name Seder."*

"Okay, maybe I should have asked... *what* are you?"

*"What I am can be answered by others in another time. Some of the more pious among the citizens of Trimoria can explain."*

"Pious? Are you... God?"

*"There is a creator, but I am not He. I am something else. There was a philosopher from your world who nearly described an absolute truth about the universe. He stated that 'Any sufficiently advanced technology is indistinguishable from magic.' I would myself say, 'Any sufficiently advanced being is indistinguishable from one's perception of God.'"*

"You're quoting from my old world. How do you know about that?"

*"Because it is I who facilitated your travel to this new world. You bring... a unique perspective to it."*

Jared was stunned. "You... brought me here? Intentionally? Why?"

*"I have been watching you and your family for what would seem to you a long time. I generally avoid influencing things directly, but my brother has been directly trying to influence the threads of destiny for several of your centuries, and I needed to respond in kind. You and your family are... tools of that response."*

Jared stiffened at the word "tools." He was no one's *tool*, and his wife and sons were certainly not to be used in some brotherly squabble.

His face heated with anger. "What right did you have to treat us so? You ripped my family out of our world, our life!"

*"Would you have preferred that I let nature take its course? The earthquake you experienced in your world collapsed the cave you were in. Had I not acted, all of you would have perished. Is the fate I chose for you not preferable to death?"*

Jared paused. It took some time for the idea to sink in that his entire family should have died.

"What do you want from me? From us?"

*"As I said, your family is a tool of a prophecy. I have foreseen the need for your sons to gain training from the elves. As such, I have spoken with the elder in the elven city of Eluanethra, and he is on his way to meet you. Tomorrow morning, he will arrive at your smithy. Make the necessary arrangements. If your wife needs convincing, you may share this dream with her."*

Jared felt something stir within him, and then that same overwhelming calm washed over him once more. "How do I know this isn't all just a dream?"

*"When you wake up, I will arouse a new skill in you. This will confirm that this exchange has been more than a dream. But I want a pledge from you. I pledge that you will take seriously the task of forming the academy. You and your wife must ensure the training of those with magical aptitude. You must*

*also reinstate the Conclave of Wizards—a conclave composed of the strongest of your wielders of magic. These things must come to pass if Sammael's plans are to be thwarted."*

"Sammael? That's the name of the hidden orb."

Jared felt Seder's amusement. *"No. Sammael is the common name for what might be known as my brother. If I were known as a spirit of order, Sammael would be considered a spirit of chaos. In time, you will learn more about such things.*

*"One parting word of caution: Sammael has influenced someone in Trimoria. I cannot directly see the things my brother does, but I can see hints and trails of his influence. Sammael has gained a replacement for his minion, Azazel. Be careful."*

---

The sun hadn't yet burned away the morning's dampness, and the air was thick with the scent of freshly turned soil as Ryan walked toward the smithy with his brother. Dad had told them to ignore their normal training today, and instead meet him at the smithy as soon as they finished breakfast.

Aaron skipped along, beaming. "This'll be the first morning in weeks when Throll doesn't trick me with a new sword sweep and Ohaobbok doesn't knock me into the next town."

"Aren't you supposed to be as strong as an ox?" Ryan said. "I thought you could handle Ohaobbok."

"Oh, I have strength, but Ohaobbok weighs about ten times what I do. It's a miracle I don't get killed on a daily basis."

Ryan chuckled. "At least you don't have to spend all day making super-skinny metal straws with magic. Dad says it's to practice my control, but my eyes really start crossing after spending all morning drilling holes through rods."

"Yeah, but if you mess up, all you have to do is start over. If I mess up, I could lose my arm."

They were approaching the smithy, and Dad's voice sounded from inside. "Your mom will heal your arm if you lose it during training. Now both of you get in here. We have guests."

The boys stepped inside to find that the fires were banked, and a table had been set up where the cooling barrels normally were. Gathered around the table, along with Dad, was a trio of elves. Their hair was light blond, their skin was deeply tanned.

"Hey!" said Aaron, nodding to the elf in the center, who appeared to be the oldest by far. "You're Illisandre's grandfather! It's good to see you again."

Ryan knew that Aaron had once traveled into the elven domain, two years ago.

The elf smiled at Aaron. "It's good to see you again as well, young warrior." He gestured to the elves on either side of him. "I don't believe you've met Eglerian and Castien."

Eglerion nodded to Aaron without taking his eyes off of Ryan. "Xinthian, you're always full of surprises. A new pupil… I do think this arrangement should pose an interesting challenge—for him."

"Boys," said Dad, "you know that you're both going to be facing some rather daunting tasks in the near future. So I want you properly prepared. And that means training with the best."

"Aren't I already doing that?" Aaron asked. "Throll is the best fighter we know. I've mastered all thirteen basic motions, and he says I can beat anyone in single combat, except for him."

Dad held out his hands as if requesting calm. "Yes, you've worked hard. You both have. And I mean no insult to Throll, but there's always more to learn." He gestured to the youngest elf. "Castien is the sword master of Eluanethra, and the elves are celebrated swordsmen. He has skills you need to learn."

The youngest elf nodded at Aaron.

"And Ryan," Dad continued, "I've done my best to work with you so far, but let's face it, we're learning together. That's going to change now. Eglerion has been teaching the basics of magic for seven hundred years. So…"

He smiled. "Boys, meet your new teachers."

Xinthian gave Ryan and Aaron a sympathetic look. "I'm sure this is overwhelming, and we're sorry to spring this upon you. But it's necessary—for all of us. As the head of the elven council, I'm responsible for the welfare of my people, and our fate is locked with the fate of the rest of Trimoria. Thus it's critical to the elves that your missions succeed.

"Make no mistake: we *will* broaden your skills. You're being offered an opportunity that has never been given to anyone outside the elven community—to learn some of the secrets that my race holds dear. Ryan, Eglerion Mithtanion is Eluanethra's lore master. His expert training is typically reserved only for our royalty. And Aaron, Castien Galonos is not only Eluanethra's sword master, he is one of the best to have ever graced our people. He will train you in the way of our warriors."

He paused, meeting both boys' eyes. "So. What say you, young men?"

Aaron spoke quickly. He already thought himself the greatest warrior in the world, and Ryan knew his brother would never pass up a chance to become even better. "Yes. I'm eager to begin.

"I'll do what's necessary. But I don't quite understand what that means. Will we be training here, or in Eluanethra? And for how long?"

Xinthian smiled. "And you, Ryan?"

Ryan was more cautious. He understood the need to be trained, but had questions about what that entailed.

"I agree to train with your people as well. But I have questions."

Xinthian nodded. "Please… ask."

"Well, for starters, how long is this training?"

"A good question. Unfortunately, we don't have the time we would normally take with new apprentices. It usually requires ten years of training before Castien allows his apprentices to practice with sharpened blades—"

"Ten years!" Aaron exclaimed.

"Aaron," said Dad, "mind your manners."

Xinthian continued patiently. "But given your situation, we'll have to settle for a vastly accelerated training. You'll both spend the next two months in Eluanethra. Then you will rejoin your family and we'll integrate what you've learned with your current training. But be aware, two months doesn't begin to approach the time necessary, so we cannot waste a moment of it. Your training will be non-stop from the moment you enter Eluanethra to the day your fate leads you to the battlefield."

He leaned forward. "I would also point out that while you are among my people, you would do well to earn their respect. Without that, they will not follow you, regardless of what the prophecy might say."

Aaron nodded. Ryan was still uncertain, but he nodded as well.

"When do we start?" he asked.

It was Dad who answered. "We're leaving as soon as we get back to the farmhouse. I'll go with you at first. But then you'll be on your own." He rose from his seat. "Come on, let's head home. Your mother should be packing our things right now, and will insist we give her a proper farewell."

Xinthian stood. "We'll meet you at the edge of the forest. Aaron, you remember the location?"

Aaron nodded. "I sure do. I think this is going to be a lot of fun."

Xinthian laughed loudly. "Youth," he murmured. "How naïve and refreshing."

## ASSASSINS

As Ryan walked with his father and Aaron back to the farm, Dad filled them in on his dream of the night before.

"I'm not sure what Seder is, other than a... an entity of some kind," he finished, shaking his head. "Honestly, ever since we arrived in this place, I've set aside all of my preconceived notions about what I believe; I'm just taking things in. Like I said, this Seder doesn't claim to be God, but if he knows about our world... if he's truly the one who *brought* us to this world... it certainly makes one wonder."

"What about the power he mentioned as proof?" Ryan asked. "Do you really have a new power?"

"In a way, yes. Although it's something I could have done before, if I knew how... and have thought of it. Here. Let me show you."

He scrunched his face in concentration. After a moment, a shimmering effect obscured him from view. When it turned translucent, he said. "Okay Ryan, throw something at me."

Ryan hesitated, but Aaron didn't. With a grin he grabbed a pebble from the ground and tossed it at Dad's chest. Except it didn't quite get there. About six inches from Dad, it bounced away with a spark, as if it had hit a solid barrier.

"It's a shield," Ryan said in wonder.

"It's *awesome* is what it is," Aaron said. "Can I throw something bigger?"

Dad smiled. "Sure, but don't go crazy."

Aaron found a fist-sized stone. When he threw it at Dad, it bounced off just like the pebble.

Aaron retrieved it. "I'm going to try throwing it harder this time."

Dad looked a bit dubious. "Well… okay. But aim away from my face. I'm not sure how strong this shield is."

Aaron's tongue peeked from between his lips as he took aim and threw. Ryan cringed. Even Dad looked nervous.

The stone connected hard with the shield, exploding on contact and sending Dad staggering backward.

"Whoa," said Aaron.

Ryan rushed to his father. "Dad! Are you all right?"

Dad broke into a wide smile. "Perfectly fine. It was a strange sensation. I felt the pressure of the stone hit the shield, and the impact almost knocked me off balance, but I felt no pain. When you boys finish your training with the elves, we'll have to experiment a little more. And Ryan, I can teach you to do it too. It's not hard, once you learn the technique."

"I'll be the designated thrower," Aaron said, grinning.

By then they were approaching the farmhouse, and the door flew open. Arabelle and Sloane stepped outside with their hands on their hips.

"Aaron!" snapped Sloane. "Did you think you were going away without even *telling* me?"

"Wha—? I—I—" Aaron stammered.

Arabelle's reaction was much different, but as far as Ryan was concerned, more painful.

Tears formed in her eyes. "Ryan, were you going to leave without seeing me first?"

Ryan stepped up to her and put his hands on her shoulders. "No, of course not. Never."

Mom appeared behind them, Rebecca perched on her hip. "Good answer, Ryan," she said with a smile.

Dad stepped in. "Don't blame the boys. They didn't even know about this until just now. It came on all of us as a surprise. Including me."

"And me," said Mom. "But we packed for you, like your father asked. All of us did."

Ryan looked at Arabelle. "You packed for me? Including… my underwear?"

"Of course," she said, laughing. "You're going to be my husband. Why wouldn't I pack your things?"

Despite the seriousness of what he was about to undertake, all of a sudden all Ryan could think about was that his future wife had seen his underwear with the rips in it.

"It's not a big deal," Sloane said. "I've seen Aaron in his undergarments plenty of times."

"Only because you're always walking into our room while we're changing!" Aaron huffed.

Sloane grinned. "Oh, like you haven't peeked when *I'm* changing."

"Give me a break, you *want* me to peek. That's why you're always changing with your door wide open."

"All right, kids," Dad said. "Everyone has underwear, and eventually someone will see you in them. Occasionally, I even let your mom see me in mine."

Mom gave him a playful elbow in the ribs, then pulled him in for a kiss. "I guess all three of my boys are leaving me."

Dad held her tight, then gave Rebecca a kiss on the head. "Just for a little while."

Arabelle took Ryan's hand and kissed the ring on his finger. "You'll keep wearing this, right?" she asked.

"Of course. I'll always be listening."

The rings were another of his father's discoveries—communications rings. When one ring in a set was tapped or squeezed, all other rings in the same set would vibrate, allowing the wearers to communicate across long distances in Morse code. There was one set of eight rings that had been distributed to the four Rivertons, the three Lancasters, and Ohaobbok, but after Ryan's betrothal to Arabelle, he'd asked his father to make a private pair just for them. When she was away with the caravan, it was the only way he could talk with her.

Ryan hugged Arabelle, and while his hands were behind her back, he tapped out a message.

She pulled back and said, with a shy smile, "Maybe you could say that out loud for once?"

Ryan blushed hotly and put his lips to her ear. "I love you," he whispered.

---

It took all of Gerald's self-control to overcome his gag reflex as he entered the shadowy room. The air stank of human waste and spilled ale. Beside him, his brother Roland merely curled his lip in disgust.

A gray-hooded figure sat at a desk, writing something on a piece of parchment, lit only by a single flickering candle. But as Gerald shut the door behind them, the figure snapped his fingers, and two candles on a wall shelf flared to life. He then motioned for Gerald and Roland to sit, which they did.

"I understand that you are the best in your business," the figure said. "Is this accurate?"

Roland was still looking at the candles. "Cheap tricks do not impress me," he growled. "Nor do I appreciate my skills being questioned. You. Explain why you asked for the help of the assassin's guild."

The figure pulled back his hood, revealing flaming eyes. The man wasn't even… human.

Gerald blanched. *Oh no, Roland. What have you gotten us into?*

The room grew colder, and two darts of light shot from those flaming eyes at Roland. Roland cried out in pain, fell to the floor, and began convulsing.

The figure turned calmly to Gerald as if utterly indifferent to Roland's agony. "Forgive me. I haven't properly introduced myself. My name is Dominic. And you are…?"

Gerald tried to keep his breathing steady. "I'm Gerald."

"Gerald." Dominic smiled. "What are your thoughts on what I've done to your friend?"

*Stay calm… stay calm…*

"If I had your abilities and was insulted like Roland insulted you," he said, "I would've taught him some manners as well."

The laughter that erupted from the gray-robed figure was harsh and grating. "Lucky for your friend, I need *two* assassins. So…"

He snapped his fingers, and Roland's convulsions ceased.

"I do hope you can appreciate my *cheap tricks* a bit more now, Roland," Dominic said. "Now get up. I expect you to listen to what I have to say."

Roland was shaking and, had to use the chair to help himself off the floor. He had soiled his pants and vomited over himself. "Yes, sir," he said. "I'm listening."

Dominic smiled warmly. "See? Isn't that much better? Now… I believe I asked if it was accurate to call you gentlemen the best in the business."

Roland jerked a nod. "Yes, sir. My brother and I have worked in the shadows since we were ten. We are both experts with bow and knife. I am also a master of poisons, while Gerald is trained in opening locks."

Dominic watched them with a wooden grin, and Gerald wiped away a bead of sweat, feeling as if the room had grown warmer.

"I need to have two people killed," Dominic said. "But they need to be killed simultaneously. And I will warn you that these targets are not defenseless shopkeepers or fair maidens. One is a young but skilled warrior, and the other is a wizard's apprentice."

Gerald tried to look calm even as he panicked inside. *A wizard? This man is crazy.*

But Roland scratched his chin. "By 'simultaneously,' do you mean the same day or literally the same time?"

Dominic leaned forward on his elbows. "I not only mean at the same time, I mean at *precisely* the same time. They and their associates have a means of instantly communicating across great distances. If one dies before the other, many people will be alerted, and your mission will fail."

"Not a problem," Roland said, sounding confident, though Gerald couldn't imagine how they would possibly achieve such a thing. "What are their names? Do you know anything of their habits?"

"I know that they leave the same home in the morning to train for the day. This may be the only time they are reliably together. They are brothers, and their names are Ryan and Aaron Riverton."

Gerald's worst fears were confirmed. Roland remained stoic, but Gerald could read the panic behind his brother's eyes.

"These would be the boys who are living with the king and queen?" Roland said. "The boys who have an ogre living on the premises, and who were involved in destroying Azazel and making his troops disappear?"

At the mention of Azazel's name, Dominic's smile fell into a grimace. "Yes, these are the very same boys. Is that a problem, Roland?" He leaned closer.

Roland smiled weakly. "Not at all, sir." What else could he say?

Dominic drew two pouches from his robes and tossed them at the assassins. "This is your first payment. If you are quick and accurate, you will receive your second, much larger payment."

Gerald opened his pouch. The coins inside had what looked like elvish runes on them. He'd never seen the like. They must have been hundreds of years old.

"Do not think of absconding with my coin. If you fail to achieve the mission I have assigned you, I assure you, you will die. On the other hand, if you succeed, I will make you very wealthy. But act quickly. Today something changed in the Riverton boys' routine. That makes me nervous, and it should make you nervous, too."

"When patterns change, it is often best to slow down and

apply keen observation," Gerald said before he could stop himself.

Dominic lurched forward, his haunting eyes flickered in the darkness of the room. "It must be done *now*. The need is great. Now go. And remember… I'm always watching."

# ELUANETHRA

As Xinthian and the two elven teachers escorted the Rivertons into the heart of the elven city of Eluanethra, Ryan turned to his father. "Can you believe all of this was just a few hours from where we've been living the whole time?"

Dad craned his neck as he examined his surroundings. "No, it's amazing."

The buildings were a lesson in woodcraft as they seamlessly blended into the forest that surrounded them. Vines clung to the buildings' scaly bark, cloaking them in a camouflage of greenery. It seemed as if each structure grew naturally within the matrix of the deep woods. In fact, the town was so well integrated with its surroundings that if all of the elves simply stopped moving, the city would likely disappear from view.

But the elves didn't stop moving. The city buzzed with

activity. Groups of elves passed on their daily errands, and elven children playfully chased each other through the streets. And of course, everyone noticed the newcomers. Several stepped forward to greet them warmly, but most carried their greetings in their smiles and gave only polite nods to their escorts.

Ryan closed his eyes and listened to the hustle and bustle. Birds chirped in the treetops, and branches groaned as a warm wind blew through them. He sniffed the air, picking up the scents of pine and sweet flowers. There was something very comforting about this place. As much as he loved home, he knew that it would require an adjustment when he had to go back to the smells of humanity.

When he opened his eyes, he saw Xinthian watching him. The elder smiled and swept his arm across the city's landscape. "Perhaps you now understand how we remain so well hidden from your world. It isn't only the natural camouflage that we employ, but there's an inherent magic that dwells in this ancient forest. The mist that surrounds Eluanethra prevents those who are unwelcome from finding us. Of course, your family is most welcome here."

"It's wonderful," Ryan said. "And… I feel something else, too. I can't quite explain it—it's a buzzing in the air, almost like electricity. It's like I can feel waves of energy."

Eglerion nodded. "That's because magic here is not as affected by the perversions that the demons wrought in Trimoria five centuries ago. There was a time when those who were in tune with the ways of magic could feel what you're sensing now throughout all of Trimoria. Things are a bit purer here. The magic runs deeper and more true."

Xinthian held up a hand. "There will be time for lessons once our guests are settled. Please escort them to their sleeping quarters so they can unpack. Ryan, you'll go with Eglerion, and Aaron, you with Castien." He turned to Dad. "As for you, Lord Riverton, I would consider it an honor if you would join the elder council for an informal dinner. There are many in Eluanethra who would like to meet you during your brief stay."

"I'd be glad to talk with anyone who wants to meet with me," Dad said. "Also, please call me Jared. This 'Lord' business doesn't feel right. I'm just a simple engineer who likes to work in a smithy."

Xinthian shook his head. "Let someone who's been alive for nearly a millennium give you some advice. In public, you should accept these titles and honorifics even if they feel like an unfamiliar burden. Not only are you now the eldest wizard in Trimoria, you're also blessed by Seder. Your title should not be looked upon as undue flattery. It's as deserved as it is necessary."

Dad nodded politely, but Ryan could tell he wasn't yet convinced.

"All right then," said Castien, clapping his hands together. The man exuded a twitchy energy, quite the contrast with the calm and patient Eglerion. "Let's get you unpacked so that we can begin your training. We've got an extraordinary amount of work to do, and not nearly enough time in which to do it. The sooner we start, the sooner we can see what we have to work with."

---

Ryan barely had time to set his things down before Eglerion led him briskly through the city to begin his training.

"I'll expect you to concentrate, work hard, and take this time you have with us very seriously," Eglerion said, stopping in front of a building that had no obvious entrance. "Don't question my requests. Listen to what I say. And don't ask me to repeat myself, because if you didn't have the courtesy to listen the first time, I won't waste my breath a second time. Do we have an understanding?"

Ryan nodded. "Yes, sir. That's pretty much my father's attitude as well."

A young female elf approached from behind the building. "Is this him?"

"Yes," said Eglerion. "I'm about to give him his first lesson."

The young elf turned to Ryan. There was something otherworldly about her. She exuded an unpretentious self-confidence that was somehow both relaxed and intimidating.

"Welcome, Ryan Riverton. I'm Labriuteleanan—and I vividly remember the lesson you're about to endure. In fact, I was annoyed with Eglerion for decades afterward."

"Decades? How old are you?"

The woman shook her head. "Humans are so cute. Let's

just say I'm quite young for an elf, but much older than your grandmother."

"Well, it's a pleasure to meet you, Labriutil... Labritel..."

She laughed. "Call me Labri. We're classmates, and will be spending a great deal of time together while—" She stopped suddenly, held up a hand, and let out a thunderous sneeze. When she'd collected herself, she blushed. "Sorry. I'm pretty sure I'm the only elf ever born with an allergy to tree pollen. I can't wait until the season changes."

She turned to Eglerion. "Do you mind if I stay and watch?"

"You may do as you like, as long as you don't interfere," the lore master said.

She sneezed again, then sat down cross-legged on the path.

Eglerion turned to Ryan. "Now, it's time to begin our first lesson." He swept his hand across the odd building. "Get into your classroom. No magic, no fire, no chopping. Now go."

"Just... go inside? That's it?"

Eglerion stared at him, stone-faced.

Ryan grimaced. "Ah. Don't question your requests. Right."

He shifted his attention to the building, walking all the way around it. It was about fifty feet long and thirty wide. A thatched roof stood about two stories off the ground. The walls were made from wooden planks. There were no obvious openings, no doors, no windows, nothing.

Ryan scratched at his close-cropped beard. "Am I allowed to ask questions about the building?"

"You may ask," Eglerion said. "But you might not find me willing to answer."

Ryan grinned. "Like, if I ask you how to get into the classroom…"

"You would not receive an answer."

Ryan shrugged. "It was worth a try."

He walked around the building again, this time searching the ground for clues. He stopped in front of Eglerion.

"There are tracks all around the building. Did you have someone walk around the building to obscure any hints about where the entrance might be?"

Labri looked up at Eglerion. "He's not as stupid as he looks."

"Hey!" Ryan objected, glanced at Labri, who shot him wink.

Eglerion frowned at her before turning to Ryan and giving him a silent shrug.

Ryan walked around the building a third time, tapping on the walls and listening carefully to the sound. Near the end of his circuit, he passed a spot where his taps produced a slightly different sound. He knocked a few more times, isolating the spot. Then he pushed against the planks.

Nothing happened.

"Am I staring at the entrance to the building?" he asked.

"That is a question I will not answer."

Ryan studied the spot, and found several knots in the wood. When he pressed on one, it gave slightly. Interesting. A puzzle?

He checked all the other knots, pressing against each one. There were nine in total, but only three of them shifted when pressed.

Ryan pressed all three at once.

With a click, a door swung open.

Labri clapped her hands excitedly. "He did it!"

"Well done, Ryan," Eglerion said. "It didn't take you nearly as long as I feared it might. All right, children. Now that we know young Mister Riverton has some of the basic problem-solving skills he'll need, why don't we enter the classroom and start discussing what magic is really about?"

As they marched into the building, Labri whispered to Ryan, "I'm glad you're here. At least now I have someone to share my boredom with."

## THE TRAINING BEGINS

Aaron chased after his teacher, straining to keep the elusive elf in sight. Castien ran through the woods at breakneck speed without the slightest sign of fatigue. Aaron, by contrast, was gasping for air. And falling behind.

"Follow me wherever I go, and don't lose sight of me." Those had been Castien's instructions. And then he'd added, ominously, "Or I'll consider you to have failed your first test."

That last statement had motivated Aaron to prove himself. Failure wasn't something he could even consider.

Of course, he also hadn't considered the elf would be so *fast*.

For the first twenty minutes, Castien had at least stayed on a well-trodden forest path. And despite the impossible pace he set, Aaron managed to keep him in sight, if only barely. But now Castien had veered off the path and was running right through the heavy brush in the forest. And when he took another turn and started up a steep hill, Aaron could only shake his head.

Castien made it look easy. He dodged between bushes and unerringly ducked vines and tree limbs. Aaron opted for the less elegant method of plowing straight through the forest's obstacles. But despite Aaron's determination, it eventually happened: the elf disappeared from his sight.

Grumbling at himself, Aaron pushed even harder up the slope.

He broke through some foliage to find Castien waiting for him atop a rocky overhang. The elf looked satisfied—and not the least bit winded. Aaron, meanwhile, collapsed to his knees, sweat pouring off him.

"You did better than I expected," Castien said. "I only had to slow my pace to that of one of our less capable children."

Aaron's stomach was threatening to heave up its contents. "You've got to be kidding. That wasn't full speed? I feel like I'm going to die."

Castien chuckled. "We definitely need to work on your endurance before I can take you through the more advanced exercises. One of your most obvious problems is that you keep fighting your surroundings. Look at yourself. You have cuts all along your arms and face. Your clothes have practically been shredded."

The elf put his hand on Aaron's forehead and pressed hard. "Ow!"

"You also have a nasty bruise on your forehead. I expect

the entire forest heard the crack when you smashed into that tree branch. Lucky for you, humans have thick skulls. Yours more than most, I suspect."

He gestured to the pack on Aaron's back. "Eglerion explained to me that food replenishes your energy at an accelerated rate. So eat. You'll need it."

Aaron shrugged the pack off his back and tore into a loaf of bread. He soon felt the energy returning to his limbs.

"By the time I leave here, do you think I'll be able to keep up with you at your full speed?"

Castien laughed. "If you could achieve that feat, I would be very impressed. For now, let's just build up your endurance and work on your ability to move in a more natural manner. I promise that with dedicated effort, you'll see significant improvement. Perhaps you'll even be able to to surprise me, but I doubt it."

Aaron finally caught his breath enough to notice his surroundings. The rocky outcropping overlooked a shady vale touched here and there by slanting rays of sunlight.

"What is this place?" he asked. "It's beautiful."

Castien sighed. "This is a place I enjoy coming to when I want to clear my mind. Now hurry up with your food. I smell rain coming. If you think you had difficulty before, wait until you see the course when it's wet."

Aaron wolfed down a second loaf of bread and a flagon of water. "Oh yeah, that sounds fun," he said weakly, and not at all convincingly.

# TOOLS OF PROPHECY

Jared relaxed in the cabin, looking through a few books on wizardry that Eglerion had left for him. He had to admit, it was a great place for study. The lodgings were opulent compared to the utilitarian accommodations he'd grown used to in Aubgherle, with furniture carved from some very dark wood that reminded Jared of ebony.

It was surreal when he stopped to think about it. Here he was, sitting in an elven city in an ancient forest, studying wizardry. *I'm pretty sure no school counselor ever predicted "wizard" as a career path for me,* he thought wryly.

The books were fascinating, though, and he quickly learned something about elves he'd never have otherwise known. They had only one wizard among them at any given time, and all the race's collective magical powers were somehow invested in that one wizard. When he or she died, that same power would pass on to an heir.

Eglerion, it turned out, was not the current wizard. So although he knew more about wizardry than probably anyone in all of Trimoria, he couldn't actually *do* any of it. For him, it was a purely academic pursuit. But he took his work seriously. One of the books had been penned by him, laying out the teaching methods and practices he used with his pupils. Jared had already determined he was going to ask to borrow this book, beg if he had to—it was just what he needed to help him set up a curriculum at the new magic academy.

In fact, while he was here, it made sense that he take a

look at Eglerion's classroom. Besides, he had only a short time in the elven city, and he didn't intend to spend the entire time with his nose in a book. So he set the books aside, left the cabin, and took a stroll toward the town center, absorbing every detail.

When he passed an elf carrying a bundle of kindling on his back, he waved him down. "Excuse me," he said, "can you tell me where I can find Eglerion's classroom?"

"Ah, you must be Lord Riverton!" The elf's face brightened. "If you follow the path you're on and veer to the left as you approach the market, you'll see a large structure with no entrances. That is our lore master's building."

Jared raised an eyebrow. "Did you say a building with no entrances?"

"Yes, m'lord. Our lore master is a bit unusual. He spends most of his time in there or with his student, Labriuteleanan, who is to be our queen. Rumor has it that he does little apart from studying wizardry."

"Well, thank you," Jared said. "I'm sorry to keep you."

"No trouble at all."

Jared walked in the direction the elf had indicated, and soon he found a building that was just as the elf had described. But as he stood outside, wondering what to do next, a hidden door popped open in the building's side, and a beautiful elven girl poked her head out.

"Please come in, Lord Riverton."

Jared sighed. "I was kind of looking forward to figuring

out the puzzle. Are you Eglerion's student... Labrut... that is to say, are you the future queen?"

The elven girl smiled. "Guilty as... ahh... AHH-CHOO!" She sniffled. "Sorry. Yes, guilty as charged. Call me Labri."

The door led to what was obviously a classroom. Its walls were full of charts of facts and figures, illustrations of anatomy, and various diagrams that Jared didn't understand. Shelves held bottles containing various animal and plant specimens suspended in liquid, and among them were what looked like snarled puzzles of wire. And of course there were books. Books everywhere.

Ryan was seated at a desk, with Eglerion hovering over him, both of them analyzing a diagram of a human brain, but Ryan looked up as soon as Jared stepped inside.

"Did you say just 'future queen'?"

Labri laughed. "You didn't know?"

"You didn't tell me," Ryan countered. "I thought the queen was trapped by the Seed of Trimoria."

"She is," Eglerion said. "And when she dies, her power will transfer to Labri."

Ryan gazed at Labri with a wide-eyed expression.

Eglerion turned to Jared. "Your son is having trouble understanding why he needs to learn the basics before he practices. It seems he's used to just... randomly testing his theories."

Jared winced. "Sorry, that's my fault. Experimentation was the only way we were able to learn."

"Well, I'm afraid that bad habit will have to be broken.

Just because a toddler can carry a torch, that doesn't mean it's a good idea for him to walk around with fire in his hand."

"I'm not a toddler…" Ryan grumbled.

"Ryan," said Jared, "your teacher knows more about magic than you and I could ever learn in a lifetime. If you aren't listening to his every word, you're just embarrassing yourself. Eglerion is ensuring that you understand the theory and precautions before you do something that could cause harm."

Ryan's face flushed.

"He has the exuberance and impatience of youth," said Eglerion. "Perhaps an illustration of why we must be cautious is in order. Lord Riverton, would you indulge me?"

"Whatever you need," Jared said.

"Good. Let's head outside. I don't want to burn the building down."

"Burn the building down?" Ryan asked, sounding nervous.

But Jared grinned and followed Eglerion as the lore master led them down a path to a wide clearing. The teacher pointed for Ryan to walk to the center of the clearing while the rest of them stood along the tree line.

The lore master then shouted to Ryan. "You are familiar with the concept of pushing a thread of power at something like a rock, or a buzzing fly near your head, yes?"

Ryan nodded. "Yes, I know how that works."

"Good. And I understand that you can create a web of power?"

Ryan smiled. "You mean like this?"

A thin thread of sparkling energy erupted from his hand

and split lengthwise. Those threads in turn split into finer and finer threads, until a hazy wall hovered before him. A few insects that had the misfortune of flying into the haze fell to the ground, stunned.

Jared felt his heart swell with pride at his son's ability.

"Very good," Eglerion said. "A web like the one you wield is tremendously useful. For although a wizard is powerful, he is as vulnerable to physical attack as anyone else. One punch to your head, or anything else that sufficiently disturbs your concentration, and you are helpless. Which is why it's critical that a wizard be able to shape such a web into a shield."

Jared nodded. There had been no time yet for him to teach Ryan this new skill himself, but he was eager to see how Eglerion went about it. This would be as educational for him as it was for Ryan.

The lore master went over the technique, and Ryan quickly got the hang of it. Soon Eglerion was repeating the exact same experiment that Jared had done with Aaron—flinging pebbles.

*We really are a lot alike*, Jared thought.

At first Ryan's shield held, knocking away the pebbles, and Ryan smiled victoriously. But Eglerion didn't stop there. He had grabbed a whole handful of pebbles and sent them rapid fire at Ryan's shield, one after the other. And each time a pebble hit, the web was pushed and tilted. Finally one of the pebbles slipped through and struck Ryan's forehead. Instantly his entire shield collapsed in a loud whuff and explosion of flame.

As Ryan stomped out the small grass fire burning at his

feet, Eglerion said, "As you noticed, your shield moves when struck—even from mere pebbles. Which is why you must anchor it. This time, push more energy into it—much more. The more energy, the more rigid it will be. Also, I want your next shield to surround you. There is no point in being shielded if someone can merely come up on you from behind."

Ryan nodded, then created a new web. This one was like a cocoon, completely surrounding him.

"I did it!" he said. "But now I can't see anything. Everything's hazy."

Labri called across the clearing. "Keep pushing more power. The shield will eventually become transparent."

Eglerion glared down at her. "Young lady, do you want to teach this class?"

She shrugged. "Was I wrong?"

The old elf grunted.

Ryan concentrated, and the haze gradually faded. He smiled, but Jared saw that his son was struggling to maintain the required flow of energy.

Eglerion set aside the pebbles and hefted a rock the size of a baseball. "Ready?"

"Yes, sir," Ryan said confidently.

Eglerion threw the rock. When it hit Ryan's shield, it was knocked aside with a giant spark.

"Whoa! I felt that!" Ryan shouted.

Eglerion smiled. "I would suggest you ensure your shield is tightly woven. That will better spread impacts across your body. Right now, your shield is like chain mail. It will prevent penetration, but you'll feel the blows and can still be injured by them. With practice, you'll be able to turn your shield into something more like plate armor. Even then you'll still feel the impacts, but not so much that they injure you."

Interesting. Jared hadn't thought of it that way, but it completely made sense. He resolved to practice this technique himself. But at the moment, he wanted to try something else.

He turned to Eglerion. "May I attempt a magical attack?"

The elf frowned. "I have never had two wizard students, so have never been able to try that. But according to theory, the shield should be effective against magical attacks." His frown turned to a smile. "When you're ready, Lord Riverton."

Jared sent a shimmering bolt of energy at Ryan. It struck the shield, which shimmered all over, popping and crackling as the bolt's energy was dispersed.

"It worked!" Ryan shouted.

Eglerion erupted with laughter. "Very good. But don't be overconfident. You are not invincible. If a mountain falls on top of you, I don't care how strong a shield you can generate, it will not be sufficient. Also, you'll need to build up your energy stores. In times of war, times we know lie ahead, you must be able to maintain a shield even as you fight."

Jared raised his hand like he was another of the lore master's pupils, which he supposed he was. "I didn't know we could expand our energy stores. How is that done?"

"Through practice, of course," Eglerion said simply. "It's no different than any other form of exercise. The more you use your energy, as long as you do so regularly, the more stamina you build. This is one reason why elven wizards have superior stamina—long life. Labriuteleanan, for instance, has been practicing her mental exercises for over a century now."

Ryan, obviously tiring, lowered his shield and rejoined the others. "Clearly I have a lot to learn. And practice. I'm willing to do whatever is needed."

Eglerion raised an eyebrow. "Good. To begin with, put that shield back up, and keep it up. I want you to maintain it during all waking hours—from the moment you rise to the moment you go to bed. I'll test you unexpectedly, and so will Labriuteleanan. Failing the test will mean you get hit in the head with a rock. Or perhaps in more uncomfortable places."

Labri threw a pebble at Ryan, almost hitting him in a spot where he'd rather never get hit.

"Hey!" Ryan shouted, then joined in her laughter—and very quickly restored his shields.

---

"Welcome to my humble abode, Lord Riverton," Xinthian said. "Please come in."

Jared stepped inside—and felt like he'd entered a library. Shelves filled every wall from floor to ceiling, all of them crammed with books.

"Xinthian, are you also Eluanethra's librarian?"

Xinthian smiled. "Lord Riverton, what in the world would make you say that?"

"Well, I would say that the bookshelves might be a hint. And please stop with the 'Lord Riverton' stuff. We're not in public. If I can call you Xinthian, you can call me Jared. I insist."

"Of course, Jared. Let's go upstairs to sit and relax. I may not look like I'm approaching one thousand years old, but I feel it in my bones, and have grown to appreciate a nice fireplace and a comfortable chair."

Xinthian led Jared upstairs to his study, where once again the walls were filled with books. Jared smiled as he breathed in the warm scents of leather, parchment, and wood. In one corner, a small fireplace was burning bricks of what looked vaguely like peat moss. A wooden desk stood against one wall, while two overstuffed chairs were positioned near the hearth.

Xinthian went to a cart that held a carafe and several opaque glasses. He poured two glasses of an amber liquid and handed one of the glasses to Jared as they sat in the chairs by the fire.

"This is a wine that we make in Eluanethra. I hope you enjoy it."

Jared sipped. The wine had a crisp, refreshing taste, with a hint of honeysuckle. "This is wonderful."

Xinthian took a much larger swallow. "I tend to agree," he said with a wink. "Now. I presume you're here because you have questions for me."

"Well, yes, as a matter of fact. Mostly about Seder."

The elf nodded knowingly, as if he'd expected this to be

the topic. "Ah, yes. I'm sure it was quite startling to have him visit your dreams for the first time."

"The first time? You mean… this wasn't the first time he spoke to you?"

"It's the second. The first time was over five hundred years ago, just before the demons invaded Trimoria. It was only thanks to his warning that our armies were not completely destroyed. We were able instead to fend off the demon attack and seal what remained of Trimoria against further incursion."

"It seems a visit from Seder is a sign of dark times ahead."

Xinthian nodded somberly. "It was then, and I fear it is once again."

Jared sighed. "Not that we didn't know that already, thanks to the prophecy. But now… now I know I have a lot of work to do. Seder told me I must create an academy of learning, and greatly expand the presence of wizardry in Trimoria. I'm also supposed to resurrect the Conclave of Wizards… which seems impossible, given that I know of only three wizards in this world. Me, Ryan, and your queen. And she may not be… suited to a conclave."

Jared paused, choosing his words carefully so as not to offend. "Based on some journals we found, I believe Queen Ellisandrea is trapped within an orb possessed by an extremely evil presence. And that experience may have corrupted her."

Jared watched Xinthian carefully, watching for a reaction.

"Your assessment of our queen is not far off the mark," he said softly. "What happened to her is a long and sad story. But let us speak of that another day. What else did Seder tell you?"

"Well, he mentioned a creature called Sammael, a spirit of chaos—and Seder's brother. I'm supposed to undo some of the actions that Sammael has set in motion. Do you know anything about this Sammael?"

Xinthian sipped at the wine and pursed his lips. "Sammael is everything that Seder is not. He is known by some as the Destroyer of Souls, while Seder is known by many as the Creator. I think if we wanted to generalize things, some might say Sammael rules those with evil in their hearts, while Seder is a guiding light for those who favor all that is good. If you would like, I can ask our scholars to search our histories for more information."

Jared nodded. "I would be indebted to you for any help or guidance you can provide."

Xinthian leaned back in his chair. "I can give you one piece of guidance right now: Trust your instincts, and don't let worry drive your actions. I've known several people who have received messages from Seder over my lifetime. The messages always seem cryptic at first, but time brings clarity to such things."

Jared smiled. "So far, worry has served me well in this world. I sometimes believe only the paranoid survive."

---

Jared rubbed his belly contentedly as he headed back to his sleeping quarters. The dinner with the council of elders had been very productive. He'd managed to get them to agree to aid not only in the construction, but in the operation of the new academy of magic. Although he suspected the main reason they agreed was that he already had Xinthian's backing.

He arrived back at the cabin at the same time as Ryan, who looked exhausted. As soon as they both went inside, Ryan collapsed on his bed.

"I think my head is going to explode, Dad. I've been pummeled. I've had sticks dropped on my head. I've been made to memorize steps for using my powers in ways that Eglerion says I'm not ready to attempt. On the plus side, I nearly caught a tree on fire."

Jared suppressed a grin. "You think you can handle two months of this?"

"Honestly? I have no choice. If it doesn't kill me, I think I'll look back at what I know now and be appalled at my ignorance."

"I doubt Eglerion will let you die."

"I don't know, Dad. I thought you pushed me hard before, but Eglerion makes your demands seem like a vacation."

"Well, good," Jared said. "Because I've arranged to borrow Eglerion to teach at the academy when the time comes. So guess what? Even after you're done here, you'll continue to enjoy the special benefits of his teaching."

Ryan groaned. "Not helping, Dad." Then he looked up as if something had just occurred to him. "Does that mean Labri would be coming, too?"

"I can't imagine she and Eglerion would part company."

Ryan groaned again.

"What's wrong?" Jared asked. "Do you not like Labri?"

"No, she's fine. She's nice, when she's not throwing rocks at me. But did you know that elves bathe in public, and think nothing of being naked in front of others? Arabelle is not going to be happy to have me hanging around with a naked elf."

Jared burst into laughter. "I guess it'll be up to you to educate her on human customs. Just tell her that nudity makes you uncomfortable and might get you into trouble with your betrothed. She'll understand."

The door banged open and Aaron staggered in. At least, Jared thought it was Aaron. He looked more like a bedraggled, mud-covered human-shaped lump of flesh. And just like Ryan had done when he came in, Aaron collapsed onto his bed.

"Had an easy day playing in the forest," said Ryan, brightly. "But you didn't need to bring half of it in with you."

Jared chuckled. "Ryan, help your brother off his bed before he makes a mess of it. It's time to eat. I brought a bunch of food from dinner because I wasn't sure what you'd be getting."

As soon as the word "eat" left Jared's mouth, Aaron bolted upright.

Jared set out the food, and his boys wolfed it down. He'd thought there might be enough for breakfast, too—for all three of them—but when they were done, not a morsel remained.

"Well, Aaron, now that you've shoveled down a day's

worth of food, how about you explain why you're covered in mud from head to toe?"

Aaron shook his head, grinning. The food had clearly brightened his mood. "You wouldn't believe how strong Castien is, Dad. And he moves like a deer through the woods. I guarantee you, he could defeat Throll without even breaking a sweat. The next couple of months are going to be *awesome*."

Jared laughed. "It seems like the harder things get, the more difficult the challenge, the more you enjoy it." He ruffled Aaron's dirty hair fondly.

"Oh! I have something I want to show you guys." Aaron suddenly dived for his mud-splattered backpack, and pulled out two round stones. "I'd fallen in a mud pit—I did that a lot today—and these rocks seemed totally out of place. I'm not sure, but I thought it might be damantite, Dad. It's got that red and black thing you described."

Jared weighed one of the stones in his hand. It was lighter than the metal he'd found in Azazel's tower. "It does seem metallic, but the weight isn't quite right for damantite. I have no idea what it is."

Ryan leaned in. "How about we see if they can hold a charge? And how much?"

"Still an experimenter," Jared said, handing the stones to his son. "I don't think that's a habit Eglerion is going to be able to break."

Ryan grinned. "Eglerion is an experimenter too, he just won't admit it."

He set the stones on the table and pushed two tiny threads of power at them. They both began to glow.

"Start counting!" Aaron said with excitement.

Jared was just about to, but right then both stones began to spark.

Ryan sat back. "Darn. They're full already."

"Weird," said Jared. "Maybe they aren't actually solid, and that's why they're so light? Or maybe they have lots of impurities."

"Can I keep one?" Ryan asked Aaron. "I'd like to study it. At a minimum, it'll do as a nightlight," he added with a chuckle.

Aaron nodded. "Sure. Maybe I'll use the other as a nightlight too."

Jared laughed. "Look at my boys. Both of you are practically married, and yet you still need nightlights." He raised his communication ring. "Should I send a message to Sloane and Arabelle and tell them you're both afraid of the dark?"

Aaron's eyes went wide. "Dad, you wouldn't."

"Tell you what. Go wash up—thoroughly—and I'll keep this our little secret."

Jared had never before seen his youngest son move so fast.

# A DIFFERENT KIND OF SCHOOL

Today was Sloane's day off from chores, so she went with her father to check on the progress of the wizard's school. She hadn't been down here in a few days, and she was impressed by the flurry of activity. Dozens of craftsmen were hard at work, and it looked like they'd almost completed the barracks.

Jared met them in the yard. He'd come back from the elven city a couple of weeks earlier. "Good news," he said. The foreman says they're ahead of schedule. The school will almost be ready by the time Ryan and Aaron get back."

Sloane cut in. "And um… when will that be?"

She hated to admit how much she missed Aaron. She'd barely been able to talk to him, as the elves had limited their use of their rings. Apparently talking with one's betrothed was considered a distraction from their training.

Jared smiled sympathetically. "One more month to go."

Father pulled her into a one-armed hug. "I know you miss them. I'm sure they're fine." To Jared, he added, "I didn't like losing my pupil, but it was a good decision to immerse them in a completely different environment. And there's no doubt the elves will help their training. I feel sorry for their mother, though. It's clear Aubrey misses them."

Jared nodded. "She's never been away from the boys this long. It's probably a good thing that Rebecca is demanding so much of her attention."

"And you?" Father asked. "Are you keeping busy?"

Jared laughed and gestured to the construction. "Are you kidding me? I don't get a moment's rest! Plus, we've had our first students arrive just this morning. Four of them. So it looks like training will have to begin whether we're ready for them or not."

"Can we meet the new rams?" Sloane asked.

"Rams?"

Sloane smiled. "Oh, you haven't heard? That's what some of the citizens are saying. Riverton Academy of Magic, R-A-M. So the students are rams. I was thinking maybe we could find a ram to keep on the grounds of the school. You know, as a mascot."

Jared laughed. "I like that idea. And yes, I was just on my way to meet the new 'rams' myself, so please join me. Honestly, I'm just delighted we're finding anyone at all, given Azazel's efforts to destroy anyone with even a hint of magic."

"Well, it looks like my edict is having some effect," Father said. "Everyone is required to screen themselves within the fountains, and if they light up the orb, they're to come here for training. All that started just a week ago, so you're just seeing the first batch—likely the locals. Who knows how many more we may find once word spreads throughout Trimoria?"

"I just hope they're not all infants. Or old men with one foot in the grave."

They strolled across the field to the building that would one day be the main schoolhouse, when it was finished. Sloane was surprised to see that someone had painted, or attempted to paint, a red ram on the door.

Father led the way into the schoolhouse's central great room. Or at least, it would eventually be a great room. For now it was a mess of tools, wood, and sawdust... and arguing.

Two dwarfs stood at the other end of the room in heated debate. One had glasses and a braided black beard; the other was built like a soldier—broad chest, muscled arms and legs—and wore a guard's outfit with a short sword belted on his waist. He was also tall for a dwarf, standing just over four feet.

"There is no way those dice are right!" the shorter dwarf yelled. "Let me see them! You couldn't have won six times in a row!"

The taller dwarf bristled. "Are ye calling me a cheat?" He launched himself at his kinsman.

But before the two could meet, a sizzling web erupted between them, enveloping them in an immobilizing blanket of energy.

Jared turned to Sloane's father. "Can you believe they

didn't even acknowledge their king as he entered the room?" he asked with mock incredulity. "That kind of thing has to be punishable by... what? Painful torture? Dismemberment?"

Her father scratched his chin, looking pensive. "I can forgive them for not recognizing their new king, but I would think they might have acted with more restraint when the school's headmaster entered the room."

"Excellent point." Jared turned to the dwarves, levitating them off the ground. "When I let you two go, I expect better behavior."

He snapped his fingers, the web of energy disappeared, and the two dwarves crashed to the floor before scrambling back to their feet and bowing quickly.

The smaller dwarf spoke first. "I'm terribly sorry, Your Highness and Lord Wizard. I had hoped to meet you under different circumstances. I've read tremendous amounts about magic, but I've never seen it used in my presence. I'm thrilled to become a RAM student."

"What's your name?" Jared asked.

"Yes, Headmaster," the dwarf replied. He looked confused. "How did you know?"

Jared looked even more confused. "What?"

The dwarf nodded. "Yes, Headmaster?"

Jared and Sloane's father looked at each other and shrugged.

The taller dwarf spoke. "Headmaster, he's trying to tell you his name *is* Wat."

Sloane suppressed a giggle.

"Ah," said Jared. "Nice to meet you, Wat. And what is your clan's name?"

"I have no clan," Wat mumbled, bowing his head in shame. "I was abandoned as a child, and raised in a human orphanage in Cammoria. But some of my friends called me Wat Crazybeard. For obvious reasons."

"Looks like a bunch of snakes on his face, if ye ask me," the larger dwarf mumbled.

Father frowned. "No insults, please. And you are?"

The larger dwarf kneeled. "My name is Oda Rockfist. I was part of Master Honfrion's caravan guard. When yer law was announced, I was forced to come for testin'. Though I don't understand what I've done to deserve dis."

"You went to the fountain?" Throll asked.

Oda nodded.

"And did the orb light up?"

Oda sighed. "Yes. But I didn't mean fer that to happen. I didn't do anyting wrong."

Father laid a hand on the dwarf's shoulder. "You've done nothing wrong, Oda. The fountain identifies people who have magical talents. And the orb doesn't lie. You gentlemen, both of you, are blessed with innate magic."

Oda grimaced. "I have no magical talent," he said, as though the words left a sour taste in his mouth. "And I'm certainly not a man."

"You have something against men, then?" Father asked.

Oda stopped short as if remembering who he was speaking to. "I—I'm sorry, Yer Highness. I guess I'm not very used to… genteel conversations. And to be honest, I feel like I've been put in a role I'm not suited for. What do we even do here? Am I supposed to be drawing pretty pictures of cows like Snake Face over there?"

Wat scowled. "It's a ram!"

Jared eyed the crazy-bearded dwarf. "So you're the one who painted the ram on the door?"

Wat looked at his feet. "I-I hope it's all right."

"It is more than all right. In fact, I think your picture will help the school spirit quite a bit."

Wat puffed his chest out proudly.

Jared turned to the taller dwarf. "And Oda, I understand your frustration, and I understand you didn't wish to be here. We'll do our absolute best to figure out a role that makes sense for you. But… I will *not* tolerate disrespect."

Oda blanched. "Yes, sir."

The headmaster turned to Sloane's father. "Would you mind if Oda trains with your soldiers while the school and its members are getting ready?"

Father passed the question to Oda. "Is that something you would want to do?"

For the first time, a smile crossed the dwarf's face. "Are ye kidding? Oda 'the One-Dwarf Army' is ready! Lead me to da soldiers! Er… I mean, please lead me to da soldiers, if'n it please yer royal sensibilities to do as such, Yer Highness, sir."

Sloane's father chuckled and slapped Oda on the back. "Follow me, Mr. One-Dwarf Army. I have some people for you to meet."

"So, Wat," said Jared, "I was told there were four new students. Where are the others?"

"Oh. They're outside. Follow me."

As Wat led him out the back door, Jared watched the braids on the dwarf's face sway crazily. Truly, he'd earned the name Crazybeard.

They found Ohaobbok sitting on a pile of wood outside, idly tossing pebbles into a bucket.

"Ohaobbok!" Jared said. "What are you doing here? I thought you'd be training with the soldiers."

"That's one of the other students," Wat said. "The other one is a girl. I hope he didn't eat her."

Jared couldn't believe it. Ohaobbok was the last person he'd have expected to be one of his students. An ogre wizard? Then again, why not?

Ohaobbok looked bored. "I tested at the fountain just this morning. And it lit up. So… here I am. I just hope I still get to train with Aaron when he comes back. I like knocking him down."

"I'm sure we'll find time for you two to bruise each other," Jared said drily. "And where is our other student?"

Ohaobbok shrugged. "Oh, Arabelle's around here somewhere."

"Wait—did you say *Arabelle*?"

At that moment she came around the corner of the building, accompanied by several merchant soldiers. And she was crying. When she saw Jared, she ran to him and buried her face in his chest.

"They made me bathe in the fountain," she sobbed. "The orb lit up."

Jared patted her awkwardly.

One of the guards stepped forward, bowed respectfully, and handed Jared a folded piece of parchment. "Lord Riverton, the sheikh has asked that I give this to you."

The parchment was sealed with the mark of Honfrion, the merchant king. Jared broke the seal and read.

*Jared,*

*I know you will understand when I say that I take my role as Arabelle's guardian very seriously. And when she lit up the orb in the fountain, destining her for a place at your academy, I was forced to make a decision I do not take lightly.*

*It's my duty to watch over my daughter. But it's also my duty to protect the welfare of my people. To do the former, I would stay with her wherever she must go. However, to do the latter, I must stay with my caravan as it moves on its trading routes.*

*Thus it is with great hesitance, but equal trust in your stewardship, that I put Arabelle in your hands, dear friend. Please take care of my daughter as I would while I'm doing what I must. I will cover any expenses that that entails, and I'll never forget such a kindness under such trying times.*

*Please know that Arabelle has an important role in this world. My dearly departed wife knew this before Arabelle was even born. She saw in Arabelle the future of my people.*

*That future now lies with you.*


*Your brother-in-law to be,*
  *Honfrion*


Jared tightened his arms around the distraught girl. "Arabelle, you have nothing to worry about. Your father will return when he can. Please… look at this as a new chapter in life. Things happen because they are meant to be."

He then turned to the soldier. "Sir…"

"Tabor."

"Tabor. Please tell Honfrion that I'll take full responsibility for Arabelle. She'll be safe in my hands."

Tabor banged his fist to his chest in salute. "Thank you, Lord Riverton." He turned to face Arabelle and gave her a bow. "Farewell, Princess. I will see you again at the end of the season when the caravans return."

And with that, Tabor and his men turned and departed.

Arabelle looked up at Jared, still sniffling, but drying her tears. "When will Ryan return?"

Jared smiled. "He'll be back from Eluanethra in a month.

And I can assure you, he'll be delighted to find out you're here."

That brightened her outlook a bit, as he'd known it would.

"Now, let's talk about quarters. Most students will be staying here at the academy, but Ohaobbok, I see no need you should move from Throll's, since it's just a short walk away. And Arabelle, I'll make arrangements for you to stay with Sloane. As for you, Wat…"

"I'll stay in the barracks, as is expected, Headmaster. But… might I ask for something to read? I already miss the library in Cammoria."

"That can be arranged," Jared said with a chuckle.

---

It was late, and the house was asleep, but Jared couldn't get his mind to rest. Too many things were still undone. Rising from his bed, he went to the crib in the corner, where Rebecca slept, sucking on her fist as she often did.

Jared smiled at her peaceful expression, though he was worried about her, too. Not surprisingly, the fountain had identified her as a potential magic user as well. He hoped, for her sake, she would turn out to be a healer like her mother, not a war wizard like him.

Reluctantly, he lay back down in bed, though he knew he wouldn't sleep. Aubrey never had a problem with insomnia. She slept contentedly no matter how much work she took on —which lately, was quite a lot. In addition to taking care of the baby, she'd been teaching some of the local children how to read, which was an uncommon skill for the people of these lands. She'd started with just Gwen and Sloane, but eventually her class had grown to over a dozen, including a few adults.

Although it was late, Jared decided to tap out a message on his ring.

*Jared here. Goodnight, boys. I miss you.*

Moments later, a message came back.

*Aaron here. Ryan sleeping. Things going great. Ryan learning tricks. I'm way stronger. Think can maybe beat Throll now. Going sleep. Love you. Goodnight.*

And then another message followed.

*Throll here. I have more tricks you haven't seen. Good luck trying to beat me. We all miss you. Hurry back.*

Jared chuckled. Using the rings to communicate was like always being on a conference call. There was no such thing as a private message. Perhaps he should have made more paired rings, like the ones Ryan and Arabelle had. He imagined having a hand full of rings, each for a different person. Things would get complicated quick.

And there were so many more important things to be done. His conversation with Seder, as well as the visions of the upcoming war, suggested his responsibility wasn't to fight, but rather to prepare those who would fight. And building a new force of wizardry out of raw, untested recruits was a daunting task. It was almost enough to make him yearn for the days of Azazel. At least back then, he only had to concentrate on a single evil target.

Not an entire demon horde.

---

Ellisandrea was surrounded by an inky blackness, a trap of Zenethar's creation. But she was content, for she had the Seed. The Seed of Trimoria. And it was far greater than a beautiful orb of crystal.

The Seed contained a piece of Sammael himself.

He spoke to her. He gave her powers. He understood her like nobody had before.

Only occasionally did Ellisandrea think of the outside world, away from Sammael. They were not fond memories. She remembered in particular the elves, of whom she'd been born. Her hatred for them permeated every cell of her being. And she would, one day, exact her revenge. Sammael would insist upon it.

*Ellisandrea, we must finish what we started.* His voice spoke all around her. *Azazel has failed. Zenethar must be destroyed. After all this time, he still maintains the barrier. It must go down.*

"I know, my dear Sammael," the elf queen replied. "Dominic will follow our plan. He will destroy the intruders from beyond Trimoria, starting with the children."

*We do not have the time to wait. A change comes. The strings of destiny are vibrating, and we must ensure they vibrate in the desired manner. Which is why I have infused*

*Dominic with a part of my essence. He will need this power to compete with the forces arrayed against him.*

Ellisandrea felt a pang of jealousy. After all her work, *Dominic* was the one to gain an essence from the one she loved?

*But Dominic alone is not enough,* the voice continued. *We need more like him. You must attract them here so that I can touch them. Influence them. Only then will we bring the barrier down. And I will rule the land, with you as my right hand.*

"People avoid the forest, my love. And my influence can only reach so far."

*Then let me show you something new. A way to transmit magical influence through sound.*

Ellisandrea shuddered as oily tendrils of Sammael's being invaded her mind. At once she felt exhilarated and horrified as he *adjusted* her. A new perception snapped awake in her mind like a torch blazing in a shadowy corner.

"I understand," she said. "I'll do as you wish. They'll soon learn the meaning of suffering."

# TRAINING

After a long day of training, Ryan was lying in his bed, staring up at the earthen ceiling, when the world suddenly turned white. The ceiling was gone, the bed, everything. Even himself. When he reached out with his hand, he couldn't see it.

And then a voice spoke. *"Ryan, I know your father has spoken of me. You can address me as Seder."*

He recalled what his father had told him about this spirit. Was it God? Something else?

*"Ryan, I'm here to give you a warning, and a gift."*

"What warning? What kind of gift?"

*"You are aware of an agent of destruction called Sammael. He has influence on your world that I cannot explain. Currently, his minions are stalking you and your brother. They*

*intend to kill you both, and they intend to do this simultaneously."*

"What? Seder, wake me up! I need to warn Aaron. I—"

*"You are safe in the elven city. My warning is for the future. Your danger lies outside of Eluanethra."*

"How do you know this?"

*"I sense the thoughts of all creatures in Trimoria. And I feel things through you as you feel them."*

"But—Azazel is dead. We—"

*"Sammael has adopted a new servant to replace the one he lost. And that servant has already hired two others to assassinate you and your brother. And before you ask it, the answer is no, I do not know who the servant and assassins are. I know only that they exist."*

Ryan groaned. "You mentioned a gift?"

*"Your education is progressing much faster than your teacher believed possible. That is because you are what the wizards of a different era labeled an Archmage. You have the potential to be the most powerful wizard Trimoria has seen in many millennia.*

*"Because of that, I am able to grant you a skill that other wizards might not be able to handle. When I release you, you will have the ability to manipulate minds."*

"What does that mean?"

*"You will see how the mind and magic are linked. You will learn to influence those links. But I caution you, you can do irreparable harm to someone by carelessly playing with their mind. Study the mind. Study how it works. And consult with*

*Eglerion. He possesses knowledge you will need. Use your time in Eluanethra wisely, for when you reenter the larger world, more than just your own lives will be at stake."*

---

The next morning, as Ryan walked to the lore master's classroom, the world seemed different. Or more specifically, the people seemed different. Whenever he focused on a person, he saw a faint aura around their head, a nearly transparent shimmer, like the shimmer of heat waves over a campfire.

*What did Seder do to me?*

Realizing that his conversation with Seder hadn't been a dream and the spirit had turned something on within him, he ran to Eglerion's classroom and told the lore master about everything.

Eglerion remained silent for a long moment, then smiled. "Interesting." He curled his finger at Ryan and pointed at his own head. "Tell me what you see."

Ryan came in close and applied his new vision. "Well... it's kind of weird. It's like your head is glowing with a very faint light." He stepped closer and really focused. "Hang on... I see... whoa, it's little dots. Pinholes. Across almost every square inch of your head. Across the top of your skull, along the back and sides. And... wait, it's like the longer I look, the more I see. Each of these dots has a different shape. Almost like—a bunch of keyholes!"

Ryan stepped back as everything became crystal clear.

"It's not an aura at all. It's more like… a dense web of strings. Out of each of those tiny keyholes, a thread emerges and loops back into another keyhole. It's just that there's so many, they form a kind of general glow. This is really, really weird."

"It's amazing," Eglerion said. "I cannot begin to tell you how exceedingly rare this gift is. There are reports of such abilities in the most ancient of our histories, but I'd never hoped to encounter one such as yourself."

"So you know what this is? What I'm seeing?"

"Yes. Those ephemeral threads you're seeing are what makes a person who they are. A physical manifestation of their inner selves."

"You mean like a computer's programming?"

"I… don't know what that means."

"Sorry. I mean… do these threads tell me what kind of magical abilities a person has?"

"They tell you much more than that. You see, we are all, each of us, but a shard of a much greater power, and that power imprints upon each of us a unique identity. What you see is a hint of that ephemeral connection to the greater power."

"I'm not following."

"You will, in time. But for now, suffice it to say that these threads can show you not only abilities—magical, physical, mental—but identity. It's all a matter of discerning the patterns. Which means it's a matter of practice."

"Is that a good idea? Seder warned me it can be dangerous."

Eglerion's voice took on a serious tone. "With the sight you now have, you could literally reconstruct who someone is—simply by manipulating the connections you see. You could give sight to the sightless, or improve a tracker's skill at woodcraft. Or... you could make a person forget how to breathe."

"Forget how to breathe?"

"Hence the danger. Seder is right. Use of this ability will require careful study."

The lore master turned to a bookshelf and scanned through the titles until he found what he was looking for. He pulled a book down, flipped through it, and showed Ryan a hand-drawn illustration: a man with a cloud of threads sprouting from various spots on his head, like a rat's nest of wiring.

"Study this book. You may not appreciate some of what it says, because it speaks of the spirit world, which doesn't follow the rules of magic that you and I know. But it will teach you much about the source of the mind's power, and in many ways, the source of life itself. And it will teach you about those threads, the patterns they make, and the resulting colors that emerge—some of which go beyond the normal range of colors we have words for."

Ryan frowned. "Thank you. I'll study and read every word of it."

"Good. And when you're done, read it again. Then we will go over it together. With a skill such as this... we cannot be too careful."

"Can't sleep?" Aaron asked.

Ryan looked over at his brother, his face visible in the glow of the nightlight rocks. It was late, and they should both be asleep. Most nights they passed out the minute their heads hit the pillow. But tonight…

Ryan sighed. "I don't know. My mind is just… racing with everything I'm learning. I'm trying to sort it all out. Why are *you* awake?"

"I don't know." He chuckled. "Actually, that's the problem: I don't know. I thought I was a great fighter, and now… I realize how little I actually know. Every time I finally think I'm mastering something Castien is teaching me, he introduces a completely different wrinkle to it and I realize just how much I suck."

"I'm sure you don't suck. Castien is just in a completely different league than anyone else. He's been practicing for centuries. If he isn't the best fighter in Trimoria, I can't imagine who might be."

"Well, I won't argue with that."

"And you're getting better, right? And stronger?"

"Oh, I'm definitely getting stronger. My endurance is better too, though I have to eat like a horse to keep up with Castien. I swear, he *enjoys* making me fail."

"Or maybe he's just doing what he thinks is best for you—and for all of us," Ryan said. "I mean, let's face it, that damned prophecy… we're not ready for all that. And we need to be."

"Eglerion give you a hard time too?"

"He's definitely pushing me. Hard. Lately he's not only been making me hold my shield and cast spells at the same time, I have to do it while balancing on uneven logs—and with Labri chucking things at me. Which I *know* she enjoys. I feel like I've got Master Yoda telling me to 'feel the Force' and Princess Leia laughing at my incompetence."

"How can he tell you to feel the Force when he can't even feel it himself. I mean, like you said, Castien is good. *Really* good. But Eglerion... I don't get how he can train you if he can't even do any of it himself."

"Yeah, I had my doubts about that as well, but he really knows his stuff. It's like... well, imagine an old fighter who knows all the forms and what they should look like, but he's too fat or too broken to do them anymore. He can still teach."

"But Eglerion has never been a fighter—or magic user," Aaron said.

"I know. Which makes it all the more impressive that he's learned what he has. He can describe to me what I'm feeling, just by having studied it so much. And it's definitely helping. I mean *definitely*. At first I could barely hold the shield up for a couple hours before I was completely exhausted. Now I barely notice the power drain anymore."

"I wonder how our teachers feel about us," Aaron said. "They probably see us as a couple of knucklehead kids, and yet they're supposed to shape us into these great warriors in two months." He laughed. "Master Yoda never did seem too happy with Luke, did he?"

Ryan laughed too. "Well, Luke didn't do too bad in the end. All we can do is our best."

"Wait," said Aaron. "If we're Luke, then Dad is…"

"Vader!" they said together, and burst into laughter.

A loud *CRACK* interrupted their laughter, silencing them both. Both brothers bolted upright in their beds.

"What was *that*?" Aaron said.

Ryan realized that his side of the room had become dimmer, and he turned to the glowing rock on his nightstand. Only it wasn't glowing anymore.

"My rock broke!"

"What do you mean it broke? Did you hit it or something?"

"No, I didn't touch it. But it has a big crack right down the—"

The rock quivered.

"Uh… Aaron… you saw that, right?"

Aaron gulped. "Yep."

Ryan picked up the rock. It definitely had a crack in it, and it was getting wider. It also felt hot.

He dropped it when another *CRACK* sounded. It must have been Aaron's rock, because the room was suddenly cast into darkness.

"What's going on?" Aaron said.

Moonlight spilled in through the windows, and Ryan's eyes gradually adjusted to the lower light. And when they did, he couldn't believe what he was seeing.

The two sides of his stone had fallen away, revealing what looked like a newborn baby lizard.

Ryan tried to stay calm. It was just a baby, after all. But when it looked directly at him and belted out a high-pitched squeal, he instinctively raised a shield.

"Holy crap, Ryan... it has *wings*."

The lizard walked toward Ryan, and stepped right off of the nightstand. Without thinking, Ryan put his hand out and caught it. It weighed almost nothing. Just a baby lizard. Or a baby...

"Dragon," he whispered.

He gingerly stroked the top of the lizard's head with his thumb. It responded with a sound that was almost a purr.

"Ryan!" Aaron exclaimed. "I've got one coming out of my rock as well!"

Sure enough, the two sides of Aaron's rock had been pushed apart by another baby dragon, which looked up at Aaron and made a high-pitched squeal of its own.

"What do I do?" Aaron asked.

Ryan laughed at the bizarreness of the situation. "Pet it?"

Aaron cautiously stroked the creature's head, and it purred in response.

"Ryan remember when those ducks imprinted on us because we were there when they hatched? I'll bet you these guys think we're their dads!"

*I'm a dad*, Ryan thought. And for the moment anyway, all of the world's troubles vanished as he focused on his new role.

After cleaning the goopy mucus from the two baby dragons, the boys set them on the floor to explore their new surroundings. The cabin was now lit with candles, though they were placed up high where hopefully the newcomers wouldn't get burnt.

They were interesting creatures, about the size of kittens. And like kittens, they had a tendency to pounce—at dust, shadows, or nothing at all.

"They're actually cute now that they aren't covered in slime," Ryan said.

"Did you notice how they look black, but when the light from the candles hits them, it creates red highlights? Just like the rocks."

Ryan held out his hand and called to his dragon. "Come here, Squeak."

The dragon that had imprinted on him looked up from exploring the corner of the room. It waddled over to Ryan, squeaked, and curled up next to him.

"Only minutes old and he already knows his name."

Aaron frowned. "Do you think we'll get in trouble for having them? Should we keep them a secret? What do they eat? How big do you think they'll get? Will—"

Ryan held up a hand. "Enough. But you're right, we know nothing about dragons, baby or otherwise. I think it's time we go ask Eglerion for some answers."

## TOOLS OF PROPHECY

The lore master shook his head with amazement at the two dragons, who were in the middle of his classroom plunging their faces into bowls filled with minced venison and munching away contentedly.

"Living dragons," he whispered. "Beautiful."

"So they're rare?" Ryan asked. "I figure they must be, because we've been in Trimoria for two years now and no one's ever mentioned dragons before."

Eglerion chuckled. "Rare? The last natural dragons were believed to have died in the chaos of the demon wars. Not a one has been seen since… until now."

He leaned down to Squeak. "*Aht tsame?*"

Squeak raised his head and squeaked something that sounded like, "*Ken!*"

Eglerion pointed toward a bucket in the corner of the room, and the dragon waddled clumsily over to it and began slurping up some water.

"Did you two just have a conversation?" Ryan asked.

"Of course. Dragons are a majestic race of highly intelligent beings. Don't ever fool yourself into thinking they are simple animals. They speak a variation of the old tongue."

"And what did you say to him?" Aaron asked.

"I simply asked *her* if she was thirsty," Eglerion said.

"Wait—her?" Ryan said. "Squeak is a she? Er… how can you tell?"

Eglerion ignored the question. "Her name is not Squeak." He turned toward the dragons, both of whom were now drinking at the bucket of water. "*Ma hashemot shelchem?*" he called.

The dragons turned and uttered noises that sounded to Ryan like high-pitched squeaks, but to Eglerion it evidently made perfect sense.

"The one you called Squeak is Rubyrend," Eglerion said. "The other is a male who knows his name to be Crimsonpyre."

"Crimsonpyre…" Aaron said, grinning. "I mean I thought 'Squawk' was good, given 'Squeak' and all… but Crimsonpyre is way cooler."

"How can they know what their names are?" Ryan said.

"When a mother dragon lays her eggs," Eglerion explained in his professorial tone, "she instills in the unborn egg its identity and other abilities. Unlike those of us of lesser races, born knowing nearly nothing, a dragon is born with pre-existing knowledge and the ability to communicate. Collected within that innate knowledge, of course, is the dragon's name."

"I guess we'll need to learn how to speak dragon," Ryan said.

"I doubt you need to worry about that," Eglerion said. "Dragons have a keen intellect. These two will most assuredly learn Trimorian long before you two have learned even the basics of the old tongue."

Aaron smiled widely and turned to his brother. "Hey, remember how I always asked Dad for a talking parrot and never got one? How much better is a talking dragon?"

"Remember," Eglerion said sternly, "these are not animals, and certainly not pets. They're smart. You would be wise to treat them as friends… if not superiors."

"I always treat my pets like friends," Aaron said. "Pyre! Come here, Pyre!"

The male dragon turned from the bucket and waddled eagerly over to Aaron before ducking its head to be petted.

Aaron scratched just above the dragon's wings. "See? He already has a nickname. We're going to be great friends. You'll see."

By the shocked look on Eglerion's face, Ryan knew it was time to go.

---

When the boy's last week in Eluanethra arrived, Eglerion announced that it was time to measure Ryan's progress with a test. The task sounded simple enough—maintain his magical shield as he walked along a predetermined path, and to capture the flag at the finish line without sustaining any injuries. But this time, it seemed like all the elves in Eluanethra were participating. They'd been instructed to distract, injure, and if possible, incapacitate Ryan along the way.

He just hoped Labri wasn't among them. She would have too much fun.

The path started deep in the woods outside the elven city. Ryan had no trouble maintaining his shield here in this peaceful place, and he'd honed his senses to detect any hidden elves or traps. Eglerion had even taught him a trick that allowed him to make time seem to move more slowly. So when the arrow came flying at him, he was ready.

He sensed it long before it ever reached him. He heard the whistle of the feathers as they cut the air. And then he saw it. At least it didn't have a sharp tip, just a metal ball. Whoever had shot it didn't want to kill him, just hurt him. Not that he couldn't deflect even a sharpened arrow with his shield.

As he stepped nimbly aside, dodging the projectile, he sent a tiny spike of energy toward the spot from which the arrow had flown. A yelp of surprise indicated he'd struck his target.

*One down,* he thought. *Who knows how many more to go?*

---

Enduring his own test, Aaron ran after the elusive sword master. He soon realized they were following the exact same route he'd taken on his first day in Eluanethra. But today was different. Aaron was much more in tune with his energy reserves, and he didn't waste effort fighting his surroundings. He instinctively ducked and twisted around obstacles, as agile as an elf—if not quite as agile as Castien.

But then Castien took a new route. He veered off to one side and slipped through some underbrush. Aaron followed, and when he burst through the bushes on the other side, he couldn't believe what he was seeing.

Castien had just leapt across a ravine.

Aaron instinctively came to a stop. How wide *was* that ravine, anyway? Much too far to jump it.

But he had to try.

He took a few steps back, roared, and then sprinted with all his energy toward the ravine. Right at the edge he pushed off, using his preternatural strength to launch himself forward. When he landed softly on the other side, he breathed a sigh of relief. But he didn't slow. He landed at a run and continued racing after the elusive sword master.

He was determined that on this day he was going to do something he hadn't even begun to do on that first day in Eluanethra.

He was going to make Castien break a sweat.

---

Ryan had eliminated many different traps, he'd incapacitated a few sword-wielding elves who'd jumped out of the shadows, and he'd more than frustrated the efforts of a half-dozen archers. With his senses stretched, he found he could easily see the auras of the elves in the trees and underbrush all around.

*They can't hide from me.*

And now he'd finally reached the edge of the clearing. The flag stood just ahead, at its center. He could see it fluttering in the breeze. He was almost there.

He took a step forward…

Several bowstrings twanged all at once. Six, his senses told him. And time slowed once again. He studied them, all six, each coming from a different direction.

Yet their aim was off. All of them. Instead of heading for his shield, they were heading to either side—three to his left, and three to his right.

He cursed his foolishness. The arrows were trailing a very fine mesh between them. But it was too late to act. They passed him, and the mesh wrapped all the way around his cocoon-like shield. Sparks erupted everywhere, blinding him. And then the blows fell. Heavy blows aimed directly at his head. He ducked and dodged, unable to see his attacker. Or attackers.

He felt his panic build. His shield wouldn't withstand this onslaught for long. And if it failed, so did he.

With a wild shout, Ryan stood tall and sent a heavy pulse of energy in every direction. Two screams sounded in reply. The pounding stopped, and the mesh fell away in burning wisps.

Ryan wobbled unsteadily. But his shield was still intact, and he was uninjured. He staggered to the center of the clearing and captured the flag.

"Very impressive," shouted Eglerion from the trees. "You succeeded." He stepped forward into the light, a wide smile across his face. "But I do hope a *few* lessons were learned along the way."

The sword master jumped and ran as if he were part kangaroo and part gazelle, but Aaron kept after him. The problem was, his energy reserves had reached their bare minimum, and he could no longer afford any bursts of speed. If Castien had another trick like that ravine in mind, Aaron would lose him.

But he sensed they were reaching the end. They'd looped around, and were now heading back up the same slope where Aaron had lost the sword master during their first such race. This time Aaron didn't rely on strength or energy, but on skill and agility. He ducked branches, hopped over roots, and moved his arms and legs with cold efficiency.

He was keeping up with Castien.

But he wanted to win.

Despite his exhaustion, he exerted one last burst of speed in an effort to pull alongside Castien.

It didn't work. Aaron had come a long way in his time here in Eluanethra—a very long way—but outrunning Castien Galonos was a bridge too far.

Still, he'd at least made Castien work for his victory. When his teacher reached the summit, he took a seat in the grass. He wasn't breathing particularly hard, but there was a bead of sweat on his brow. Aaron was sure of it.

"You did very well, Aaron," Castien said as Aaron arrived.

Aaron collapsed to the ground. "No longer at a child's level, eh?" he said proudly.

Castien shrugged. "Perhaps a particularly athletic child."

Aaron rolled his eyes. "I figured you'd say something like that."

Castien chuckled and put a hand on Aaron's shoulder. "You did very well, Aaron Riverton. You have been a most satisfactory pupil."

Aaron beamed.

## LEAVING ELUANETHRA

Ryan and Aaron gathered in the Eluanethra council chambers with Xinthian, Eglerion, and Castien, to talk about their upcoming departure. They'd brought the dragons with them as well, which might not have been the best idea. The dragons were now the size of dogs, and played just as roughly. Before the discussion could even begin, their wrestling had sent them rolling into a table, knocking a bowl of fruit to the ground.

At least Ruby had the good sense to look sheepish, Ryan thought. Pyre looked proud of himself.

"If they continue to grow at this pace," Xinthian said, "they'll be the size of a house within a year or two."

"Yeah," Aaron said, "but they're very friendly."

Xinthian shook his head. "Friendly won't do you much good when they're grown. It is *you* who should be friendly with *them*. Those cute puffs of steam they emit will soon enough turn into gouts of flame, and you'll need to make arrangements for them to be housed somewhere safe."

"Don't worry," Ryan promised. "We'll take good care of them. These dragons are like our own kids."

Aaron smiled. "Our own *scaly* kids."

"Well," said Xinthian, "we should get on with our discussion. Eglerion and Castien, please tell me how your charges have progressed in their training."

Eglerion looked directly at Ryan as he spoke. "Young Ryan Riverton started off with a few failings that one might expect for a young man of his age. His attention oftentimes wandered, and he had some trouble taking instruction from those who knew more than he did."

Ryan felt his face warm with embarrassment. He wasn't proud of his headstrong attitude during the beginning of his training.

"However," Eglerion continued, "I believe those difficulties have been largely overcome. Ryan is now an apt pupil quite hungry for knowledge. He devours information at a rapid pace, and not only does he now have an excellent grasp of his skills, he has learned quite a bit about what I might consider more advanced topics of mind analysis. He also has an unusual amount of raw power."

The old elf fixed Ryan with his steely gaze. "So much power, in fact, that I think it would be dangerous to allow him to leave us without at least several more years of intense tutelage. At that time, he might ultimately reach the highest echelons of wizardry. He may even match the abilities of the greatest of all human wizards: Zenethar, whom the humans call the First Protector."

Ryan barely even heard the complimentary words at the end, because he was too hung up on three words in the middle.

*Several more years.*

He felt as if he'd been hit between the eyes with a hammer.

"Thank you, Eglerion," Xinthian said. "Now, Castien? What do you have to say about your charge?"

Castien, never one to stay still, had been pacing throughout Eglerion's report. But now he stopped and studied Aaron for a long time. The only sounds in the room were the scratching of dragon claws on the floor as Pyre and Ruby resumed their wrestling match.

Finally, the sword master spoke. "Aaron Riverton came to me as a wholly unprepared pupil. He was overconfident, uneducated, and his physical conditioning was atrocious. He was barely capable of taking a casual jog through the forest without collapsing due to exhaustion."

*Wow*, thought Ryan. *This is not going well.*

"But…" Castien continued, a twinkle in his eye, "Aaron has proven himself to be an immensely hard worker. His physical progress has been quite remarkable. He's learned not to rely only on his incredible strength at the expense of proper technique. He's now a competent swordsman and could likely outduel many of our citizens. Most importantly, he's earned the respect of many of the citizens in Eluanethra for his ongoing interest in their welfare and culture."

Aaron smiled broadly. Ryan got the feeling these were the first compliments Castien had ever given him.

"That being said, he must get better," Castien finished. "Much better. I believe he will require years of further training as well."

"But—" Aaron began.

Castien held up a hand. "Do not make me reevaluate my assessment of your performance."

Aaron sat back in his seat, his shoulders slumping in defeat.

Castien turned to Xinthian. "There is something more." He paused. "I was visited by Seder last night."

Eglerion sat up straight. "And?"

The sword master sighed. "I was told that I must continue Aaron's training until he has mastered everything I can teach him. I was also told… that I must leave Eluanethra."

"Leave Eluanethra?" said Aaron. "I don't understand."

"I believe I do," Xinthian said. "I think Castien has just informed us that his responsibility for the training of soldiers will expand beyond the borders of Eluanethra, to include the rest of Trimoria. Eglerion informed me of a similar intent prior to this meeting. He intends to join the academy of wizardry that Lord Riverton is forming."

He turned to the Riverton brothers. "Which means, you will be departing as scheduled. But you will not be going alone."

Only now did Ryan get it. "You two are going with us," he said to Eglerion and Castien.

They both nodded.

Xinthian smiled. "You will also be accompanied by our future queen. After all, she cannot be parted from her teacher."

"Labri's coming, too?" Ryan said.

"Is that a problem?"

Ryan shook his head. "No, sir. I just have to explain some things to my betrothed."

Aaron grinned. "He's afraid his betrothed will get upset because he's seen Labri naked while bathing."

Xinthian laughed deeply, then sobered.

"Tomorrow is the first step toward the showdown between good and evil," he said. "I only hope to live to see the outcome."

---

Everything was planned perfectly. Gerald and his brother Roland were in position, ready to do what they'd been hired to do.

Their spot had been carefully prepared. They were on opposite sides of the road, not only hidden behind shrubbery, but literally dug into holes in the ground, with flaps of grass on top that hid them from view. Looking through special devices of Gerald's own invention—they looked like tubes bent with two ninety-degree angles—they could observe the road without even removing their heads from their holes. Even if someone looked directly at the spots where they hid, all they would see was a tiny tube.

The only problem was: their quarry hadn't shown up for weeks.

Roland was losing his patience. He'd always been the more impatient of the two. But by now even Gerald was getting tired of lying in this hole eighteen hours a day. It was not the life he'd imagined when they first entered this profession. True, they'd chosen this career path only because they were desperate—and hungry—but he'd assumed it would have its share of glamor as well. Not lying in the mud, creepy-crawlies in his britches, some of them burrowing into his skin…

But there was nothing for it now. If they didn't complete their mission, and kill those two boys, Dominic would kill *them.*

*Or maybe something worse.*

As Gerald looked through his tube and waited, the sky lightened, indicating dawn was coming, and the king's daughter would soon be passing by to oversee the tending of the fields. Gerald recalled how curvaceous, young, and vulnerable the princess was.

*If I'm doomed to a painful death,* he thought, *I might as well enjoy myself before I go.*

## A RETURN HOME

Clankton Hammerthrower led the other dwarves through the tunnels that led from the mountain range they called home. They were in good spirits as they reached the cave that opened onto the lands of Aubgherle. The cave walls bent in gentle slopes above them, providing a canopy of dry, dark rock, and beyond the mouth of the cave, the sun was dipping low on the distant horizon. Clankton took comfort in that.

"All right, boys," he said. "Let's scout da surrounding area while there's still light, and ensure there are no dangers. Go in pairs. We'll set out for Aubgherle upon first light of da morning."

The members of the Hammerthrower Clan scattered to carry out his request.

Clankton was acting as emissary for the Hammerthrower

Clan, and had been tasked with reporting to the recently crowned king in Aubgherle. It was his own father—Mattias, head of the Hammerthrower Clan—who had given him this responsibility, and Clankton knew his da was hoping Clankton would prove he possessed some leadership ability. He'd been shy as a youth, and his father's disapproval through the years had been palpable.

"Clankton," his father had once said, "ye should consider lettin' yer sister be the head of da clan after I pass. Ye don't command da respect a leader should."

While his dwarves scouted, he built a fire, and it had warmed the cave nicely when the first pair of scouts returned.

"All is clear in the direction of Azazel's tower," one reported.

Clankton nodded. "Start preparing the evening meal. I think a nice joint of mutton would be tasty along with the fall ale." Then he returned to his maps, plotting a course for the morning.

Two by two, the other scouts returned to report the all-clear. But the last pair was delayed, and in the end, only one returned. He looked ragged, tired, as if he'd endured a long journey.

"We done scouted to the south like planned," the weary dwarf reported. "It be darn spooky there. Neither a sound nor sight of nothin' alive there, I can tell ya. Heck, all I saw was forests, mists, and rocks. I aimed to return, but Halas refused. He said he heard a beautiful song and wanted to follow it to da source. I couldn't hear none of it, and told him so. Halas ignored what I said. I think his brain done gone funny. He was just walkin' and payin' no mind to me. So I returned to let you know."

Clankton exploded. "You left yer partner to wander off in the haunted forest? What in da name of all dat is holy made you tink dat would be a good idea?" He shook his head. "All right, Hammerthrowers. Bank da fire. We need to find our cousin, and find him now."

---

*Halas was standing in a clearing in the midst of a misty forest. Before him stood an ancient-looking house, its windows dark, and yet somehow bathed in green light. The odd thing was, Halas couldn't recall how he'd gotten here. He remembered scouting with his partner, and then... and then he was here.*

*He heard a voice. Or... a melody. And it carried visions along with it. He saw himself embracing a beautiful woman. She was ridiculously tall and thin, with blonde hair. Not at all like the women who normally caught Halas's attention; she wasn't even a dwarf. But she was beautiful, and she would be his.*

*And then Halas was moving forward, walking around the house. Ahead of him stood a simple stone altar, and somehow he knew the beauty was hiding there. His life would forever be blissful with her; he simply had to find her.*

*A hand grabbed his left arm. Then another seized his right.*

*"Halas! Has yer brain gone soft? Time to leave dis cursed place."*

*Halas screamed and struggled against his captors. "Leave me be!" he shouted. "She needs me, I tell ye, and she wants only me. None of ye are gonna cheat me of dis!"*

---

"What do you mean I was in the forest? Why are ye holdin' me like a prisoner?"

They were back in the cave, and Clankton stood over Halas as his clan mates tied him up for his own safety. "Halas, I think we all just saved yer life. Ye had fallen into the clutches of da witch's wiles. Heck, even I had visions of her."

They had been enchanting visions, too. Clankton had seen himself entwined in bed with the beautiful elf witch. And as revolting a thought as that was—a dwarf with an elf!—it had been one of the most intoxicating things he'd ever felt.”

"What now?" asked one of the other dwarves.

"We must delay our trip to Aubgherle and return home to warn the other clans. We must warn them of what we've witnessed, so that no others fall victim to da witch's lure. The clan leaders will determine if there's something further to be done."

The dwarves around the fire nodded acceptance, and Clankton nodded to himself with satisfaction. *I gave direction, and the men accepted it unquestioningly. We saved one of our lads, and will warn our people of a possible danger. That seems like leadership to me.*

---

More than two months had passed since Gerald and his brother had taken on this assignment, and they still hadn't so much as seen their quarry. Gerald was about ready to give up; he'd had enough of living in the dirt. He wanted to return the fee to Dominic through a courier and run away. But Roland was convinced the wizard would find them and kill them if they ran.

Gerald wasn't convinced the wizard wouldn't kill them either way. He didn't seem like the type who would leave witnesses to his actions.

He was watching through his periscope, as always, when a troop of armed elves came down the road toward the farmhouse. What were elves doing here?

And then he caught a glimpse of their targets, right in the midst of the elves. Finally!

If only the boys were alone.

The group continued on up to the farmhouse, and the two boys went inside, followed by two strange winged dogs. The elven troop mustered in front of the farmhouse, clearly setting a guard. That would complicate matters.

Roland sent him a quick flash of reflected light. That meant, *Be alert.* Well of course he would be alert. This was the first thing that had happened in two months.

He smiled. At last, their waiting had come to an end. And soon, so would the boys' lives.

---

As Ryan walked with the elves to the farmhouse, he smiled. He would miss Eluanethra, but he was delighted to be back home with its familiar sounds and smells. But at the same time everything was subtly different, because one thing had changed: himself. He now felt the power surging through him like no time in his life.

And not just him. Aaron had changed, too. His features were now chiseled and lean, his body significantly more muscled. Yet at the same time, he seemed lighter on his feet, with the gait of an elven warrior.

As they neared the farmhouse, the door opened, and Ryan's mother appeared in the doorway, tears of joy forming in her eyes. Ryan had sent a word of caution, so she didn't step outside, but the minute the guards escorted the brothers to the door, she wrapped them in her arms and covered them in tears and kisses.

Ryan then received the same greeting from Arabelle, whose hug was even tighter. Even after everyone gathered at the table, she refused to let go of his hand.

Through the communication rings, he'd already told everyone most of what he knew—including that he'd spoken to Seder and learned that he and Aaron were in mortal danger.

But he hadn't given them details, until now. When everyone was settled, he explained.

"Seder informed me that after Azazel's death, Sammael replaced him with a new servant. This person has hired assassins to try to kill both Aaron and me. I don't know who the servant is, or the assassins, only that the danger is real. And that they intend to kill us both simultaneously."

"Well, they won't succeed," Dad said with determination. "Especially now that everyone has new armor. Speaking of which, Ryan, I'll need you to charge a few things."

"New armor?" Aaron asked. "What was wrong with my old armor?"

"Nothing was wrong with it, but I realized we could do better. So while you boys were gone, I arranged to begin trading with Silas Redbeard. Ryan, you remember him from the caves near Azazel's tower. So I've got some new metal to work with. I'll think you'll be pleased." Dad winked and grinned.

Aaron opened his mouth to say something more, but at that moment Ruby waddled up to Ryan and screeched, "Hungry!"

Arabelle's mouth fell open. "They can *talk*?"

Ryan fished a piece of dried meat from his pocket and tossed it to his dragon. "They could talk when they were born, but it's a dragon language. Now they're learning Trimorian. It's wild."

That was when Silver chose to finally make his entrance. Ryan had worried about this moment—about how the giant swamp cat and the baby dragons would react to one another, and if things might turn violent.

For a moment, things seemed tense. Silver eyed the dragons with suspicion, and they returned the look. But then the dragons started making strange sounds Ryan hadn't heard from them before. It wasn't Trimorian, or the squeaky dragon tongue, it was more like a series of clicks.

And to everyone's surprise, Silver clicked right back. It was the same noise he used to make when he was an ordinary housecat and saw a bird through the window.

This continued for a minute, and then Silver lay on the floor, and the two dragons curled up next to him, all three of them purring.

"For a second there, I thought we were going to have either toasted cat or shredded dragon for supper tonight," Throll said.

"I'm glad we're not," Aaron said. "Elven food is fine and all, but for two months now I've been looking forward to some good old-fashioned Trimorian food made by the best cooks I know."

As if to emphasize the point, his stomach rumbled, and Mom and Gwen both laughed.

"Some things never change," Sloane said, shaking her head.

When dinner was over and the plates had been cleared, Ryan studied everyone's aura. And he realized that there was something odd about Sloane's. Normally all of the thin threads that extended from a person's head looped around in a tangle, connecting one part of a person's brain to another. But one of Sloane's filaments was hanging loose, connected at one end but not at the other.

"Sloane, do you trust me?" he asked.

Sloane frowned. "That's a strange question to ask."

"Sorry, it's just… I see something unusual about your aura, and I want to explore it a little bit. I'm pretty sure you won't feel a thing. Is that okay with you?"

"My aura?"

"It's a long story, but yes… do you trust me?"

Sloane looked hesitant, but nodded. "I guess."

Ryan went to stand behind her and studied her head. He once again found the loose thread, and tried to grab it with his hand. His hand went straight through it. Then he tried pushing energy at it. This time it moved.

"Did you feel that?" he asked.

"I didn't feel anything, except you hovering over me."

Holding the thread still with his magic, he traced it back to its source, and studied the shape of the keyhole from which it emerged. From Eglerion's book, he'd learned that these connections were usually like a puzzle, with the two ends of a thread attaching to keyholes of the same shape. So when he'd identified the shape of the source hole, he then scanned her for an unoccupied hole of the same shape. It took him several minutes, during which Sloane fidgeted and Aaron grumbled, but finally he found a match—not on her scalp, but deep within her mind.

With the slightest touch of energy, Ryan manipulated the disconnected end into that matched location. It locked into place as if it had been meant to go there, a new glow sprang to life around Sloane's head.

Sloane gasped.

"Are you okay?" Aaron said. "Did he hurt you?"

Sloane put a finger to her lips to signal for quiet, then her eyes darted around the room, moving from one person to the next. When her gaze settled on Aaron, she blushed.

Then she leapt to her feet and gave Ryan a rib-crushing hug. "Oh thank you, thank you, thank you!"

"What's going on? What did you do, Ryan?" Aaron snapped.

Ryan would have answered, but he didn't even know. He'd just done what had just seemed right and obvious.

"You're worried about me!" Sloane said excitedly.

"Well of course I'm worried. I don't—"

Sloane spun to face Arabelle. "Ryan is really worried about you being jealous about Labri and hopes you understand. Nothing ever happened. Isn't that sweet?"

Arabelle looked confused. "What?"

"Wait a minute!" Ryan said. "How can you—"

Sloane turned to Gwen so quickly that her blonde hair whipped Aaron in the face. "Mother, the baby is awake, but he's just listening to us talk." Then to Mom she said, "Aubrey, Rebecca is dreaming about feeding."

"Oh, wow…" Ryan said. "You're reading people's minds."

As a test, he quickly thought up something ridiculous. *The password is Bubba*, he thought.

Sloane frowned at him. "Bubba?"

"She just read that out of my head!" Ryan exclaimed.

Sloane put her hands to her mouth. "Oh! I can even hear Silver and the dragons as they sleep!"

"This is truly amazing," said Dad.

Everyone was impressed—except for Aaron, who scowled.

"Are you kidding me, Ryan? You taught Sloane to read minds? Now I'm never going to be able to get away with anything!"

## INTERROGATION

Ryan had dutifully endured Eglerion's scolding for what the elf had termed, "Experimental use of his powers on others." Although Ryan and Sloane were quite pleased with the results, Ryan had to admit that Eglerion was probably right. It was risky to have attempted to manipulate his friend's mind. But when he saw the stray thread it had just seemed obvious what he'd needed to do. Maybe there was an instinct to some of this, but he had to agree that it was probably stupid for him to have done it without some forethought and consulting with Eglerion and the books.

It was late in the evening, and everyone had gone to their bedrooms early, except for Aaron, Sloane, and Arabelle. Ryan had spent the past hour or so charging Aaron's newest set of armor made of damantite. Ryan's experience with the strange metal was limited to the one sample he'd encountered in

Azazel's tower. In Eluanethra, he was taught that this metal originated from the blood of wounded demon lords. Eglerion had taught him that in an age many thousands of years ago, the barrier between the Abyss and Trimoria was nonexistent, so the spilling of demon blood had been more common back then. Ryan wasn't sure what a demon looked like, or how it bled, but he did know for certain that this metal was relatively light, stronger than any other metal he'd ever encountered, and could soak up more energy than practically anything he'd ever seen. He'd expended so much energy charging Aaron's armor that he'd consumed the equivalent of almost twenty full meals doing it.

As he placed the final piece of brightly glowing armor on the table, he looked at the results with pride. The suit of armor glowed with a fiery red glint. Ryan heard the humming of the massive quantities of energy he'd poured into it. When Aaron saw it, all he could say was, "Wow."

Ryan smiled. "Dad was the one who actually made it. He probably spent *days* on this armor. I just charged it."

"Silver is dreaming about a man hidden under some shrubbery," Sloane said suddenly. "I recognize the surroundings. I think the hiding place is near the house."

Ryan frowned. "I wonder if that's the guy we're supposed to watch out for."

"Sloane, what are you doing?" Aaron asked.

Sloane was staring at Silver, her forehead furrowed in concentration. Silver suddenly woke and made a series of clicking vocalizations.

Ryan whispered to Aaron, "I think your betrothed is talking to our cat."

Silver laid his head back down and closed his eyes.

Sloane turned to Aaron with excitement. "He understood me!"

"And you understood those sounds he made?" Aaron asked.

"No, not the sounds, but while he was talking, I could sort of see the meaning in his mind. He said there are two smelly humans lying in the ground. He said they smelled of fear and danger."

Aaron hugged her. "You're awesome. If those humans are who I think they are, you may have just saved our lives."

"Do you know exactly where they're hiding?" Ryan asked.

"Yes. I could point you to the precise spot. It's within sight of our front door."

---

Both dragons sat up and screeched. "Food me," Pyre said at Gwen, who smiled as she held a tray out of their reach.

"Ryan! Aaron! Your dragons are begging for food. What can I feed them?" *That's odd,* she thought when there was no reply. *They must have gone to sleep early.*

The dragons were begging like puppies at Gwen's feet.

"Will you eat fried bacon?" she asked. To Gwen's astonishment, both dragons nodded.

Gwen daintily picked a strip of bacon and tossed it at the

dragons. Pyre immediately caught the strip and chomped merrily.

Ruby looked at Gwen and squeaked, "Me?"

Laughing, Gwen handed Ruby a strip. The dragon carefully took it from Gwen's fingers, then chomped quite contentedly. As Ruby ate her piece, Pyre was using his snakelike tongue to pick up any crumbs off the floor. Gwen found herself amazed by how well the dragons behaved. All the stories she'd heard of these creatures suggested that they would be marauding, stupid beasts that would destroy everything in sight. Clearly, this wasn't the case with these two.

Apparently unable to find any more crumbs, Pyre peered up at Gwen. "More?"

Gwen smiled. "Follow me to the kitchen. I'll make you an evening snack since the boys must not have fed you enough. Don't worry; I'll somehow manage to keep everyone in the house fed."

Both dragons waddled eagerly after Gwen as she walked toward the kitchen.

---

Ryan snuck through the house to avoid waking his parents. According to the plan he and Aaron had come up with, Aaron would have put on his new armor by now, and they would meet by the front door, where two of them could take care of the threat outside without anyone else having to get involved.

But as Ryan passed through the living room, a lamp flared

to life. Sloane and Arabelle stood before him, hands on their hips, and behind them stood Ryan's parents, Throll, and Gwen. Last but not least was Aaron, his neck held in Throll's grip.

"Ryan, how nice of you to join us," Throll said. "Perhaps you'd like to explain why you and your brother are sneaking about in my house in the middle of the night?"

Aaron shrugged. "Sorry, Ryan. It's hard to be sneaky in full armor."

"And it's hard for me not to hear you two scheming," Sloane added. "Your thoughts were broadcasting your plans throughout the house, you know."

"Boys," Dad said, "this is serious. Tell us what's going on."

Ryan told them about Sloane's conversation with Silver, and the plan he and Aaron had come up with to confront the two assassins.

Throll frowned. "The basis of your plan is sound. But you *will* be getting my assistance."

"And mine," Dad said.

Mom nudged him in the ribs. "Both of ours."

Ryan suddenly had a thought that hadn't occurred to him before. "Sloane? Do you think you could communicate telepathically with people that are camped outside the house? For instance, Ohaobbok? Or Castien?"

"Of course!" Aaron said. "What a great idea. We'll get the elves to help!"

A look of concentration crossed Sloane's face. When it

passed, she opened her eyes and shrugged. "I *think* I just yelled at Castien and Ohaobbok to please come to the front door. I have no idea if they heard me."

Moments later, there was a knock on the front door.

Throll laughed, his white teeth flashing behind the threads of his thick beard. "I think it worked."

He unbarred the door, and in walked Castien and Ohaobbok.

Ryan quickly filled them in.

"Neither of you are going to risk your lives," the elf said when Ryan was done. "This is a job for stealth. No matter how good you think you might be, you stand no chance of sneaking up on someone lying in wait for you."

"You are confident you can manage?" Throll asked.

Castien nodded. "I can, and so can a couple of my scouts."

"Can you capture the men alive?" Ryan asked. "We need to find out who hired them."

Castien frowned. "That might be difficult. It can be quite difficult to prevent an assassin from committing suicide, as they often do."

"I could come with you and immobilize them," Ryan offered.

"Stealth, remember?"

In reply, Ryan concentrated on a style of shield he'd been working to perfect. He built his power up, wrapped it around himself, and snapped it closed. "What about this?" he said.

"Woah!" said Aaron. "Where'd you go?"

Ryan smiled. "I guess it worked. I've been thinking about

how I can wrap light around me so it looks like you can see through me. Instead, you're really seeing around me."

Dad whistled. "Invisibility. I'm impressed. I have to try that."

He assumed a look of concentration. From the sound humming in the air, Ryan sensed that his father had activated a shield, but it didn't turn him invisible. Instead it created all sorts of flashing lights and distortions that made Ryan dizzy.

"I think I'll need more practice," Dad said, letting the shield drop.

"Ryan, you can come along," Castien said. "Remember, just because someone cannot see you, that doesn't mean they cannot still hear you approach. Walk on the balls of your feet, and stay very quiet."

Ryan nodded.

"If you're responding non-verbally, I can't tell."

"Oh, sorry," Ryan said. "Yes, I understand."

"Then follow me," the elf said.

Mom had tears in her eyes. "Be careful. I'll be right here if you need me."

Arabelle held Sloane's hand. "Sloane, can you please keep track of what Ryan sees and tell us? I'm worried."

Ryan smiled as he realized that being invisible made everyone think he was already gone. Everyone but Castien.

"Just stay behind me on my left-hand side," the elf murmured as stepped outside. He made a signal with his hand. "When I provide this hand signal, that's your cue to immobilize the target. You got it?"

"Got it."

---

Gerald was waiting and alert. The sun was a few hours from rising, but he'd seen the ogre guarding the front door to the Lancaster home, and the elf that had gone in and come back out. This was unusual, and he'd been an assassin long enough to know that anything unusual could be dangerous, or a possible opportunity.

A single spark flew from a piece of flint where Roland hid. Roland had had the same thought.

Suddenly Gerald's world turned to pain. His muscles spasmed, no longer under his control, and he was dragged from his hidden bunker. Two rough hands grabbed his mouth and pried it open while another dug around and found the capsule of poison between his cheek and gums. His clothes were ripped from his body, his weapons removed.

*I'm going to be tortured,* he thought.

His arms and legs were roughly bound. He was dragged toward the Lancaster home.

*I wonder if Roland escaped.*

---

Ryan and Castien dragged the naked assassin into the house. The only people in the living room now where Throll, Aaron, and Sloane.

"Sloane," Throll said, "I'm allowing you to be here only to use your new ability. Maturity please."

Sloane rolled her eyes.

"Where's the other one?" Aaron asked.

Castien lifted the man onto a chair and tied him to it with a length of rope. "The other one managed to commit suicide," he whispered. "There was nothing we could do. The poison was fast-acting. Your brother immobilized this one before he could act in a similar manner."

Sloane spoke directly into Ryan's mind. *"Right now all he can think of is his own pain. Are you doing something that's hurting him?"*

Ryan let go of the trickle of energy he'd been pouring into the assassin. The man sagged in the chair with relief.

*"Ask him whatever you want,"* Sloane projected. *"Whether he answers you or not, I can tell you what he's thinking."*

Ryan stood in front of the assassin. "Who are you? And who hired you?"

A flash of surprise crossed the man's face before being replaced by disdain. He said nothing.

*"His name is Gerald. The man who hired him is named Dominic. His visual of the man is very disturbing."*

Dominic? Ryan thought. *It couldn't be the same Dominic, could it?*

He smiled at Gerald. "You know, I've been looking for my good friend Dominic for years. I owe him for a knife wound."

Gerald struggled against his bonds until Castien smacked him in the back of the head.

"How many people did Dominic hire?" Ryan asked.

Gerald still said nothing.

*"Only two. The man who died was Gerald's brother. Roland."*

"I'm sorry Roland died," Ryan said.

That got a reaction. Gerald may have been a killer, but judging by the look on his face, he was truly devastated to learn his brother had died.

"What instructions were you and Roland given?" Ryan continued.

*"They were hired to kill you and Aaron. Their only special instructions were that the two of you had to be killed simultaneously."*

Ryan nodded. "Last question. Where is Dominic?"

*"Hang on,"* Sloane projected. *"Okay, yeah, I recognize the place. It's in one of the seedier parts of Aubgherle."*

Ryan smiled. "Gerald, you have been a fountain of help. Thank you."

"Right," Throll said smartly. "Do we have any further need of him then?"

"No. I think we have everything we need."

Throll sent a tremendous blow to the side of Gerald's head, not only knocking him unconscious, but sending both him and the chair to the floor.

"What do you plan on doing with him?" Ryan asked.

"I plan on executing him at first light at the town square,"

Throll growled. "We cannot tolerate attacks against a future prince of Trimoria."

"Prince?"

Sloane sighed. "You're as dense as your brother. I'm a princess now, right? And I'm marrying your brother, so…"

Ryan and Aaron looked at each other, the realization hitting them both at once. "Oh," they said in unison.

# SCHOOL STARTS

Jared fumed as he walked to the academy grounds. He'd spent the morning searching for Dominic, but all he'd found was a hastily abandoned room filled with unspeakable evidence of death and human waste.

Throll had promised to send word to every garrison in Trimoria, stating that there was a significant reward for Dominic's capture, dead or alive. Castien also promised to keep Aaron under protection of an armed elven escort at all times.

It wasn't enough. Someone had come after his boys. That someone had to be stopped.

He found Aubrey, with Rebecca on her hip, watching the very first classes begin. The main school building was almost finished, but work was still being done on the roof, so for now the students would be working outside. Farther afield was the ram that Sloane had donated, grazing in a fenced section, along with a few ewes to keep him company.

"What do you and Rebecca think of the new school?"

"It's a lot bigger than I'd pictured. Call me naïve, but when you talked to me about being a teacher at a school for magic, I was thinking of a one-room schoolhouse. I mean, it really wasn't that long ago that I could count on one hand all the people we knew of with magical skills."

Jared laughed. "Things have definitely changed. How's our Archmage doing with his class?"

"Ryan is growing up so quickly. He's actually a very good teacher."

---

Aubrey looked on proudly as her eldest son stood before a group of twenty young people sitting cross-legged in the grass. Arabelle was among them, looking stunningly beautiful despite the cross-eyed look she was giving to a piece of ore she held in her hand. Ryan was trying to teach his students how to infuse energy into an inanimate object, but it was clear that this particular lesson wasn't taking with Arabelle.

Sitting behind her was Ohaobbok. Even sitting cross-legged, he towered above the rest. He, too, had a problem with the ore in his hand—he'd accidentally crushed it to dust.

Aubrey laughed under her breath at the sheepish look on the ogre's face.

Ryan walked over to Ohaobbok with a chunk of metal. "Try this instead," he said. "And don't squeeze."

He turned to the rest of his students, sounding remarkably professional as he continued the lesson.

"Okay, let's change things a bit. I would like you all to place the ore on the ground before you. This is so you don't burn yourself from holding a red-hot rock. Now imagine you're pushing waves of energy at the ore. For some of you, you'll find that the ore starts giving off some heat, some of you will affect your target more than others. And for some, you might not sense any change whatsoever."

Aubrey gasped as sparks erupted from the rock resting at Zenethar's feet. Clearly frightened, the boy fell back and started to cry. Ryan ran to the king's son and stooped over what was now a pile of molten slag. He whooped as he picked up the toddler.

"Zenethar, my boy," he said. "I think you overwhelmed that poor chunk of ore. We now know you aren't a healer." He set the boy back on his feet. "Come on and give me a high five. It looks like you're going to be a war wizard, just like my father."

The chubby little boy high-fived Ryan and then hugged his leg.

Unfortunately, it soon became clear that some of Ryan's students would never be able to send killing energy at their samples of ore. In some cases, the rock glowed slightly with inner heat. For others, he noticed the a few waves of heat rising from the sample, maybe a few puffs of smoke from burnt grass, but Arabelle wasn't among those who'd managed to affect her ore. She looked devastated and on the verge of tears.

Aubrey stepped forward and kneeled beside her.

"Don't fret, my dear," she said. "It could be that you're a healer, like me. Supposedly, it's a rare gift."

"Mom," Ryan leaned over and pointed at a few students who hadn't managed to get anywhere in the last round of tests and said, "Can you help test for healers?"

"Of course," Aubrey smiled. She stood and raised her voice a bit. "Everyone who wasn't able to heat their ore, come here, we'll test to see if we've got some healers in our midst."

Aubrey walked over to a table and passed each student a cup of water and a clay pot containing a very sick-looking plant.

"This lesson will be similar to the one with the ore. Do the same thing with the water—just attempt to push energy into it. If you are a strong healer, you might even feel vibrations returned to you. This means that the item cannot hold any more of your healing energy."

Everyone stared at their water. Before long, two of their lot gasped. One was Arabelle, and the other was a young boy.

"I felt the vibrations bounce back at me!" Arabelle cried happily.

Aubrey clapped. "That's great! Okay, now pour the water on your plant. If it carries any healing energy, we should see the plant react."

Arabelle poured the water on the shriveled brown plant.

Almost immediately, the plant turned a bright green, and a flower bloomed.

"We just found another healer!" Aubrey announced.

---

Sloane watched Aaron spar with two fighters from the local garrison and two elves from Eluanethra. As always, she'd prepared a huge snack for him since these workouts always wore him out, and she felt that it was her responsibility to make sure he was well cared for. Her duties had increased a lot in the past two years. Not only did she help her mother with the farm and tending to the household chores, she had a husband-to-be to look after, as well as a little brother.

Things had changed for Aaron over the past two years, too. Especially after he came back from the elves. He looked older somehow, more mature. Of course he looked stronger, and his movements were definitely faster, more precise, but there was something more, too, some self-possession that hadn't been there before.

She smiled as he ducked a slice from the wooden sword of one of the garrison guards and kicked the man's leg out from under him. Even as the man was falling backward, Aaron spun around to meet an elf fighter's overhead chop, using his full strength to toss the elf away from the action. As Aaron was circled by the two remaining fighters, Sloane's father called out to him.

"You did well with your riposte, but your slice motion needs more work!"

He then turned to the elven sword master standing beside him. "I like that move where he knocked an opponent off his feet as he ducked from the attack. Did you teach him that?"

Castien gave a faint smile. "Effective, wasn't it? Quick like a cat, but sneaky as a weasel, he is."

Then he, too, called out to Aaron. "You must stop depending on your strength to compensate for your laziness in counterattack. Some demons are as large as Ohaobbok, and strength will not be enough!"

"But I'm winning the fight, aren't I?" Aaron complained.

"That's not the point!" Throll and Castien hollered at once.

---

Over the next several weeks at the academy, Ryan and his father trained the novice wizards, and Mom trained the novice healers. The only thing that caused some grumbling among the students were the non-magical lessons. Mom insisted everyone learn to read and write, and Eglerion made it his personal mission to ensure every student had sufficient knowledge of Trimorian history—at least, when he wasn't giving private lessons to Ryan and Labri.

But the day came when Dad decided it was time for an all-academy meeting. Every student gathered in the yard, and Ryan was pleased to see that the students hadn't grouped off by magical ability, as he had feared. The hedge wizards, war wizards, and healers all intermingled. That was a good sign.

There was, not surprisingly, one student who sat off by himself. Charlie Carbunkle. Charlie was nine years old, and possessed a great deal of raw magical power, but he was also an arrogant troublemaker and a bully. Ryan was already starting to dislike the kid.

"What is this meeting about?" Arabelle asked at Ryan's side.

"I'm not sure. I think we'd find out if everyone would stop chatting and listen."

Dad stood up front, waving his arms for attention and not getting it. Finally he sent a ball of plasma into the air. When it exploded, that made everyone suddenly go silent.

"Thank you," Dad said. "Now that I have your attention, I have two announcements to make. First, I will soon be starting a competition among the RAM students. The king has agreed to donate a prize for the winner. One hundred gold pieces."

The students murmured in excitement. That much gold was a few years' income for a farm worker.

Arabelle turned to Ryan and asked, "Is your father going to allow you to compete?"

"I don't see why not. Sure, I can do some things that others can't, but as to raw power, there's some students who are total beasts. And besides, if I win, I'll buy you something awesome with the prize money," Ryan whispered to Arabelle.

She frowned. "I don't want you spending money on silly

things. If you win, then we should discuss what we'll do with the money. You know, like adults."

"The contest will consist of several categories," Dad continued. "You will be measured on use of magic, accuracy, knowledge, and popularity. The winner in each individual category will be awarded ten gold pieces."

Oda raised his hand, and Dad nodded to him. "Yes, Oda?"

"How is dis a fair contest for us hedge wizards? I can't possibly compare my magic skills against even da baby sitting next to da giant."

Zenethar, who'd been sitting in Ohaobbok's lap, hopped up on his stubby legs. "Not a baby! Am big boy!"

"Sorry." A smile creased Oda's face. "I apologize. Da big boy over there can beat most of my magic skills. Why should I even compete?"

"I'm very glad you asked. Come up here, please. I want to introduce you to Castien. He is sword master of Eluanethra."

As Oda stepped to the front, Castien tossed him a metal staff, then twirled a wooden staff of his own. "Attack me," he said.

Oda apparently needed no reason to start a fight. He rushed forward, chopping with the staff as if it were an axe. Castien deflected the strike, but Oda continued, spinning and hacking. Castien blocked, deflected, and dodged. Finally, Dad called the exercise to a halt.

"I fail to see what dis proves," Oda grumbled. "Give me an axe and I will show dis elf what a dwarf can do."

"You will indeed show him what you can do," Eglerion

said, stepping forward, "but you will do it with that staff." He turned to face the assembled students. "Hundreds of years ago, before the time of the First Protector, hedge wizards were used as members of an elite warrior force."

Ryan had learned about this, but clearly many of the students had not, as another murmur passed through the students.

"Oda," Eglerion said, "push your energy into your staff."

Oda concentrated. Ryan sensed the dwarf's energy, though weak, heating the metal. It was always interesting to watch another magic user, because each student's magical glow was slightly different, like a signature.

"Enough!" Eglerion called.

Oda stopped. The glow of the staff immediately vanished.

"Now attack Castien again," Eglerion said. "But this time, I want you to push energy through your staff at the same time."

Castien held out his staff and nodded. Oda smirked as he rushed forward with a vicious overhead swing. The two staffs connected, and in a shower of sparks, Castien's wooden staff shattered.

Oda looked at his staff with a huge grin. "Can I do dat again?"

Dad laughed and took the staff from him. "As a matter of fact, you and your classmates will be practicing this a great deal. Hedge wizards use their magic in different ways."

Oda shuffled back to his seat, looking quite pleased.

"That gives you some insight into the use of magic category," Dad said, addressing the students once more. "And we are exploring some ways to vary the tests for hedge wizards and war wizards as well. The accuracy category is self-explanatory. The knowledge contest will be based on your lessons, in both magical *and* non-magical subjects. And the popularity contest will be determined by a vote among the students. It is you who will decide which peer you most enjoy working with."

"And no," Mom said, "you cannot vote for yourself."

"You're going to vote for me, right?" Ryan whispered to Arabelle.

"Only if you're nice to me. Are you voting for me?"

"Of course. Even if you're mean."

"I think that's it for the contest, though more details will come in due time. We won't actually begin for a while just yet. My second announcement is somewhat related. Starting today, each and every one of you will be eligible to receive combat training. Swords, bows, axes, whatever your teacher determines is best suited to you. Castien will be leading those classes."

Castien, as usual, wasted no time. "All of the hedge wizards!" he yelled. "Stand and form a line! Your lesson begins now."

Dad smiled. "And the rest of you report to your usual classrooms. Castien will get a crack at you soon enough."

# DOMINIC STRIKES

Ryan sat on the edge of his bed, comparing notes with Aaron on the progress of the hedge wizards during their first several months of combat training. Aaron spent most of his waking hours working with either Throll or Castien or both, and much of that involved training of some kind right along with the hedge wizards.

"You should see it when Oda fights with Ohaobbok," Aaron said with a laugh. "A five-foot-tall dwarf against a twelve-foot-tall ogre. Just seeing them square off brings a smile to my face."

"So how does Oda do?" Ryan asked. "Does Ohaobbok knock him to the moon?"

"Oh, not anymore. At first, yeah, Ohaobbok would toss the poor guy across the training arena. But then Castien switched Oda from the sword to a mace and flail, and taught him some techniques for competing with larger opponents. And now Oda can hold his own, believe it or not."

"You mean he can beat Ohaobbok?"

"Not yet. He's still lost every fight with the ogre, but they are actual fights now, not complete mismatches. I predict he'll eventually fight Ohaobbok to a stalemate. He'd do better if he'd keep his mouth shut. He's constantly shouting things like, 'What do you need to bring down a giant? An army, of course. Oda the One-Dwarf Army will bring you down!' That just makes Ohaobbok mad."

"I hope he isn't making an enemy."

"Oh, don't worry about that. Those two like each other. And respect each other's skill. At this point I'd say Oda is the second best fighter in the class, after Ohaobbok."

"Wow, he really is holding his own. How about the rest of the hedge wizards?"

"They're going to be a fearsome force. When they power up their weapons and we make contact, the impact makes my blocking arm feel all tingly, like a bunch of fleas are crawling all over it. It took a while for some of them to learn that the pointy end of a sword is the dangerous part, but now that they have some basic techniques down, the main thing they need is more conditioning."

Ryan laughed. "I'm sure Throll and Castien will take care of that."

"Maybe Throll. Castien will be too busy making me miserable. Tomorrow we're going into the woods to work on my stealth and tracking. Both of which he is ridiculously good at, and he doesn't mind showing me up at every opportunity. Which means I need to get a good night's sleep so I can be on my toes." He lay back in bed. "Good night, Ryan."

"Good night."

---

*The hulking remains of a ruined castle rise from a windswept cliff overlooking an ancient battlefield. On the other side of the battlefield, past scraps of decayed siege engines and rusted armor, looms a shimmering white mist.*

*A door opens at the base of the castle, hidden in the growths of ivy and mold. Emerging from within is an elf in leaf-green attire, wielding a staff. He looks out over the battlements, toward the distant, shimmering wall.*

*"How long?" he asks aloud.*

*A disembodied voice replies. "It has been five hundred sixty-four years since the raising of the barrier."*

*"Any changes in the barrier?"*

*"None, Bryan Greenwalker."*

*"Is the royal line still intact? Are the Thariginians still alive?"*

*"I would not be here if that was not the case," the voice responds.*

*"Then all is not lost."*

. . .

Ryan awoke with the dream clear in his mind. Was that a real event? It didn't feel like the prophecies, but nor did it feel like an ordinary dream.

There was one person who would know for sure exactly what this dream meant.

Eglerion.

---

Eglerion's reaction to hearing of Ryan's dream was extreme, to say the least. He insisted that he and Ryan return immediately to Eluanethra to speak to Xinthian directly. Yet he refused to explain any of the dream to his pupil.

"It's not my tale to tell," was all he would say.

So it was that several hours later Ryan found himself in Xinthian's study, face to face with the elven elder, reciting the events of his dream for the second time that day.

"What does it mean?" Ryan asked when he was finished. "Who is Bryan Greenwalker? And where is he? I can't explain why, but I felt like this castle was on the other side of the barrier."

Xinthian sighed sadly. "Bryan Greenwalker was our lore master and healer in the days before the schism."

"Schism? You mean the Great Departure?"

Eglerion had told him about that ancient time. Many thousands of years ago, a faction of elves, influenced by an unknown entity, departed, forever separating the elves. Over the centuries, the remaining elves had often sought out the missing faction, but had never found them.

"Ah, Eglerion has taught you well. But no, I do not refer to the Great Departure, that it was indeed a schism. I refer to the battle that occurred five hundred sixty-four years ago. In a land south of the mist barrier, at the castle of King Zenethar Thariginian."

"The First Protector," Ryan said. "You're talking about the great battle that all Trimorians dream about. Or used to dream of, before the new prophecies came along."

"Yes. As you know, the three races battled together against a demon horde. The commander of that horde was a general named Malphas. In the course of the battle, our forces were split in two. Many of our people were with Zenethar at the last. But many were fighting another horde of demons to the south. And when Zenethar erected the barrier and destroyed the nearest demons, although he saved me and all those near him, he sealed us away from us those of our people who were further to the south. They were left to face the remaining demons alone."

Ryan's throat tightened at the thought.

"That is the Schism to which I refer," Xinthian continued. "And until today, we have had no knowledge of what became of our people. Until today. This vision… it gives me great hope that at least some of my brethren have survived."

"And what about that voice Bryan was talking to?" Ryan asked. "Do you know what that was?"

"I do, and it may explain how those elves survived. The

castle you saw is endowed with a powerful spirit tied to the ruling family of Trimoria. That spirit not only protects those within the borders of the castle, it can also provide food and water through its access to the land's natural resources."

"Why do you think I had this vision?" Ryan asked. "Why me? And why now?"

Xinthian shrugged. "I don't know. Perhaps these are questions that you'll have to puzzle for yourself."

"Maybe I can ask Seder."

Xinthian laughed. "Good luck with that. I have never heard of Seder responding directly to a summons. But who knows? We live in strange times."

---

Dominic knew exactly what had become of his two assassins. Once he had marked them, he could, when he chose, see what they saw. When he felt that Roland had died, he immediately looked through Gerald's eyes. He had watched as that damned Riverton wizard extracted information from his agent by magic. And there was nothing he could do about it. Had he been able, he would have snuffed out Gerald's life. Instead he was forced to flee the city before the king's guards could capture him. And since then, he'd had to stay on the move. The king had sent his description to soldiers far and wide, and it wasn't safe to stay in one place for too long.

Now, weeks later, he was perched on a stool in a caravan tavern when he overheard a conversation that interested him.

"We need to get more recruiters," a voice said. "This new king and his troops are hunting us down, and our numbers are dwindling."

"I agree," said a second voice. "But the last few folks we brought in got zapped to dust by Anarane."

"That dark elf probably found too much good in their hearts or something," the first grumbled.

Dominic zeroed in on the source of the voices. Two hooded figures hunched over their drinks in the corner. He gathered up his mug and strode over to join them.

*Anyone who speaks in such a way just might be of use to me,* he thought.

He didn't bother with pleasantries or permission. He just plopped down in the empty chair at the men's table.

"Sorry, spook, we aren't looking for company," one of the men growled.

*Spook?* Dominic liked that.

"Actually, I think you do," he said. He told them about the assassins he'd hired to dispose of the two famous Riverton boys, and he explained his subsequent troubles with the king's soldiers. "So I do believe we're on the same side," he finished. "Or at least, we're both on the side that desires to avoid the attention of the king and his minions."

The smaller of the two men narrowed his eyes. "You make many claims. For all we know you could be a spy for the damned king."

With a slow smile, Dominic pulled back his hood slightly,

just enough to reveal his flaming eyes. The two men drew back sharply.

"What *are* you?" the larger man asked. "Why do you have flames where your eyes should be?"

"Best not to ask questions to which you would not like to hear the answers," Dominic replied. "Suffice it to say… would a king's spy look like this?"

The hooded men exchanged a long look, then both nodded.

"Fine, spook," said the smaller man. "But if we're going to have this conversation, let's go somewhere with fewer ears."

Dominic nodded. "Please. Call me Dominic."

---

It turned out the two men worked with slavers. Their job was to assemble small groups of soldiers who were willing to capture unprotected wanderers in Trimoria and sell them into slavery.

The larger of the two men explained as they walked through the dense forest surrounding Cammoria. "The problem is, it's slow work finding the right people, and there's only two of us. Anarane has insisted we either up the pace or bring in some new recruiters. Sounds like you'd be perfect for the job, but be aware… she has a way of looking inside people. And she doesn't always like what she sees."

"Who exactly is this Anarane?" Dominic asked. "From where does she come?"

"That's a mystery. To all of us. But we're almost there, so feel free to ask her yourself. Just don't expect an answer."

The trees thinned, and the larger man stopped before the mouth of a cave. "Stay here," he said. "I have to signal our arrival."

From a crevice near the cave entrance, he retrieved a container of some kind of powder, then sprinkled the powder across the entrance to the cave. Finally, he pulled out flint and lit the powder. Flames of the deepest purple flickered upward, and a thick smoke formed overhead, making the area as dark as night.

A few minutes passed in silence and then suddenly, two ogres emerged from the cave and took up positions on either side of the cave's entrance. Guards. Then a few moments later, a third figure emerged. An elven woman, painfully beautiful. Her skin was smooth and wrinkle-free, with a milky white tone that almost glowed, and thick, luxuriously long raven black hair fell over her shoulders. Her violet eyes indicated power and confidence, the eyes of someone who was used to being obeyed. Hanging from her belt was a flail adorned with multiple serpents. No—these were not adornments. They were actual snakes, alive and wriggling.

As she stepped out among the trees, the two recruiters and both ogres knelt.

Dominic refused to do the same. But as he stood, he felt the prickle of magical power forcing him downward. He resisted the compulsion. A contest of wills, then.

"I presume you are Anarane," he said.

The elven woman glared at him. The magical force dissipated, and she smiled coldly.

*Was that a flash of fangs I saw?*

"My, my…" she said. "Who do we have here?"

Dominic was surprised to find himself feeling a bit intimidated. "Just a person looking for work. I have a few issues with the king's soldiers, so the normal jobs are unavailable to me. I heard you might be hiring."

Anarane stepped forward and sniffed the air—then looked at him with alarm. "Remove your hood," she said. "Let me see your face."

Dominic complied.

At the sight of his eyes, Anarane backed away and let out a snakelike hiss. Her lips peeled back, and yes, she did indeed have fangs, with beads of a yellow liquid at their tips.

"You have the stink of the Abyss and of Sammael on you," she said. "I cannot help you. Lilith forbids it."

"Lilith?"

"Lilith will not deal with the minions of Sammael. I cannot help you." She dug into a pocket and produced a pouch of coins, which she tossed at his feet. "Take that and leave. And do not return."

Dominic picked up the pouch, weighed it, and smiled. "Very well, Anarane. I'll leave."

*And I'll speak to Sammael about this.*

As he turned to depart, he called back over his shoulder, "Blessings of Sammael on you."

Another hiss escaped the pale elf, and Dominic picked up

his pace.

---

Dominic cursed under his breath as he neared the entrance to the misty forest. An entire encampment of dwarves was set up, cooking food, drinking ale, and patrolling the vicinity. What on earth were they doing here? They certainly didn't look like they'd be going anywhere soon. Dominic didn't want any witnesses observing his trek into the woods—which meant he'd have to find a way around.

A tap on his shoulder startled him. He'd been concentrating so completely on what was in front of him that he had failed to detect the scouts approaching from behind. Two heavily armed dwarves had crept up and glared at him suspiciously.

"Why are you skulking behind this tree?" one asked.

Dominic tried to maintain an even tone. "I was just curious, is all. What is that group of dwarves waiting for?"

Both of the dwarves leveled their spears at Dominic's chest. "Hold your hands where they are," said the second dwarf, the one with the red beard. "What's your name?"

He tilted his head politely. "My name is Dominic."

And before either of the dwarves could so much as yell to warn the others, Dominic grasped them with his otherworldly power. The only sound that escaped his hiding spot was the whoosh of the dwarves' last breaths as he squeezed the life from them.

# THE HUNT

Aaron stretched in his bed and smiled. He'd been looking forward to this day for several weeks.

An actual day off.

No training, no teaching, no chores.

Instead, he was going to spend the day with Sloane. He'd promised to show her what he'd learned from the elves when it came to bow hunting.

He'd barely started getting dressed when she knocked on his door. "Come on, Aaron! I've got a whole day with you, and I want to make the most of it."

"Come on in!" he called. "I'm mostly dressed."

Sloane opened the door just as Aaron slipped on his shirt. She was fully outfitted in her hiking attire, which consisted of form-fitting pants, walking shoes, and a blouse with extra pockets. Although her clothes were more practical than stylish, Aaron noticed the tightness of her pants. Her legs were long and lean, her backside supple…

"Stop driving yourself crazy," she snapped. "It'll be a couple years before we're married."

Aaron scowled. "I'm never going to forgive Ryan for giving you the power to read my mind."

"If I couldn't read minds, those assassins might have gotten you."

"Sound like a fair trade to me," Aaron grumbled.

"Very funny. Would it help if I told you I think the same things when I see you without your shirt on?"

"Actually, yes. Er… but maybe no. Oh, I don't know. Let's change the subject. Are you ready for a hunt in the woods?"

"As long as you promise not to make me look like a fool. While you've been practicing nonstop, I've been working the farm and babysitting."

Aaron smiled. "I promise. After all, you were my first teacher. It would be rude to show you up."

Sloane rolled her eyes.

"Hey, I heard your father talking about a large hare that's been evading him for months. Maybe we'll be able to get it."

"Oh, sure, that would be smart. Capture the one quarry my father has been looking forward to capturing himself. He loves to talk about how close he's come to getting that stupid thing."

Aaron frowned. "You make a very good point. Maybe we should just bag a deer instead."

They walked hand in hand to the kitchen, where the dragons were asleep on the floor.

"Hi, Ruby! Hi, Pyre!" Sloane said.

The dragons both cracked an eye open and then went back to sleep.

But then came the sound of little feet pounding down the hall. "Ruby! Payar!"

Zenethar tore into the kitchen, and the dragons hopped to their feet and ran to him.

"Aren't you supposed to be in school with Ryan?" Aaron asked.

"I have heg-ache!" he said, laughing as Ruby bit his leg.

"Oh, a headache," Aaron said drily. "I can see you feel terrible."

"Okay, Zenethar," said Sloane. "If you and the dragons are going to play, take it outside." She opened the door, and the three young playmates scampered out.

"Those dragons are getting big," Aaron said. "I think Zenethar could ride them. Pretty soon they won't be able to fit through the door."

"That might be for the best," Sloane said. "Lately they've been starting to exercise their wings. Mother was furious when they tried that in the house."

"Is that why all the furniture in the living room is piled into a corner?"

"Yup. They blew everything into a heap. At least they said they were sorry."

Aaron stood in the doorway and watched the two dragons with Zenethar.

"Am I pretty?" Ruby asked.

Zenethar hugged the dragon. "Sure. You nice dragon!"

Pyre nudged Zenethar with his nose. "Am I fat?"

Zenethar patted Pyre's big belly. "Only a little."

---

Sensing movement ahead, Aaron paused on the trail, pulled an arrow from his quiver, and expanded his senses as Castien had taught him to do. He felt Sloane's presence directly behind him, of course, and not surprisingly he also sensed four elves in the brush behind him. Even on Aaron's day off, Castien insisted he have an elven guard to protect him from any would-be assassins. At least they stayed hidden so he could *pretend* to be alone with Sloane.

A breeze blew, and Aaron picked up the musky scent of deer.

He nocked the arrow, pulled back on the string, and waited. Ten seconds passed. Then twenty. After a minute, a buck lifted up from the foliage. But Aaron didn't yet have a clear shot.

The breeze shifted. The buck would soon detect his scent, and Aaron would be in danger of losing his quarry.

Sure enough, the buck turned his head, made eye contact with Aaron, and flared his nostrils.

Aaron held his breath, motionless.

The buck moved away from the foliage, and Aaron had his shot. He loosened his fingers on the string…

Sloane pushed his arm. "No!"

Aaron's arrow flew above his target and disappeared harmlessly between the trees. The buck bolted.

Aaron turned to Sloane, angry at her for ruining his shot, until he saw the tears streaming down her face.

"Sloane? What's wrong? Is it the deer? Forget about it. There'll be others."

Sloane looked him in the eye, obviously distraught. "Aaron... I'm sorry. I can't do this. I *felt* that poor animal's fear when he saw you. He knew he was going to die. I—I can't hunt with you, Aaron. I'm sorry. And to be honest, I don't think I can stomach the idea of eating meat. Not after feeling what that poor thing felt."

Aaron felt a knot form in his throat. He pulled Sloane into his arms. "It's okay. We don't have to hunt. We can just go home, or... anything you want."

She squeezed him tightly. "Maybe we could take a walk? Just the two of us?"

"You mean just the two of us alone with four stealthy elven warriors?"

She chuckled into his shirt. "Yes. Them too. The armed guard is very romantic."

"Sure, let's walk. I don't really want to hunt anyway. I just wanted to spend the day with you."

She pulled back and smiled. "You *did* want to hunt, but thank you. I tell you what: when it's time for lunch, I'll eat the vegetables, you eat the chicken sandwiches."

He laughed. "Deal."

Ryan sat in Eglerion's history class with thirty other students. Today's lesson was less dry than some, as Eglerion was sharing with them some maps and artifacts he'd brought from Eluanethra. Particularly interesting were the maps that extended well beyond the borders of the Trimoria everyone knew today, and showed the entire continent that existed before the barriers were erected by the First Protector. The really amazing thing, as far as Ryan was concerned, was that Eglerion was actually old enough to remember the time before the barriers were erected.

Unfortunately, Charlie Carbunkle, the ten-year-old bully, was also in this class. And lately the mischievous boy had discovered the joy of spitballs.

Ryan looked on as the boy ripped off a bit of parchment, chewed it in his mouth, pulled out a wad of juicy pulp, then flicked the wad at a younger student two rows in front of him. Fortunately, the spitball missed. But of course Charlie simply went to work making another one.

Ryan had had enough. He summoned a tiny thread of energy to his fingers, and surreptitiously, he let fly a red-hot needle of energy right at Charlie's backside.

Charlie yelped and hopped up from his chair. And judging by his coughing, he'd inhaled his own spitball.

"Someone attacked me!" he announced angrily.

Eglerion's eyes narrowed. "And why would someone attack you, Charlie?"

Another student spoke up. "He's been throwing spitballs."

The lore master's gaze darkened. "In that case, Mister Carbunkle, it seems to me the other students are kindly trying to help you learn self-control. And if they fail… well, you can rely on me to come up with my own solution. You aren't the first discipline issue I've had in the last thousand years. We'll get you straightened out. As a matter of fact…" He tapped his chin. "Why don't you go dunk your head in a bucket of water? When you return, you'll feel right as rain."

Charlie's eyes went wide and his face turned red. Then he bolted from the room.

As Eglerion continued the lesson, Ryan smiled. Unlike the other students, he'd seen this side of Eglerion before. Now everyone knew what he already knew: *Don't mess with the elven lore master.*

---

"How about we collect some mushrooms for Mother to cook?" Sloane asked as she and Aaron walked.

"Sure," Aaron said. "I know where there's a large patch. Spotted them when we were doing endurance runs—in full armor, of course."

Sloane linked her arm in his. "Lead the way."

As they walked, Aaron continued to use his senses in the way Castien had taught him. He felt the moisture in the air from yesterday's light rain. He smelled the scent of freshly aerated soil. And he heard the soft footfalls of the elves who shadowed them.

But then he heard something else—something that shouldn't be there. It was just the slightest of whines, followed by the crunch of dried leaves trampled underfoot.

Using the hand signals he'd learned in Eluanethra, he called for the elves to circle into a defensive pattern around Sloane, then pulled out his bow and nocked an arrow.

"What's going on?" Sloane whispered.

"Something's stalking us from the edge of the woods," he whispered back. The breeze changed, and he sniffed the air. "I smell wolves. Get your bow out just in case."

Aaron continued to watch the woods. There—to the north. A hint of gray fur.

"You are more elf than human," one of the guards whispered. "I didn't even detect the pack."

The beasts began coalescing at the edge of the woods. Young wolves, at least a dozen. And judging by their protruding rib cages and the hungry gleam in their eyes, they were starving. That made no sense; there was plenty of game in these woods.

He glanced over at Sloane, who was in deep concentration.

*Oh no,* Aaron thought. *She's talking to them.*

Yips sounded from the pack. Then again. And then the wolves moved away, loping westward, some of them looking back over their broad shoulders.

"We have to help them," Sloane said, tears rolling down her cheeks. "Their father and mother were trapped by a falling tree, and their father is injured." She didn't wait for a reply; she just pulled at him to follow as she started jogging after the pack.

Aaron had no choice but to trot after her.

---

They chased the pack for a good fifteen minutes before it slowed near a remote cave. A massive tree had fallen directly in front of it.

"We're here," Sloane said. "I can sense the pups' nervousness."

"And I smell an infection," added Aaron. "I'm going in to see what I can do. Can you tell them not to kill me?"

Sloane focused silently for a long moment, and as Aaron watched, the young pups moved aside and sat together, all of them starting at Aaron.

"What did you say?" Aaron asked.

"I told them that my mate would help free their parents, and that they needed to calm down and sit at a distance."

"And they listened?"

"Better than you ever do."

Aaron gestured for the elven escort to follow at a safe distance as he and Sloane moved forward to the fallen tree. Her mind-reading was right. There were two wolves beneath the tree, a male and a female. The male's back half was crushed beneath the tree's trunk. The female had either freed herself or had only been struck by the branches, but she too lay still, her breathing shallow. Both of them were thin with the late effects of starvation.

Sloane touched the male's front paw. "He's in a fever-dream," she sobbed. "They both are."

Aaron turned to the elves. "I need some of my mother's healing items." The elves who accompanied Aaron always carried plenty of food infused with his mother's healing energy, in case he exerted himself and need to recharge. They now rummaged through their packs and handed over bundles of jerky and flasks of milk.

"Tell the she-wolf that I'll be giving her some of this dried meat, and she needs to eat it," Aaron instructed Sloane. "It should help with the fever. Then tell her that I'm going to move the tree to help her mate. Also remind the young wolves what we're doing."

"Okay, one thing at a time."

Sloane adopted her now-familiar look of concentration, and the she-wolf growled, whined, and snapped her jaws in midair.

"Well?" Aaron said.

"The she-wolf isn't a fan of yours, I'm afraid. You smell of the hunt, and apparently she's been shot by arrows before. But she'll accept food from me."

"Even better," Aaron said, handing Sloane the jerky.

Sloane approached cautiously, but the she-wolf wasn't a threat to her, and very gently took the meat from Sloane's hand. She swallowed, then yipped.

Sloane laughed. "She says thank you, even though she

prefers deer. But she thanks me and my mate for providing food."

Aaron smiled. "Tell her that now is the difficult part. We have to lift the tree, and it may hurt her mate."

After more yips and whines, Sloane nodded. "She understands. I think she is resigned to having her mate die, since it's better to die than be a burden to the pack."

Aaron motioned for the elves to help, and they all got into position to lift together. Aaron called out, "One… two… three… lift!"

Aaron lifted with all his might, his body straining with the effort. The trunk barely moved. But it was enough. As soon as the male wolf was free, the female bit his scruff and dragged him to safety.

"Drop it!" Aaron called.

The tree fell back with a thud.

Aaron straightened up, his back cracking and popping. "Oh, I'm going to regret that in the morning."

Sloane took one of the flasks of infused milk and slowly approached the injured male. Kneeling before him, she dribbled as much as she could onto the injured wolf's lolling tongue. The wolf awakened from its fever just long enough to cry out in pain.

"He says his leg is hurt, and his ribs," said Sloane. "He wants us to leave him here to die."

"Tell him the milk will heal him," Aaron insisted.

After another moment of concentration, Sloane returned to

dribbling the milk on the wolf's tongue. This time the wolf lapped at it a bit, consuming at least some of it.

One of the elves stepped forward with a bowl he'd produced from his pack. "Maybe this will help." Aaron looked around and realized two of the other elves had disappeared. Perhaps they were once again assuming their role as hidden guards.

"Thank you," said Sloane. She filled the bowl with milk and placed it under the wolf's snout. Though the wolf still didn't lift his head, he was now able to drink more efficiently. Sloane slowly refilled the bowl as the wolf drained it. When he'd finished two full flasks, she stood back.

"He says he's going to try to move."

Slowly and awkwardly, the wolf moved onto its belly. Sloane gave him some of the jerky, and he ate it eagerly. Soon he was standing on four legs, though he still looked shaky, and was as thin as ever. The she-wolf came over, licked his face, and nuzzled him.

Sloane then turned to face the half-grown pups, who were still waiting obediently. She tossed the rest of the jerky pieces to them, and they immediately dove in and chomped happily.

That was when the two missing elves returned, and now Aaron understood where they had gone and why. In no time at all, they had tracked and hunted a deer, and now they dragged the carcass behind them. Aaron was relieved to see it was not the same buck that had made Sloane cry earlier.

"Tell the wolves that this deer is a gift from the elves and humans," Aaron said to Sloane. "Their family is obviously in great need of food. We want them to eat and get well."

Sloane silently talked with the pack. Then she turned back to Aaron. "I explained that my mate sent part of our pack to bring them a gift of food, and that our pack wishes their pack peace and health.'"

The male wolf stepped up to Sloane and rubbed his head against her hip. Then he looked up at her and yipped.

"He says his name is Grey Wind," Sloane translated.

The wolf yipped again.

"He says that we are pack friends now, and that he will spread word of this kindness."

The rest of the pups then rushed in and practically swarmed Sloane, yipping as she rubbed their necks. She looked up at Aaron with tears in her eyes. "Aren't they adorable?"

Aaron smiled. "Can I pet them?"

Sloane shrugged. "They say we are pack friends. Why not?"

"I don't know what that means," Aaron replied, feeling a bit concerned.

"It's fine. Come here you big baby." Sloane motioned for him to approach.

Aaron cautiously walked closer, held out his hand, and several of the pups came over to sniff him. He rubbed their heads, and they playfully nipped at him.

"We should go," Sloane said, standing. "I know they want to eat, and I don't want to be here to watch that."

"I understand." He took her hand, and as they turned for home, the elves spread out around them, on the job once more. "I can't believe we've just been befriended by a pack of wolves. Really, Sloane, you never cease to amaze me. If you can win the animals to our cause, you may end up being the most powerful one of us all."

## PRACTICING SKILLS

"Quiet, Ryan. I can't tell you how hard it is to energize this amount of milk," Arabelle said. "I need to concentrate."

Ryan sat back to watch his betrothed work on the task his mother had set for her. The two of them were alone in the classroom, where a huge container of milk was set on a table, along with several leather flasks that she was to fill once the milk was infused with healing energy.

As Arabelle's forehead furrowed with concentration, Ryan used his visual abilities to watch what she was doing. He'd noticed before that some of her mind-filaments vibrated when she used her magic, and they activated in certain groupings, like musical chords. There was one chord that he now knew drained healing energy from Arabelle, and another that transferred that energy into the milk.

By the time she was done, her energy level was much dimmer, but a glow now emanated from the milk.

"You should eat something now," he said. "You look exhausted."

She began filling the flasks. "I will, as soon as I finish loading these up. Aren't you going to be late for your lesson with Eglerion?"

Ryan looked out the window at the position of the sun in the sky. "You're right! I gotta run." Eglerion was not one to stand for tardiness.

He headed for the door, but Arabelle stopped him. "Hey! Are you going to leave without giving me a kiss?"

Ryan smiled and gave her a peck on the lips. "You're going to make me even later?"

"Hey, I didn't keep you here watching me for the past thirty minutes."

"I love you," he said, then ran for the door. "Eglerion's gonna have my hide!"

---

"In battle," Eglerion said, "you'll find all sorts of distractions. Today we'll be learning one way to prevent such distractions from breaking your concentration. Ryan, move to the center, please."

The war wizard students were sitting in a circle outside, and as Ryan rose and walked to the middle of the ring, he was nervous. You never knew what Eglerion had in mind.

Eglerion took a wooden ball from his pocket and tossed it. "Charlie, catch."

Ryan noticed that Zenethar was sitting with Charlie once again. Somehow, the two of them had become friends. It had been some time since the spitball incident, and Charlie had since turned a corner and had been making an effort to get along with people. Somehow the toddler had been one of the first to accept the new Charlie. Perhaps because they both shared a certain mischievousness.

"Charlie," Eglerion said, "I want you to take careful aim at Ryan's head. When you're ready, throw that ball at him as hard as you can."

The class tensed, and Charlie looked uncertain, but Ryan wasn't worried.

"It's all right," he assured the boy. "Go ahead and throw it."

Charlie stood, still looking worried, but he took careful aim and tossed the ball—lightly—at Ryan's forehead. It met Ryan's shield, which he was now used to maintaining at all times, and bounced off with a slight spark.

The classroom erupted with excitement. They'd never seen a shield employed before.

"Did you see that? It didn't touch him!"

"I think it hit his forehead!"

"Did you see the spark?"

Eglerion silenced the class with a wave of his hand. "You have now witnessed one of the main differences between a regular hedge wizard, who can conjure mean tricks, and a true wizard, who can shield himself from the physical intrusion of others. Today, the only practitioners of such shielding are Ryan and the headmaster." He smiled. "That is about to change."

As Eglerion organized the class and began going through some tests and exercises with them, Ryan was free to sit back and watch. He chuckled as he leaned back in the grass. These guys had no idea what they were in for.

But he also used his unique powers of observation to better understand what was happening. When he saw a ball crash into a student's head, it was like the threads of energy that composed a student's magical ability touched each other and sparked, causing what his father would call a "short circuit."

After a while, Ryan stood and walked over to Eglerion. "Do you mind if I try something?"

Eglerion frowned. "As long as you do not injure my students. Not badly, anyway."

It had been Wat Crazybeard's turn to work on his shield while the others threw things at him. Ryan walked up to him.

"Don't worry, I won't be throwing anything at you. I just want to do… an experiment. Is that okay?"

Wat looked nervous, but he wasn't one to step down from a challenge, especially in front of the class. He braced himself and nodded, his snake-like beard wiggling in affirmation.

Ryan reached out with his powers and lightly brushed the lines of energy that crisscrossed Wat's head, making them crash into each other. The threads that only he could see smashed into each other, sending off a shower of invisible sparks. Wat's expression suggested he didn't feel a thing.

"Okay, Wat," Ryan said. "I'd like you to use your powers. To do anything you want."

"I thought you were going to do an experiment."

"This *is* the experiment."

Wat shrugged, then concentrated. The threads on his head sparked intensely, but nothing else happened.

His mouth fell open in shock. "I can't! What did you do?"

Ryan's experiment had just confirmed what he'd suspected. He'd known it was possible to stun a wizard such that he lost his ability to access his magic, but this approach to doing so... it was almost too easy.

Wat's eyes shone with tears. "Fix it," he whispered. You can fix it, can't you?"

"I'm sorry, of course. It's fine. Hold still."

He studied the lines vibrating violently across the dwarf's head, then very delicately shielded Wat's head and calmed the vibrations. When they settled down, he said, "Okay, Wat, try again."

Wat concentrated on the ground in front of him... and it burst into flame. The class erupted with applause, and Wat smiled in relief. Ryan quickly stomped out the fire.

"Please don't do that again," Wat said. "Now that I've learned to be a wizard, I'd rather lose my beard than lose my magic."

"You're right. I'm sorry, Wat, I should have warned you. But I promise, you're back to normal now."

"Well," said Eglerion, "now that we've seen know how quickly your skills can be snuffed out, let's talk about how to prevent that from happening. Now your training *really* begins…"

---

Arabelle stood in line with her fellow RAM students, waiting her turn. Jared had arranged for all the hedge wizards to learn combat with bows and throwing knives. As he'd said, "Any of you who can't kill from a distance will likely be killed from a distance."

Arabelle knew that, as a healer, her skills would best serve the cause from behind the lines, but she wasn't about to limit herself. So she'd taken it upon herself to prove her worth in other ways.

Ohaobbok was in line directly in front of her. "I'm going to be laughed at," he grumbled.

Arabelle had to crane her neck to look up at the giant ogre, even though he was kneeling. "I would never laugh at you, Ohaobbok. Why do you think anyone else would?"

He leaned down so he could whisper. "I've never handled a dagger before this last week. I prepared for this class by throwing at a target on my own. It has taken me the entire week just to get my daggers to stick to the target."

"That's good though! You're hitting the target."

Ohaobbok sighed. "My target is the wall of a barn."

Arabelle coughed to hide her amusement. "Don't feel bad.

I haven't held a dagger in a long time. I was expecting we would start with bows, so like you, I did a little warming up—I've been shooting a bow with Sloane for several days now. And now that's not going to do me any good at all."

Castien called out, "Next!"

It was Ohaobbok's turn.

Their target was a log hanging from a rope. The rope was looped around a high tree branch, and Castien's aides were yanking on the other end to make it swing and move up and down. The student was to throw a dozen daggers at the target to measure their baseline ability.

"Raise the target another six feet," the sword master ordered. "I want everyone to practice with opponents at chest height first."

When Castien nodded for Ohaobbok to begin, the ogre picked up the first dagger and weighed it in his hand. The elves began yanking on the rope, making the log swing and dance.

Arabelle held her breath and sent good thoughts Ohaobbok's way as he threw.

Twelve throws later, three of his daggers had landed solidly into the log. Not bad. But the other daggers had gone absolutely anywhere and everywhere. Some were buried deep in the ground just yards from where he stood. Some had flown far over the hill behind the target.

"A fair attempt," said Castien. "Nothing to be ashamed of. Though I wonder if we should have you throwing swords instead. These daggers look like toothpicks in your hands; with a sword you might feel the weight better."

Ohaobbok turned back to Arabelle and smiled slightly. She nodded to him; no one had laughed.

"Arabelle, you're next!" shouted Castien.

One of the elves brought her a dozen fresh daggers and wished her luck. But Arabelle's nerves only grew worse when she noticed that Sloane and Aaron had arrived to watch the practice. Sloane smiled and waved.

"Are you ready, healer?" Castien asked.

She nodded, and he yelled for everyone to clear out.

Arabelle moved into place before the target, and Sloane's voice spoke in her head. *"Good luck."*

She picked up the first dagger and felt its weight resting in her palm. As she'd told Ohaobbok, she had held daggers before—though not for throwing. And she was surprised to find how familiar it felt in her hand, almost like an extension of her arm. She identified where its center of balance lay, then held it by its tip as she watched the log sway.

With a quick movement, she let the dagger fly. And instantly knew that she'd made a mistake. She'd aimed where the log was, and not where the log was going to be. It landed a dozen feet behind the target.

Arabelle took a deep breath and cleared her mind. As she grabbed the next dagger, she watched the elves pulling the rope to move the log. She realized that she could tell what the log was about to do by watching how the elves moved their arms. By watching them, she could get a split-second advance notice of the log's movements.

She concentrated, feeling her anxiety drain away. She narrowed her vision to exclude everything but the log and the movement of the elves. Holding her breath, she threw.

She knew her throw was true even before the knife struck the dead center of the log with a satisfying *thwack*.

The other students cheered, then fell silent at Castien's glare of disapproval. He was not a fan of celebrations.

Arabelle grabbed the next dagger, feeling looser now, more comfortable. She repeated the process exactly as she had just done, and threw.

There was no *thwack* this time, but the clank of metal on metal. She'd struck her second dagger with her third. She'd been so precise that she'd hit the same mark twice.

"Halt!" Castien yelled to the elves swinging the log. He walked over and pulled Arabelle's dagger out of the log, then returned to his observation position. "That last hit counts as a center shot. Please continue, healer."

For the next nine throws, Arabelle ignored everything but her target. All nine of them hit dead center.

When the last dagger struck, the students, who had remained tensely silent until then, absolutely exploded with cheers. And Castien didn't even try to shush them. In fact, he was looking at Arabelle with an uncharacteristic smile.

*"That—was—amazing!"* said Sloane's voice in her head.

And then her ring vibrated with a message from Ryan.

She'd taken off her group ring for the exercise, but would never take off her link to him.

*Aaron told us every throw as it happened. You're incredible, my love. I'll see you tonight.*

Before calling up the next student, Castien walked up to her. "After I'm done with testing, you and I need to speak about… possibilities you might enjoy."

Arabelle nodded, feeling the warmth of all the praise. She couldn't suppress the smile that bloomed across her face.

## A NEW CASTLE

Ellisandrea fumed. Her efforts to recruit more acolytes to Sammael's cause had been thwarted by those stubborn dwarves maintaining a presence just outside her domain, blocking those that she might otherwise be able to entice. Any time she gained control of one of the weaker minds bordering her woods, those dwarves would physically prevent her victim from stepping farther into her radius of influence, and would instead drag the poor soul out of her reach.

And there was little she could do from within her magical prison.

Suddenly the presence of Sammael flooded her senses, and his grating voice broadcast into her mind.

*"Ellisandrea,"* he said, *"since you have failed to gather additional assistants on this side of the barrier, we must determine a way to bring the barrier down."*

Bring down the barrier?

Vivid memories from over five centuries ago bubbled up in Ellisandrea's mind. An invading horde of demons screaming through her lands. Destroying all living things in their wake. Those demons were a raw wound that festered deep within her.

*"Somewhere within the barrier lies the wizard responsible for erecting the shield. Azazel was never able to find him, but you will. Slip into the minds of the dwarves. Access their memories of the Protector. One of them must have seen this wizard. And perhaps from them, we can determine his location."*

He wanted her to find Zenethar, her former student. She felt a twinge of guilt as she recalled all that she'd done to him, though indirectly.

But that guilt touched her for but a moment. Then she used her powers to reach out to the weak dwarven minds at the edges of her domain.

---

In a grassy field south of Aubgherle, Throll had called the first meeting of his Council of Advisors. No one but Throll knew the purpose of the meeting, or why this remote spot had been chosen as its location. But Jared was confident Throll had good reasons. Throll had always been a level-headed and fair-minded man, and though it had taken some time for him to settle into his new role, the title of king was now wearing well on Throll's shoulders.

The last to arrive was Silas Redbeard. He dismounted his horse and stomped heavily on his short legs. "Lord King, if you insist on such travel, you need to find a horse that isn't so darn large. I've lost the circulation in my legs."

Throll smiled. "All you need to do is ask. Next time, I'll arrange for a strong mountain pony."

Silas harrumphed and took his place within the circle, still rubbing his legs.

Throll stood at the center of the circle, turning to face every member as he spoke. "I want to thank everyone for the indulgence in meeting here. Perhaps we should begin with introductions. Grendel, would you begin?"

Grendel nodded. "My name is Grendel Hawthorne. I am a common man, a historian, and I was honored to accept a role as an advisor to the king."

Throll shook his head "'Advisor' is insufficient to describe all you do, Grendel. How about… seneschal of House Lancaster?"

Grendel turned red. "As you will, Your Highness."

Next, Silas Redbeard stood. "I am Silas Redbeard, head of da Redbeard Clan, and representative of the coalition of dwarf clans from da Iron Mountains. The king asked for a counselor from da dwarves, and I am he."

He sat back down, and Eglerion spoke. "My name is Eglerion Mithtanion. I am the lore master of Eluanethra. I act as advisor and historian of all matters arcane for King Throll Thariginian Lancaster."

The next in the circle was Labri. She looked uncomfortable to have all eyes on her, but spoke confidently. "My name is Labriuteleanan Sirfalas—but most people call me Labri. I am Eglerion's student from Eluanethra."

Throll cleared his throat. "You are a little more than that, Your Highness."

Labri blushed. "Well, when the time is right, I will be the next queen of my people. And when I do become queen, I pledge to continue to assist and advise in any way possible."

It was now Jared's turn. "My name is Jared Riverton. I long ago committed myself to helping Throll... er, King Throll in any way possible. I'm the headmaster of the Riverton Academy of Magic. I am also a war wizard and blacksmith."

"My kind of wizard," Silas said. "A fellow anvil-thumper."

Throll pressed his right hand to his broad chest. "Thank you all for honoring me with your presence for this council meeting. Now let me be direct and explain why we're all here. As you know from the prophecies, we will, in time, be facing a great battle—one that will require all our preparation for years to come. We are already enlisting an army of soldiers and an army of wizards, and providing training to both. Much work remains to be done, but I'm comfortable with the progress occurring on both fronts.

"However, in talking with Silas and Eglerion, I realized there is another front that we have not yet begun to prepare: an *actual* front. A defensive fortification from which our troops might wage this war.

"In the first battle against the demons, Castle Thariginian stood against the horde. Without it, we might not stand here today to tell the tale. But that castle now lies on the other side of the barrier, and nothing within the boundaries of the barrier is anywhere close to its equal. Which means… we need to build a new castle." Throll pointed at its feet. "And I propose that we construct that castle on the ground upon which you now sit."

Silas leapt to his feet. "The dwarves volunteer to assist in its construction! We constructed Castle Thariginian, what stood against da demon horde over five hundred years ago. It should be our construction dat does it again."

Throll nodded. "Thank you, Silas. We'll take you up on your kind offer."

Grendel was already thinking through logistics. "This will be quite the organizational effort. We need workers, draftsmen, designers… and we must ensure that sufficient funds exist in our coffers to pay them all. Sir Redbeard, please let me help you in any way possible."

"Just make sure that your budgets account for a proper supply of ale, and you'll have done more than you can know."

Throll turned to Eglerion. "My friend, can you please tell everyone what you told me about Castle Thariginian?"

Eglerion panned his gaze across the council. "When Castle Thariginian was dedicated almost a thousand years ago, the family line of the Thariginians was magically linked to it. As a result, the castle became something more than the original builders intended.

"I barely understand the powers involved in such a thing, but during the dedication, an enormous amount of energy was invested, enough to pierce the space between this land and the spirit realm—and the very spirit of the Thariginians was invited into Trimoria, to occupy the castle itself. In that moment the castle became a living thing, dedicated to the family line of the Thariginians, and forever linking their fates.

"And as a living thing it has a mind of its own, and even magic of its own. It can heal itself. A broken pavement stone may find itself mended the next day. A crack in a lintel, the same.

"It is also linked to the land surrounding it. It extracts water from the ground and grows an edible moss that can sustain its inhabitants. At times it can tell those inhabitants what is occurring in distant locations. And finally, the castle has its own voice. It can speak... at least it can speak with those who can hear it."

"Who can hear it?" Jared asked.

"Only those who are of the family line, plus some wizards who tuned themselves to the proper vibrations."

"Given all these benefits, I take it you intend to do something similar with this new castle?" Jared said to Throll. "Dedicate it to your family line?"

Throll smiled. "Not quite. Actually, I intend to dedicate it to *your* family line."

Jared was speechless, and he must have looked suitably shocked, for the king laughed, and so did Silas and Labri.

"Eglerion," Throll said, "please explain."

The wizened elf turned to Jared. "There is *already* a castle dedicated to the Thariginian line. There cannot be another. Nor need there be. The only requirement for joining a spirit to a family line is that the family in question be gifted with strong magic. Certainly, your family qualifies far beyond anyone alive in Trimoria in centuries. You, Ryan, Aubrey… even Aaron has a power that must be acknowledged as magic, though I don't understand it. The Riverton line is without a doubt the logical choice."

"The decision is already made, my friend," Throll said. "Strategy requires this castle of us, and our fate requires sacrifice. I ask you, both as a friend and as your king, to please allow for the gifting. We cannot achieve victory without the advantages that a sentient self-healing castle might provide."

Jared couldn't deny Trimoria's need. "I… I would be honored," he said at last. He looked to Eglerion. "What do I need to do?"

"First, you must resurrect the Conclave of Wizards. Include only the strongest of your wizards and healers. In addition to you and Ryan, I recommend the dwarf wizard Wat be included."

"You have a dwarf wizard?" said Silas. "How is it dat I didn't know about this? To which clan does he belong?"

"Wat was raised in Cammoria as an orphan," Jared said.

"He's adopted his own clan name: Crazybeard. If you saw him, you'd know why."

"I'll admit that I'd never heard of a dwarf wizard either," said Eglerion. "But he is quite powerful."

"I do want ta meet this Crazybeard," Silas said.

"I'll arrange an introduction," said Jared.

Eglerion continued his instructions. "The conclave must also include healers. Aubrey would be best suited, but Arabelle is quite talented as well. And this is just a start. Ultimately, we'll need more power to pierce the veil than we can generate even from this powerful group, but these are a good start."

"When I come into my powers," Labri said, "I would be happy to assist in the dedication."

Eglerion smiled. "Labriuteleanan, when you receive your powers, you will definitely be a boon to the conclave."

"I'll immediately send word to da clans," Silas announced. "Especially now dat I know dis is the castle for Lord Wizard Riverton, master blacksmith, I will make sure we employ damantite throughout. This castle will be impenetrable by da time we're finished!"

"And I will return to Eluanethra to consult with Xinthian and the elders," Eglerion said. "I will need to do much research before I'm prepared to give further instruction for the dedication."

Grendel raised a hand. "I will immediately set to work on planning. We can't begin construction until the dwarves are involved, but I'll find local workers to begin clearing the land." The diminutive man seemed downright thrilled at the notion of organizing a big project.

Throll nodded to all. "Thank you, everyone. We all know the importance of this task, and we all have a great deal of work to do to make it happen. Let's get started."

## SWAMP CATS

Ellisandrea sent out the tendrils of her influence across the expanse of woods surrounding her former home. She felt the warmth of the living beings within her reach, but instead of exerting her influence to obey, which usually resulted in the consciousness of the creature rejecting her, she gently brushed the minds with a suggestion to recall past events.

For the elf queen, the mind was like a series of images that, when assembled into a whole, told a story. Many of these minds were utterly useless, and it took all of her control to not lash out in disgust. But she'd had success in traversing the hideous little dwarven memories. She just had to practice patience and stealth.

Neither of which were her strong suits.

The problem was, none of the dwarves had any memories

of value. It seemed they did nothing but binge on ale, work in a smithy, and mine for ore.

Until now.

She knew the importance of the memory the instant she came across it. A cave, heavily guarded by warrior dwarves, and in that cave was a dais holding the body of an ancient man, surrounded by a scintillating aura of rainbow hues.

The dwarf whose memory she was exploring knelt reverently at the base of the platform. The aura over the body flickered, then became nearly translucent. In that split second, she could see the face of the man on the dais.

It was him. Zenethar, her former pupil. The man Trimoria now called the First Protector.

*"Good,"* came the voice of Sammael. *"Now to pass this information to Dominic. He'll find this savior and destroy him. Then the barrier will fall."*

---

Aaron was amazed at how much the dragons had grown in only nine months. Pyre was now the size of a horse, and Ruby was only a tiny bit smaller. They'd both perfected their ability to fly, and they now hunted for food on their own. At first Throll had been concerned that the dragons would start poaching the domestic animals from the neighboring farms, despite their promises that they wouldn't. It was Sloane who convinced her father that they would only hunt wild game.

After all, she could look directly into the dragon's minds and see the truth.

Aaron smiled, as he always did when he thought of Sloane. She was still the same plainspoken girl he'd first met almost three years ago; the only difference is now she didn't even have to move her lips to tell him exactly what she thought of him. She could bury her thoughts right into his head and he couldn't possibly escape.

Her voice sounded in his head. *"I heard that. Anyway, I'll be there in a second. I was just giving Silver some instructions."*

"Ruby! Pyre!" Aaron hollered. "Enough playtime. Sloane will be here in a second, so get ready to leave for the cave. I don't want to keep the dwarves waiting."

Pyre tilted his head. "That is today? I thought it was yesterday."

Ruby blasted a ring of smoke at Pyre. "You mean tomorrow, not yesterday, you idiot.

Sloane came around the corner, wearing the Trimorian version of baggy overalls. Aaron felt a twinge of regret; the overalls covered up all the things about her body he so liked to stare at.

She sniffed in annoyance. "I can't exactly wear frilly things *all* the time, Aaron."

Aaron grinned. "Doesn't have to be frilly. Just not so baggy."

She rolled her eyes and took his hand, and the four of them set out.

"What were you talking to Silver about?" Aaron asked.

"Oh, that. Lately I've had him scouting the edges of the swamps to the north. You remember."

Aaron hesitated. He thought he vaguely remembered a conversation about that. He should probably learn to listen better.

"Yes, you should definitely listen better," Sloane said. "Anyway, he found some pockets of swamp cats and was able to communicate with them. I'd like to see if we can enlist their help. After all, if the demons invade, all living creatures are in jeopardy. And swamp cats are fierce fighters."

"Are you sure Silver will be all right?" Aaron asked. "I'm nervous at the idea of him interacting with wild animals."

"Don't worry, love. He's a smart cat. He and I agreed that if there's any danger, he should just run away." She squeezed Aaron's hand. "Hey, I love the big furball too. I won't let anything happen to him."

---

Silver leapt to the top branch of a stunted oak tree and let out an identifying roar, a signal to all cats in the area. He didn't have to wait long for a response. A sleek black cat slunk out of the marshy fields, his tail waving aggressively. The black cat vocalized his thoughts through a series of clicks.

"I, too, am here," he said. "My territory is still mine. Remain in the no-tail territory."

Silver leapt to the ground, careful not to cross the odorous line that marked the edge of the other cat's territory. Except, as he sniffed again, he realized that the cat before him wasn't the one who'd made the markings.

"I request to speak to the alpha cat," Silver said. "I represent the no-tails. They wish to reach an agreement."

The black cat looked at Silver curiously. "That explains why you smell of the no-tails." His eyes narrowed. "Wait here. I'll return."

The cat turned and melted into the shadows.

Now Silver had a much longer wait. But in time, the cat returned. And not just with the alpha; at least two dozen cats converged on his location. Silver's muscles bunched in anticipation.

An enormous black cat, far larger than Silver, strode forward, his muscles rippling as he walked. This was the leader, the cat whose scent was all along the edge of the territory.

The cat stepped across the demarcation line and into no-tail territory. Silver stood patiently as the larger cat sniffed him, verifying the scents that indicated where he'd traveled. But after only a moment, the great cat leapt back.

"You have no-tail and lizard lord scent! Explain what brings you here!"

Silver patiently related the message that Sloane had given him. That the no-tails desired peace with the cats, and the warning of the battle with demons that was to come.

"I have never known a demon, nor can I scent one on you," the large cat said skeptically. "Why should I believe in them? And why do you smell of lizard lord? I thought only bones were left of the last of them."

"There are two lizard lords in companionship with the no-tails with whom I live," Silver explained. "And another of these no-tails can communicate with us. She speaks with images in our heads. I've seen images of these demons and what happened many lifetimes ago."

The black cat contemplated Silver's words for a long moment.

Then he leapt forward with a mighty roar.

---

As Sloane stood with Aaron at the base of a cliff that rose hundreds of feet in the air, she felt the entire world around her. Not just heard it; felt it, and understood it. What had once been the mere chirp of a cricket was now the call of a male cricket looking for females of his kind. The primitive messages coming from beneath the ground were ants focusing on their tasks. Her gift was truly remarkable, and she couldn't imagine being without it.

She also sensed Aaron, of course. He was actively scanning for danger and internally marking all the possible directions from which an attack might come. And yet he was unaware of the dwarves waiting for them not fifty yards away. She knew exactly where the dwarves were, because she could sense their thoughts.

She squeezed Aaron's hand. "The dwarves are already here."

He chuckled. "You're amazing. I bet you're a better tracker than Castien."

She sent her thoughts to the dragons, instructing them to wait here so as not to frighten the dwarves. They really had become intimidating to those who didn't know them, and soon they wouldn't even be able to stay in the barn with Ohaobbok. Not only did they need more space, they needed someplace that was fireproof, as Pyre had proven one night when he breathed fire during a nightmare and had nearly set the barn on fire.

Which was precisely why they were here today.

She and Aaron continued forward, looking up at the very same cliff that Ohaobbok had tumbled from two years ago. Or, rather, he'd been thrown from it by his overbearing mother as punishment for not being more like a normal ogre. During the time in which Aaron and Sloane nursed the ogre back to health, they'd had the opportunity to explore, and they'd found a number of fissures, crevices, and caves. One of those caves was the one chosen by the dwarves of the Redbeard Clan.

"Greetings, dwarves!" Aaron called out. "May we approach?"

A large-bellied dwarf sauntered forth from the entrance, then stopped when he saw the dragons in the distance.

A voice sounded from behind him. "Oy, Alebelly! You aim to lead those young'uns in or just stand there!" A second dwarf appeared beside Alebelly, his large, bushy red beard so long that it nearly dragged on the ground.

"Th-th-they really *exist*!" said Alebelly. "Thems be dragons!"

"Of course they exist, you idiot," said the second dwarf. "They're the whole reason we're here."

Sloane stepped forward. "Alebelly, is it? It's a pleasure to meet you. My name is Sloane Lancaster. Would you like me to introduce you to our dragon friends? I promise they're quite friendly."

Alebelly stared at Sloane for a long moment, then turned to his companion and smacked him on the shoulder. "Granton, you could have told me I was going to meet a princess today! I would have worn proper leggings and my new jerkin."

He turned back to Sloane and awkwardly knelt. "I'm sorry, Your Highness. I am—"

Sloane smacked the dwarf on the top of his balding head. "Glennock Alebelly. Do I look like I need anyone kneeling to me? Did I even introduce myself as princess this or princess that?"

The dwarf rose to his feet. "I'm sorry, I— Wait, how did you know my name?"

Aaron stepped forward. "Hello, Glennock. I'm Aaron Riverton. I happen to be engaged to this young lady. I should warn you, she reads minds as plainly as any book. I expect she plucked your name right out of your head."

Sloane felt herself blushing. "I apologize for smacking you. I sometimes have a bit of a temper, especially when I'm treated like a princess. Like Aaron, I'd prefer to be treated like you'd treat anyone else. How about we start over. I'm Sloane. And you are?"

Glennock straightened up to his full three and a half feet. "My name is Glennock Alebelly. Silas Redbeard asked me to attend to a matter of some cave expansion. I'm a surveyor and an expert when it comes to the structural integrity of caves."

The other dwarf bowed. "My name is Granton Redbeard. I, too, was asked by Silas to assist in acquiring a proper home for your magnificent beasts. My specialty is rock excavation."

"A pleasure to meet you both. Now, I'd like to introduce you to the dragons."

She sent a silent call to them, and they both approached.

"The dragons were hatched by Aaron and his brother Ryan," Sloane explained, "so they have a familial bond with humankind. The larger one is Pyre. He's a male. The other is Ruby. She's a female, and thus is the more intelligent of the two."

Aaron cocked an eyebrow.

The dragons scrabbled up beside her and sat proudly, their long necks stretching high.

Glennock's eyes were wide. "By Seder's long white beard! I can't believe what I'm seeing. Two beautiful dragons sitting there just as you please. Amazing!"

Pyre cocked his head. "You look tasty, dwarf."

Glennock backed away, panicked.

Ruby nipped Pyre's tail and said to the dwarves, "Excuse

my brother. He meant to say, 'You look *nice*.' He is sometimes an idiot when it comes to human speech."

Glennock didn't look entirely sure, but Granton laughed.

"I told you there was nothing to worry about, you fat rock inspector."

"I am *not* fat. This belly is all muscle."

"Well," said Granton to Sloane, "Allow *Musclebelly* and I to walk you through the cave. All in all, I think it's an excellent choice. It bears a few cracks, but they don't go deep and won't affect the structural integrity. We'll have to widen the entrance to allow for the dragons' growth, but that won't take long. I'd like to know what the dragons think, and whether they have a preference for nesting areas within the cave. So please." He waved them in. "Follow me."

---

As the dwarves showed the dragons around the cave, Sloane sensed Silver's call from somewhere in the distance. She'd taught the cat how to cry out in a way that was easy for her to sense mentally. She instructed the dwarves and dragons not to leave the cave, then excused herself.

Aaron followed her outside. "What's going on?"

"Silver is returning."

"Well, that's good, right?"

"He has company."

She felt the thought patterns of other cats with Silver. A *lot* of other cats.

"Company?" Aaron asked. "*People* company?"

"No, cat company. They'll be here soon. I think they're running."

She mentally reached out to Silver and asked if everything was all right. But he'd already arrived. He was loping along the base of the cliff, followed closely by a pack of pitch-black swamp cats. As they neared, the other cats slowed and stopped, but Silver came right up to her.

*"The leader of this pack wanted to speak to the picture talker,"* Silver said. *"He doesn't understand the danger with the demons, and wanted to see it for himself."*

Sloane put her hand on Aaron's shoulder. "Everything's fine. The pack leader just wanted to speak to me."

A truly giant black cat stepped forward, and Silver made introductions. *"I present to you the leader of this pack,"* he said. *"He is known as Midnight."* Silver turned to the lead cat. *"The no-tail with light-colored fur on her head is the picture talker. The other no-tail is her mate."*

The black cat came forward and sniffed at them both.

Sloane sent Aaron a mental message. *"He's smelling us to see who we are and where we've been. It's their way to learn about those they meet."*

Midnight backed away and sat on his haunches. He sniffed again, his fur rising a bit, and growled. *"I can smell lizard lords and other no-tails nearby."*

*"I've told them to remain in the cave so we might speak first,"* Sloane replied.

The cats reacted with surprise, though outwardly they remained stoic.

*"How is it you speak this way?"* Midnight asked. *"Can all no-tails do this? Are you their leader?"*

"I'm not the leader, but I'm the daughter of the leader of all humans. And unfortunately I'm the only one who is able to speak to you like this. My name is Sloane Lancaster."

*"Very well, no-tail leader-daughter. Your pack member Silver mentioned dangers that I couldn't scent. I would like to hear about these dangers from you."*

Sloane delivered the visual messages meant to explain the prophecies. At the images of the First Protector's battle with the demons, all the cats' fur began to bristle, and Midnight paced back and forth.

When she'd finished with the visions of the prophecy, she told the cats of the plans to prepare for the coming battle. She showed them the army coalescing, the training, the wizard school, and the students' powers. Finally, she sent images of what she hoped would come. She showed groups of wolves, cats, and dragons joining with the rest of the army, all with a common goal: saving Trimoria.

Midnight growled. "No-tail leader-daughter Sloane, I'm not optimistic about working with the wolves… but you, and your pack, you may consider us pack allies. My family will join yours in this battle."

Sloane repeated the words to Aaron. And then all the cats fell on their sides with their stomachs exposed.

*"They are showing trust by exposing their bellies,"* Silver

explained. *"I would suggest that you show them their trust is accepted."*

Sloane held a giggle inside as she rubbed Midnight's belly. She felt a purr of acceptance.

She looked up to Aaron. "Apparently, now we have to pet all the cats. Can you help? Otherwise this will take forever."

## THE CONTEST

Dominic lifted the tarpaulin under which he'd been sleeping and saw that the eastern sky had started to lighten. It was probably an hour or so before the sun would break over the horizon. He lay back down, considering his next move. For weeks now, he'd been hiding on the fringes of the caravan just outside Cammoria. He was confident no one had linked him to the deaths of the dwarves, but the king's guards remained on the hunt for him.

As he stretched out, he felt a tickle of energy at the base of his neck. He bolted upright, the tarpaulin flying off him. He saw nothing, yet was certain an energy was building somewhere nearby. A breeze stirred, bringing him the distinct odor of rotten eggs.

And then a mist coalesced before him.

*What the…*

A diaphanous female outline took form, then condensed into a semi-translucent image of the woman he'd met in the woods.

She spoke in his mind.

*"Sammael has new instructions for you, Dominic."*

Dominic was blinded by visions. He saw a cave deep in the mountains, and within that cave was his target. Blood was splattered on the walls and the dais, which now stood empty.

He understood, and smiled malevolently. "It'll be my pleasure."

---

Excitement mounted for the school's end-of-year contest. All the students were in attendance, of course, and the teachers, including Castien and Eglerion, and Throll and Gwen had positions of honor. But also many locals had come to spectate, along with some elves and dwarves. It was fortunate that the king's men had built substantial seating at the side of the field where the events were to be held.

"I can't believe how many people are here," Arabelle said at Ryan's side.

"I know," Ryan said. "I better not screw up, or I'll never live it down…"

A tremendous shriek sounded in the sky, and Ryan looked up to see Ruby and Pyre soaring toward them. They played in the air above the crowd for a time before swooping down and settling in to watch.

Finally, Ryan's father strode to the front of the gathering and motioned for silence.

"Welcome, everyone! I know we've all been looking forward to this event. Two days of contests that will not only be fun and educational, but will showcase how far the academy's students have come over the past year.

"Now, before we officially begin, I want to explain how things will work, for the benefit of our visitors. There have been a couple of modifications since I last outlined the competition's structure to our students—including an increase in the prizes."

He smiled as the students murmured.

"The contest is split into four categories: strength, accuracy, knowledge, and popularity. And, after discussion with the faculty, we've decided to split the strength category into two classes: one for the war wizards and another for everyone else. The winner of each category has been promised ten gold pieces by our king. But now the pot has been sweetened with a little something extra.

"For the winners of the strength and accuracy contests, I will personally be contributing a special damantite weapon."

A student near Ryan whispered to her friend, "Oh, I *so* want a damantite sword. I have *got* to win this."

Dad continued. "And for the winner of the knowledge contest, Xinthian, the elder of Eluanethra, has promised unfettered access to his personal library for any research the winner desires. And let me tell you from personal experience, I've never seen a more extensive library in my life."

Wat Crazybeard, who sat just behind Ryan, squeaked with excitement. "Can you imagine the riches within those books? Who cares about the money—it's the knowledge of the ages that has real worth."

"And as the students already know," Dad said, "the winner of the contest overall will receive one hundred gold coins from their king."

At this, many of the locals gasped and gossiped, and Dad had to raise his hands for silence.

"You may be wondering how that overall winner will be chosen," he said, "In each of the categories, twenty points will be awarded for the winner, fifteen for second place, and so on. The popularity contest is the exception. There, we will award forty points for a win, thirty-five for second, and so on. So I hope you all made some good friends this year. When all the contests are complete, we'll tally up the points, and announce a winner."

Dad grinned. "But enough from me. I'm sure all of you want to get started. So let the contests begin!"

---

"You are all war wizards," Eglerion began, "but not all of you are equal in your power. Today's test is very simple. You'll each be given an identical metal rod. Your task is to use your powers to cut through the rod as quickly as possible."

Ryan frowned. That sounded too easy.

Eglerion smiled as if reading Ryan's mind. "Sound

simple? Then how about this: the rods are made of damantite. It is denser and harder to cut than any metal you have ever encountered. I assure you, even the best of you will be exhausted by the time this contest is complete, and many of you will not complete the task at all."

He picked up a black metallic rod from a container beside him.

"Wat Crazybeard!" he called. "You're the first contestant. Good luck."

---

Castien paced at the center of the circle of hedge wizards. On three sides, benches had been set up for spectators. This was expected to be one of the more interesting competitions of the contest.

"The rules are very simple," Castien began. "You will be paired off randomly, and each pair will face one another in head-to-head combat. The first contestant to achieve three scores on their opponent wins. A loss means that you are eliminated from the competition; a win means you move on to the next round of elimination."

He looked from contestant to contestant. "You will be given your choice of weapons, but note that they will be dulled. We want to tap our opponents, not wound them. You've all been taught control, and I expect everyone to display it. Anyone using excessive force will be automatically eliminated, and if I find anyone in serious and purposeful violation of this rule, they'll suffer the wrath of King Throll and Lord Riverton…" He paused, his eyes uncharacteristically menacing, before adding, "And worst of all, you'll face *my* wrath."

Earlier, all of the contestants had written their names on identical wooden chips. Castien swept the chips into a bag, shook it, and then pulled out two names.

"Tessa Boutwell and Bran Sanders!" he called out. "You two have the honor of the first match."

Ohaobbok was glad he wasn't among the first called. He wanted to watch others first and get comfortable with the nature of the contest.

Tessa Boutwell was a long-limbed teenager, and very fast. She wasn't strong, but she compensated for her lack of strength with cunning and agility. Bran Sanders *was* strong, and he was a bit older, in his mid-twenties. Prior to joining the academy, he'd been a guard in the caravan that Arabelle's father led.

"Pick your weapons," Castien said, pointing to the weapons table.

Bran selected a blunted longsword and shield, while Tessa selected two blunted short swords. Both contestants took practice swings to get a feel for the weight of their weapons, and Castien reminded them once more about safety and the importance of maintaining control. Then the elf had the contestants face each other, and he blew a whistle to indicate the start of the bout.

The two contestants eyed each other and circled the ring,

Tessa remained crouched, clearly waiting for Bran to make the first move. Bran feinted a few times, trying to force Tessa to expose herself. But she waited patiently.

*Good strategy,* Ohaobbok thought. *Human males get impatient quickly.*

Bran lunged, slashing low at Tessa's legs, using his advantage of reach. It looked like he would land a touch, but Tessa somersaulted over the swing, landed, and casually tapped Bran's neck with both of her swords.

"Score number one for Tessa Boutwell!" Castien shouted.

---

Aaron watched Castien's contest with envy He wished he could join, but he wasn't really a student at the school. And it would probably have been unfair since he'd likely defeat anyone here. Except Castien himself, of course.

Ryan walked up and sat next to him, eating a loaf of bread and looking tired.

"Tough contest?" Aaron asked.

"Exhausting," Ryan said through a mouthful of bread. "I did all right though. Almost half the class passed out before they could finish, so I know I'm at least in the top half, but Eglerion didn't announce times, so I'm not sure how I did beyond that. How are things going here?"

"You just missed a great semifinal match. Tessa Boutwell *almost* beat Ohaobbok. It was incredible, tied up at two to two before Ohaobbok managed the winning touch. I knew she was good, but wow, she's come a long way since the last time I sparred with her."

"So Ohaobbok's in the finals? Who's he up against?"

"You'll see," Aaron said. "They're about to start."

The crowd was several deep behind the benches, as it seemed everyone had come to witness this final match. Castien had to wave for silence.

"Everyone, this will be the last match of this contest. But before we begin, I would like to acknowledge the young lady who just left the ring. Tessa Boutwell has placed in third—an achievement that should be congratulated."

The audience erupted with applause. Tessa curtsied.

"And now, the final match. Ohaobbok, formerly of the Bloody Fist Clan, against Oda Rockfist!"

"I've always wanted to watch the two of them go against each other," Ryan said.

"They've sparred a lot," Aaron said. "Definitely our two best. It should be a really good contest. Brute strength advantage goes to our ogre friend, of course, but Oda is much stronger than you'd think. He's also much quicker. What I want to know is what weapons they choose."

The two competitors were already at the weapons table. Ohaobbok, as usual, chose a two-handed great sword and the largest shield on the rack. Aaron expected Oda to pick the mace-shield combination he'd used in earlier rounds, but instead he chose a mace-flail combination.

Aaron nudged Ryan. "Oda's smart not to waste time on a shield. Ohaobbok is so strong that even if you block one of his hits, you'll feel a shock down your arm that's likely to make it go numb for the rest of the bout. So he may as well go for an all-out assault with two weapons at once."

The entire sparring court became silent as the contestants —one a twelve-foot-tall ogre, the other a four-foot-tall dwarf —entered the ring.

"Begin!" shouted Castien.

The two contestants began cautiously; clearly they had deep respect for the other's abilities. There were a number of feints as each warrior tried to pull his opponent from his guarded stance.

Ohaobbok broke the stalemate. With surprising speed for his size, he swung his sword at the dwarf. But Oda used his size to his advantage. He rolled beneath the blade, tumbling to Ohaobbok's right, where he tagged the ogre's elbow with his flail.

"Score! Oda!" Castien exclaimed.

Ohaobbok grimaced at his mistake as he circled the dwarf, scanning for an opening.

Again Ohaobbok swung at Oda—almost the exact same move, but from the opposite direction. And again Oda timed his roll under the blade perfectly. But before the dwarf could bring one of his weapons to bear, Ohaobbok's shield smashed him across the ring.

"Score! Ohaobbok!" Castien announced.

Oda bounced back to his feet, looking angrier than ever. Again the two circled each other.

This time it was Oda who took the initiative. He dove right

between Ohaobbok's feet, below his shield and inside the radius of his sword. Aaron knew from experience that this was where Ohaobbok's height worked against him, leaving his lower body exposed. The ogre jumped away, but not before Oda scored a hit on his ankle.

"Halt!" Castien announced.

The two contestants faced him.

"I will rate that as a score for both Oda and Ohaobbok," the elf said tersely. "No more suicide attacks," he ordered the dwarf. "Ohaobbok should have dropped his full weight on you, but instead he was kind enough to jump out of range. You may have scored a point due to his desire not to hurt you, but that was a stupid move on your part."

Oda looked sheepish. "It didn't work out how I planned."

"Whoever wins the next point wins the match," Aaron whispered to Ryan.

"Match point!" Castien yelled. "Go!"

The crowd began to roar with excitement.

"The only way to take down a giant is with an army!" Oda hollered. "I am Oda, the One-Dwarf Army!"

Many among the crowd laughed. Others cheered.

"I've told him to stop doing that," Aaron whispered. "He never listens."

The dwarf and ogre circled slowly, with Oda edging toward Ohaobbok's shield side. The ogre seemed to be trying to get the dwarf within reach of his giant sword.

"Look," Ryan said. "Ohaobbok's holding his shield much lower than before."

Aaron nodded. "Yup. He doesn't want Oda to try that trick again."

Oda suddenly swung his flail at the top of Ohaobbok's shield. The ball at the end of the chain went right over the top of the shield, and Ohaobbok instinctively pulled back. But to the evident surprise of both warriors, the flail's ball caught on the top of the shield, and Ohaobbok's sharp backward movement pulled Oda off the ground and flying right over the ogre's head. The dwarf reached down with his mace and gently tapped Ohaobbok's shoulder as he passed.

The court fell dead silent.

"Score, Oda!" Castien hollered. "Winner!"

The audience roared.

"Think Ohaobbok's going to be okay with this?" Ryan asked.

The ogre was smiling as he congratulated Oda on his win.

"Oh, he'll be fine. They're friends. But I wouldn't want to be the next person to face Ohaobbok in a sparring match."

---

The next morning, Oda and Wat walked toward the field where the archer contest would take place. Oda carried his lucky bow with a quiver full of his best arrows, and tried not to get annoyed as Wat talked the whole way.

"You're so lucky," Wat was saying. "You already *know* you won. Eglerion won't even tell us who won the war wizard contest! I think I did well. It's difficult to tell, but I really think

I have a chance. Wouldn't it be great if both of the winners of the day were dwarves?"

Oda laughed. "What would be even better is if a dwarf wins the overall competition. Specifically, me! Now dat I know I have a chance, I'm aimin' for the big prize. Can you imagine what I could buy with a hundred gold pieces?"

They arrived at the field, only to find that, if anything, there were even more spectators on hand today than there were yesterday. Apparently, word had traveled about the excitement of yesterday's matches. There were more humans and elves, but there were way more dwarves—no doubt because of Oda's dramatic victory.

"Look how many people are here!" Wat said as they joined the other students. "This is crazy."

"Don't get nervous," Oda said. "Just focus on da target. You'll be fine."

"I don't know. This is nothing like yesterday."

"Really? I figured you would have lots of people wantin' to see all those sparks and flashes of magic."

Wat shook his head. "I don't think so. Then again, I passed out as soon as I finished my task. Arabelle had to revive me."

"That girl has come a long way. Remember our first day, when she was crying for her father. Now she's the best healer in the class."

Castien waved for silence. "Everyone ready?" he asked.

The students responded with a resounding, "Yes!"

The sword master pointed toward a log suspended from a stout wooden apparatus. Ropes extended from both the top and bottom of the log, and the ends of the ropes were manned by elves. A small red dot had been painted on the center of the log, with concentric circles expanding outward from the center.

"You are all familiar with this exercise," Castien said. "The log is your target, and the job of the elves with the ropes is to make you miss your target. You will be allowed a choice of bow or dagger from our weapons rack. I have personally tested each one. No outside weapons are allowed."

Oda groaned, and he wasn't the only one. Apparently others had brought their "lucky weapons" as well.

"Each person will get only *one* shot," Castien continued. "Because in the heat of battle, you may not get a second. The closest to the center dot… will be our winner."

He shook his bag of names, then pulled out a wooden chip. "Desdin Frielander!"

Desdin was a lanky student who was known for his skill with a bow. And like Oda, he'd brought one of his own. But as he rose, he handed it to a man in the audience, apparently his father.

"Did you see dat bow?" Oda whispered. "Dat's dragonbone! Those are legendary for their accuracy and power."

"Then I'm glad he won't be able to use it," Wat whispered back.

Desdin selected a bow from the rack, then approached the mark on the ground from which he would shoot. Castien nodded to the elves manning the ropes, and they swung the log erratically.

Desdin pulled the string back on the bow, moving as if carefully tracing the motions of the log, and let his arrow fly.

The arrow thumped into the log. The elves stopped working the ropes. Castien stepped over, took great care to precisely measure the distance from the center dot, and scribbled something into his notebook.

"Six spans from the center!" he announced. "A very good shot. You should be proud."

Castien removed the arrow, shook the bag, and pulled out another name. "Arabelle Riverton!"

Arabelle stood and walked to the dagger section of the weapons rack.

"Is she a Riverton already?" Wat asked. "I thought they weren't married yet."

"Fer someone who reads so much, ye sure are dim. It's the nomad tradition to adopt da husband's family name upon da striking of a marriage contract. It doesn't matter if they aren't yet married. Da agreement is binding."

The crowd quieted as Arabelle left the weapon rack with a dagger in her hand. When she arrived at the mark in the grass, Castien nodded to the elves holding the ropes, and the log began its erratic dance.

Arabelle held the dagger by its tip and studied the motion of the log. Several long moments passed without her so much as blinking.

Then she flicked the dagger so fast that Oda almost missed it.

She struck the red dot dead center.

Castien stepped up to the log with his measuring device, but then with a shrug, decided he didn't even need to use it. "Arabelle, your shot is *zero* spans from the center mark. Congratulations. A truly amazing feat, young healer."

The crowd erupted with cheers, and Ryan sprinted out of the crowd to Arabelle and swung her around, to her obvious delight.

"Little chance I'm going to win dis event now," Oda groaned.

Wat patted his friend on the back. "All we can do is our best."

---

Ryan wrote Arabelle's name on a wooden chip, showed it to Eglerion and his mom, deposited it in the voting box at the front of the classroom, and then took a seat. One by one, every other student did the same. When they were done with the vote, it would be time to begin the academic testing.

Ryan honestly had no idea who would win the popularity contest, and he was anxious about it, because he knew it would weigh so heavily on the cumulative results. He thought he was fairly popular—he got along with almost everyone—but it was really impossible to tell.

The last student cast her vote, and Mom stepped up in front of the class. "Time for the testing to begin," she announced.

She pulled the covering off the board at the head of the classroom, revealing a series of questions scrawled in chalk.

*Question One: How many years ago was the barrier erected by the First Protector?*

Ryan snatched up his charcoal pencil and parchment, and set to work.

## AWARDS CEREMONY

It had been months since Ryan had been to his father's smithy, but this morning, he'd been asked to come by and infuse the damantite prizes with energy. And as he arrived at the building, he was amazed at how much things had changed. The smithy had been expanded to twice its size, or was in the process of it anyway; dwarves were putting the finishing touches on the roof and necessary smoke vents. More dwarves were hard at work everywhere, many of them transporting buckets of ore from a new storage area out front.

A dwarf waved at him from the roof. "Huzzah, young Lord Riverton! Welcome to da smithy. Your father's expecting you."

Ryan walked in to find just as much activity inside the smithy as there had been outside it. Several anvils were manned by dwarves, who hammered expertly on bits of metal, and another area seemed to have been established for finishing work. The dwarves there were currently polishing a set of sparkling black daggers. At the center of it all stood Dad, applying magical energy to some damantite ore that dwarves were shoveling into a crucible that glowed red with heat. Ryan was surprised it wasn't sweltering in here, but then saw the new ventilation fans in the roof. They looked to be powered by a steam-driven contraption heated by the central furnace.

But most surprising of all was just how much raw energy his father was putting out. Ryan could do many things his father could never dream of doing, but no one could match Dad for sheer power, except maybe Azazel when he was alive. He transformed the damantite ore into a bubbling pool of slag and molten metal within the crucible, and as the dwarves took over, skimming away the slag and pouring the molten damantite into a series of forms, Dad smiled at Ryan through the steam. His face was covered in soot.

"Ryan!" he called. "I told you things have changed, didn't I?"

"It's amazing," Ryan yelled over the sounds of pounding hammers and the running steam engines.

His father led him to the area where the dwarves were polishing the daggers. These, too, were damantite, with fine ivory handles. Dad inspected their work, then nodded.

"Perfect," he said. "Now go help with the forming of the other weapons. We need to deliver those swords to the king."

As the dwarves scurried away, Dad put his arm around Ryan's shoulders. "So, what do you think?" he asked proudly.

"It really is impressive, Dad. Looks like you've hired all the dwarves in Aubgherle."

"We've got more coming. Remember, we're preparing for a war. Anyway, I didn't ask you to come all the way out here so I could show off the new smithy. Though I do like to show it off." He handed Ryan the two daggers. "I figured you'd like to have a hand in infusing your betrothed's prize before we present it to her. You'll need to infuse the war wizard and warrior prizes as well."

Ryan's heart began to beat faster. "Who gets the war wizard prize?"

His father shrugged. "I might be the headmaster, but I don't actually know yet. Eglerion has been very secretive. But I'll know very soon—now that you're here, I'm going to head over to the academy, and me and the others will sit down to compute the overall winner. But hey—don't be nervous about it. You did awesome, and that's what matters. These contests were set up to boost morale and to get the students to take their studies seriously. I'm rooting for you, but in the long run… we have much bigger fish to fry."

He then yelled across the smithy to one of the dwarves. "Bintas! When the staff is ready, bring it over to my son. He'll need to put the final touches on it."

The soot-covered dwarf looked up from his work. "Understood, Lord Riverton."

Dad turned back to Ryan and pointed to a giant basket. "Tons of food, courtesy of your mother and Gwen. You'll need this. Damantite just soaks up the energy."

It felt to Sloane as if the entire town of Aubgherle was in attendance. The crowd had swelled well beyond the confines of the academy field. For once she welcomed her royal status, as it earned her a seat atop a dais the dwarves had constructed for the occasion. Aaron, his parents, Castien, and Eglerion sat along with her. And of course Rebecca sat in Sloane's lap.

A murmur erupted as the gathering parted to make way for the king and queen. Armored guards escorted them to the stairs leading up to the dais. Father held Mother's hand and led her to the bench, where she sat next to Sloane and took Rebecca into her lap.

Above, the two dragons shrieked as they flew below the clouds for the first time, showing their impressive wingspan before settling on the two platforms that had been placed for them on the roof of the academy. They sent tremendous gouts of flame up in the air, earning a gasp from the crowd, then a rousing cheer.

Father stepped up to the lectern and gestured for silence.

"Welcome, everyone! We're here to congratulate the top students, whom I expect to serve as future leaders in our society. And believe it or not, I'm just as excited as all of you to learn the identities of the winners. I now invite the teachers to come forward and announce the results."

As Father sat beside Mother, Aubrey, Jared, and the two elven teachers strode to the lectern. Jared handed Aubrey a paper adorned with a bright yellow ribbon.

Aubrey cleared her throat and projected her voice to the crowd. "Before we announce the results, the faculty decided that a special award is warranted for one particular RAM student. As the students already know, the faculty at the Riverton Academy of Magic believes strongly in the value of hard work. The headmaster reminded me of a quote that captures well the type of behavior we strive for: 'Winning isn't everything, but *trying* to win is.' There is one student who exhibits this special brand of hard work on a constant basis. Whether he excels or not, he's always doing his best."

She held up a rather fancy-looking certificate.

"I would like everyone to help me congratulate the student who most exemplifies this can-do attitude: Zenethar Lancaster."

Sloane's throat tightened as her three-and-a-half-year-old brother was escorted forward by a group of other smiling students. Sloane's mother and father were equally choked up as they smiled and clapped. Zenethar beamed as he accepted his certificate, then shook all the teachers' hands and hugged everyone seated on the dais.

Jared launched a flaming bolt of white-hot plasma into the air to silence the crowd, then stepped forward to speak again.

"Before we announce the contest winners, I just want to emphasize that I'm very pleased with *all* the students and their efforts in these contests. And now…"

He pulled a piece of paper from his pocket.

"The winners are…" he began dramatically.

The crowd quieted.

"Actually," said Jared, "might I ask the king to step forward and make the announcements?"

Sloane's father was obviously surprised at this impromptu change, but he strode forward. "It would be an honor, Headmaster."

Jared stepped to one side, and Throll stood at the lectern.

"The first-place winners are...

"In the war wizard contest: Ryan Riverton! In the hedge wizard combat competition: Oda Rockfist! In the accuracy contest: Arabelle Riverton! And in the knowledge exams: Wat Crazybeard!"

The winning students came forward, to cheers from the crowd. A dwarven contingent blew horns and stomped their feet as Wat and Oda stepped onto the dais. None of the winners could keep the smiles off their faces.

Father handed each winner a pouch of ten gold coins, and then Jared pulled special weapons from a case. For Ryan, a long metal staff with sparks of energy snaking up and down its length; and for Oda, a mace that glowed with the same preternatural energy. Finally, he pulled out two sheathed daggers, which he presented to Arabelle with a flourish.

When the crowd had calmed, the king spoke again. "You may have noticed that we failed to mention one category: the popularity contest—the one contest that was voted on by the students themselves. Well, I won't make you wait any longer. The winner is... Ohaobbok!"

The crowd roared, but not nearly as loud as the students

did. Ohaobbok came up onto the dais and sheepishly received his gold pieces.

The king waved for silence. "Is everyone ready to know the overall winner?"

The platform shook with the noise of the crowd.

The king smiled. "Well you'll have to wait just a moment for that. Because first, I'm going to announce second and third place. In fact, these two students ended up tied." He looked to the students beside him. "Wat Crazybeard and Ryan Riverton! Congratulations on tying for second!"

Aaron's shouts were matched only by the dwarves cheering for Wat. Ryan and Wat waved to the crowd and then shook each other's hand.

"And now, finally, I would like to introduce you to this year's RAM contest grand-prize winner. Everyone, please congratulate… Ohaobbok!"

The crowd roared with approval and everyone on the dais rose to their feet. Zenethar ran to Ohaobbok and gave the giant ogre a bear hug around his knee. And Father had to reach up to pat Ohaobbok on the arm in congratulations.

Jared took the lectern once more. "King Throll has arranged for a celebration feast in the town center, and I don't know about the rest of you, but *I'm* hungry. So without further ado… let's eat!"

He sent a series of crackling balls of energy into the sky. Each one exploded in a shower of sparks and a resounding thunderclap. And with that, the ceremony was over.

# THE FIRST PROTECTOR

Long banquet tables had been set up in the central marketplace, and proud RAM banners hung from the facades of every building surrounding the square. A gentle breeze blew through the market, cooling the diners who'd been suffering from the relentless early summer sun. More than a thousand people had gathered to eat, talk, and enjoy the end of a fine couple days of competition.

As the other winners enjoyed themselves, Ryan couldn't help but keep looking at his staff, and he noticed that Arabelle was likewise preoccupied with her daggers.

"You'd better watch out or you'll cut yourself, Belle," he said.

She grinned. "I'm not exactly inexperienced with sharp weapons." She made a jerking motion with her right hand and a third dagger practically materialized in her palm.

"Whoa! Where were you hiding that?"

She leaned into him. "Some secrets a girl has to keep to herself."

"It's a beautiful dagger," Ryan said, studying it. "Wait—is that damantite too?"

"I think so. My mom left it to me." She showed him the handle. "Feel the leather wrap; it's almost like sandpaper."

Ryan ran his finger across it. "That's shark skin. Where can you find a shark in Trimoria?"

"Ah, such creatures are beyond the mists, young Lord Riverton," said another voice.

"Castien!" Arabelle got up and gave the sword master a hug.

The elf smiled, which was unusual for him. "That's a very old weapon you have there, Arabelle. It's probably seen many a battle over its years."

Just then the sound of galloping horses echoed through the streets, and a troop of dwarves on exhausted-looking mountain ponies rode into the middle of the square.

Dad stepped forward. "What's all this about?"

Silas came forward as well. "You'd better have a damned good reason for riding like maniacs in the middle of town."

"We were attacked!" said one of the dwarves. "We lost two dwarves, and one poor bugger was injured badly. The maniac wizard fled into the mountains like da craven finger-wiggler he is."

"Are you sure it was a wizard?" Dad asked. He looked to the king. "It could have been Dominic."

The dwarf drew a deep breath. "I know not his name, but I'm sure he was a wizard. Before young Barnaby passed out—uh, Barnaby be da one injured during da incident—he said dat a robed man entered the Cammorian passage into da mountains, and dat, with a motion of his hands and a wiggle of his fingers, he pulled half of da cave down on dem. It took us folks that was on da Cammorian side several hours to clear da blockage and rescue poor Barnaby. The only direction the wizard could have gone was through da remainder of da passage into da mountains."

Oda shoved his way closer. "Did I hear Barnaby was injured? Barnaby Rockfist?"

The visitor nodded. "Yessir, but he'll be fine. I can't say da same for poor Lamnas and Camnas. It wasn't a good day for da Rockfist Clan."

"Revenge!" Oda shouted. "I demand retribution! I will see dis wizard's entrails strewn throughout da sewers of Cammoria! I will—"

Throll put his hand on Oda's shoulder. "Enough," he said.

Oda's eyes were watery as he looked up at the king. "I can't let dis crime go unpunished, Your Highness. I won't remain here while dat murderer dat killed my twin cousins and injured my brudder roams freely. I'll depart tonight and hunt dis craven down myself."

"I respect your wishes, son, and I understand. However, I forbid you from traipsing across the plains in search of revenge."

"But Your Highness—"

Throll raised a hand. "Oda, look at me."

Oda did as he was instructed, though the expression on his face was pure murder.

"Oda, you have a right to your revenge. It was your blood and clan that was most grievously injured. But you will not act rashly. With that in mind, I have two conditions. First, I will ask for a team of volunteers to assist you." Throll turned to Ohaobbok. "Ohaobbok, I trust your good judgment and level-headedness. Are you willing to assemble this team?"

Ohaobbok looked surprised, but nodded.

"Good," said Throll. "The second condition is that if the culprit is Dominic, as I suspect it might be, you must bring him back to Aubgherle to face justice. *My* justice. I don't want any of you to stain your hands with such a miscreant's blood. I personally owe him a proper punishment for hiring assassins to target my family."

Oda smiled grimly. "Done and done, Your Highness. However, if it is in fact this wizard Dominic, he isn't likely to come willingly."

"I have ways of stunning him into submission," Ryan said. "I'm sure we can bring him back."

---

"Father!" Sloane whined. "You can't tell me I can't go."

"I can and I will," Throll growled. "It's too dangerous."

Sloane stomped her feet. "Dangerous? We're going after one person. And it's not like I'll be going alone. I'll be in the company of Oda, Ohaobbok, Wat, Ryan, Aaron, and Arabelle."

"Then it sounds to me as though they have all the strength they need."

Sloane shook her head. "Strength, perhaps. But how do you think they're going to find Dominic in the first place?"

Throll frowned. "What do you mean?"

"I mean, we'll need to use the wolves to track Dominic, and I'm the only one who can talk to them. They *need* me, Father. I'm part of the team."

A storm of emotions brewed behind the king's eyes. He said nothing, but his expression admitted his defeat.

"Everything will be all right, Father," Sloane said. "Ohaobbok chose wisely, and you know it. This is the right thing to do."

Throll embraced his daughter and sighed. "I promised your mother that I would talk you out of this foolishness. Don't make me regret giving you my permission."

---

Ryan watched in amazement as Ohaobbok outpaced the horses and ponies. He didn't even slow until they reached the stream that they'd decided would be their resting spot for the night. And even then, he didn't settle immediately. With a single kick, he felled a dead tree and began breaking it into kindling.

Oda stomped his feet in the cold. "Will one of you wizardy

types light a fire? It's going to be a chilly night in the highlands."

"Aren't you a wizard yourself?" Wat said.

"Sure, but all you have to do is wiggle yer fingers and boom, we have an inferno. Whereas by da time I light an ember with my wizard skills, I could have gotten my tinder kit out and started a fire the regular way."

At that moment a wolf howled in the distance.

"That's Grey Wind," said Sloane. "He's saying his pack will meet us just outside the mountains.

"I wish I could talk to animals," Arabelle said.

"You can," said Sloane. "You'd be surprised how much human speech they understand. So keep talking to them. They hear you, even though you can't hear them."

Ohaobbok arranged the wood, and Ryan concentrated energy at the center of the pile. Almost immediately, there was a red glow within the mound of wood and seconds later, the first licks of flame reached into the sky.

Oda laughed. "See! You just wiggle and stuff happens." He pulled out his glowing mace and held it over his head. "I prefer to hit versus wiggle."

"Oda, stop talking and start helping," Aaron said. "If you want to eat, go get some buckets of water for the soup. We have a long distance yet to travel."

Dominic felt a pang of guilt as he watched the dwarves guarding the cave. Killing dwarves who attacked him was one thing, but these two dwarves were just sitting there, totally unaware. Yet the dark wizard's goal lay inside that cave, and that meant he needed to get past those guards.

Both dwarves were armed with maces and held spears nearly double their height. They were armored with bits of splinted mail and rough leather tunics. But Dominic was less concerned about the two dwarves guarding the cave than the unknown quantity of dwarves that might be within. In the scenes shown to him by the mysterious elven beauty, he had seen a lot of blood in there, so he could only assume he had a serious fight ahead of him.

He was just beginning to have second thoughts about this mission when his mind was hit with a wave of compulsion that momentarily blinded him. When he recovered from the influence that ravaged his mind, he found himself splayed on the ground, covered in sweat and having emptied the contents of his stomach. He sat up unsteadily, knowing that now was the time to act.

He looked to the ledge directly above the dwarves guarding the cave and concentrated on the rocky outcropping. As he strained, he felt his powers stretch, build, and exert their influence on the ledge. He felt his pulse throbbing in his neck, and the fibers in his muscles began to snap. Just when he thought he could take no more, an explosive crack erupted across the chasm, and several tons of rock fell on the two dwarves' heads, killing them.

Dominic swayed on his feet. He felt lightheaded as he climbed down from his perch and approached the cave entrance. He listened for voices but heard none. There was no sound of life or activity in the cave or the mountain pass.

*Good,* he thought. *This should be easy.*

He climbed over the rocks that partially blocked the entrance to the cave. He stumbled at one point, falling right beside the bloody hand of one of the dwarves he'd just killed. He stood and stepped on it dismissively as he entered the cave.

The cave was small—built to the dimensions of a dwarf. He had to stoop to move through. His heart racing, Dominic took his first step into the domain of the First Protector.

---

Grey Wind howled into the wind. *"Light-furred she-human, we are here. You are slow. There are tiny humans ahead."*

Grey Wind and his family rested near an entrance to the mountains. While they waited, the lead wolf listened to the pack of tiny humans speaking loudly and pointing in his pack's direction. He smelled their fear on the wind.

*"Greetings,"* came the message in his mind. *"Your pack moves as quickly as the wind. Stay where you are. I'll talk to the dwarves guarding the entrance so they understand why you're here. We'll arrive shortly."*

"Princess, you best be giving folks like us warnin' before ploppin' a bunch of dwarf-eatin' wolves on our front door," Castore Stoneforge complained.

Sloane smiled. "I didn't realize you would be here. I'm sorry about startling you. We were in a hurry to avenge our friends who were killed or injured in the passage."

Castore shook his head. "Nuttin' startlin' about a pack of wolves wanderin' into the middle of a dwarf encampment without as much as a 'by your leave' and just starin' at you with thems beady eyes of theirs. See it every day, I tell ya!"

A white-bearded dwarf put his hand on Castore's shoulder. "Seder's blessings on your mission. Lamnas and Camnas will be sorely missed. Is there anything we can do to help?"

"Can you lead us to the passage?" Sloane asked. "After that, we'll be depending on Grey Wind and his pack's nose to sniff out the miscreant. We've been commissioned to produce him for the king's justice."

Castore looked behind Sloane. "This has da makings of an epic tale dat I be witnessin'. A tamed ogre I heard tell of, a pack of nasty-lookin' wolves, a very strange assortment of humans and dwarves, and a princess at its head. Dat's some odd company, Princess, but walk this way. I'll show you the proper passage…"

---

Grey Wind growled. *"She-human Sloane, the scent of our target travels along all three passes with equal strength."*

*"How can that be?"* Sloane messaged back. *"Would it take long to scout the passes to see which is the most likely to investigate?"*

Grey Wind turned toward his mate and yipped instructions. After a few yips, barks, growls, and one large howl from Grey Wind, the pack split into three and scampered down the paths through the mountains.

Sloane turned to her fellow travelers. "And now we wait…"

---

Before him lay the legendary First Protector. As Dominic approached, the shimmering aura surrounding the reclining wizard morphed from rainbow-colored opaque to misty gray to nearly translucent. Dominic watched the constantly transforming aura, wondering what purpose it served and whether the color changes signified anything. Regardless, he decided that it was time to complete his mission and put an end to this distraction.

He unsheathed his dagger and waited. Since the colors seemed to follow a set pattern, he waited for the moment the aura turned clear.

*Rainbow… Gray… Clear… Plunge!* he thought.

As Dominic's dagger connected with the translucent barrier, time seemed to progress at a snail's pace. A blinding flash of energy erupted at the tip of the dagger, climbed up the blade and into Dominic's arm. Searing pain like that of a thousand hot pokers exploded in his arm as a shock wave blasted him across the cave, and he slammed his head against the low roof.

He must have lost consciousness, because when he woke, he didn't recall having gotten sick all over himself once again. His arm tingled and felt weak. Blisters had formed on the palm of his right hand. The dagger lay on the floor beside him, its blade having been partially melted and warped. It had been reduced to junk.

Dominic stared at the dais with the shimmering aura and felt anger welling up within him. For the first time in a long while, he found himself truly and utterly furious. The First Protector would be destroyed on this day, or he would tear this mountain down atop him. As far as Dominic was concerned, either would be an acceptable result.

He shook his arm to rid himself of the tingling sensation. At that moment, he heard a wolf's howl. The howl was followed soon after by another. And another.

Dominic paid it no mind. He was focused on his mission. But just as he returned to the task at hand, that old familiar tingling sensation flared at the base of his neck. The unmistakable warning of approaching danger. Dominic groaned, and decided to scramble out of the cave and seek refuge to plan his next step.

The wolves howled up ahead. Ryan didn't need Sloane's translation as he ran down the slope in the direction of their baying. It had taken several hours for the wolves to track and eliminate all the dead ends and loops that Dominic had left for them. But now, as the group progressed, Ryan's excitement was building. He strengthened his shield in preparation for the coming battle.

Over his shoulder, he saw that the group had formed an orderly train following behind him. He led the way because he'd made the case that he possessed the strongest of shields, and the only one fully resistant to physical and magical attacks. Ohaobbok and Oda ran immediately behind him. They had both lived in these mountain passes, and were the most familiar with the terrain. The rest of the group, along with many of the wolves, followed behind, with Arabelle bringing up the rear.

As Ryan approached a clearing, he heard whining from the younger wolves. By the time he arrived by their side, they'd begun scratching at a pile of rubble that mostly obscured what looked like a cave entrance.

*"I can't detect anyone nearby,"* Sloane messaged telepathically.

Ohaobbok approached the rubble. "This was where I first met and talked with some dwarves," he announced, his voice cracking with emotion. "They called this the cave of the First Protector."

Ryan was stunned at the revelation.

"The wolves say the quarry went in the cave and left,"

Sloane said. "There are also some dead beneath this pile of rubble."

Oda growled. "Another debt this lowlife owes to all Trimoria."

"Let's clear the cave entrance and go inside," Ryan said. "Dominic entered this cave for a reason."

---

Oda kneeled before the dais. "I just can't believe he really is here," he whispered.

"I figured his presence here was a well-kept dwarven secret," Ryan replied, his heart racing at the sight of the unmoving man lying before him. The man's beard was long and white, and his steely yet warm face was familiar from Ryan's dreams.

Oda nodded. "It was… er… *is*. I mean, I'd always heard enough rumors about the First Protector being in the mountains to make me believe that there had to be a kernel of truth to it. It's just jarring to have the legend and savior of Trimoria lying in front of me."

Ryan crouched at the dais, and using his preternatural vision, he saw the threads of magic that wrapped the First Protector in a pulsing cocoon of power. As their colors changed, Ryan sensed the tiniest gaps within the threads grow and then shrink. Energy was being siphoned from a source within the man. Suddenly Ryan understood what he was seeing.

"He's alive!" Ryan said with a gasp. "Each of those color changes represents the moment the First Protector breathes. The aura is acting as a shield. The shield is somehow powered by the pulsing of the First Protector's heart." He turned to Sloane. "Do you sense anything through that shield of his?"

Sloane concentrated for a moment before shaking her head. "I can't sense anything past that aura. It's as if nobody's there."

Ryan pondered all that he'd seen. Just when he was about to give up, a soundless vision overtook him.

*A tremendous castle lies on the plains of Trimoria. Deep within the stone structure, past hallways of the bustling castle, stands a room with a heavy wooden door. In that room are Ryan, Aaron, Arabelle, and Sloane, all of them kneeling before a flashing ball of purple energy.*

*The four link hands, forming a circle, and a sparkling white energy springs from Ryan to the others. A ring of brilliant light connects the foursome; it pulses, quickening until it synchronizes with the flashing of the ball of energy. The color of the ring deepens to match the purple of the energy near the ceiling as filaments of violet light snake from the ball above and connect to each member of the ring. The energy running through the circle of companions continues to pulse in synchrony with the sparkling ball. The circle expands in all directions with a brilliant flash before disappearing, leaving an empty room with the familiar ball hovering near the ceiling.*

. . .

## TOOLS OF PROPHECY

The vision shifted.

*Another room, this one empty but for a greenish ball of energy near the ceiling. The ball fills the scene with brilliant green light and then instantly dims, revealing the kneeling foursome with hands linked. Ryan opens his eyes and smiles as he stands.*

The vision shifted.

*The group is exiting a stone chamber that overlooks a desolate plain with a wall of mist to the north. Coming down a corridor is a tall elf wielding a thick staff. Upon seeing the newcomers, the elf kneels and begins to weep.*

The vision shifted.

*A glowing orb of purest white sits on a pedestal of glasslike black stone that rests in the center of a stone chamber. Next to the pedestal stands a similar pedestal, this one bare. All along the walls of the chamber, smaller pedestals hold statues of the First Protector with his arm raised, his hand clutching a tiny gem. A pulse of energy streams from one of the statues to the orb on the central pedestal. Moments later, a different statue sends a pulse of energy into the orb.*

*The focus of the vision pulls back, revealing that the entrance to this chamber is guarded by a snakelike creature that breathes steam. The creature is at least three feet thick and perhaps fifty feet long. A milky-white-skinned elf with dark hair sneaks across its path, and the snake-like creature strikes with blazing speed. The doomed elf disappears in the creature's maw, leaving nothing behind but the dagger that he dropped.*

Ryan opened his eyes to find himself on the floor with his companions staring down at him worriedly.

"Did you see that?" he asked.

"We didn't," Sloane said, "but I saw it through you, and I told the others."

"I'm sure that wasn't a dream," Ryan said, sitting up. "That felt exactly like a vision."

"We were all worried," Arabelle said, kneeling next to him. "When the mist covered you and you fell backwards, we didn't know what to think, until Sloane began to read your thoughts."

"The mist covered me?" Ryan asked. "When did that happen? I don't remember anything like that."

Aaron sat on his heels in front of Ryan. "You asked Sloane a question, and then a plume of mist shot out from the dais and engulfed you completely. It lasted only a few seconds. The mist evaporated, and then you fell backwards. Oda caught you before you knocked your head on the floor. You've been unconscious for nearly half an hour."

One of the wolves whined outside the cave.

"The wolves are complaining that the scent grows weak with time," Sloane said.

Ryan stretched his arms and legs. "Well, I feel fine now. I don't know if there's anything more we can accomplish here at the moment. We need to find Dominic before the trail grows cold. But I definitely want to come back here again."

Oda poked his head into the cave. "It's about time you're awake," he groused. "Some of the Hammerthrower Clan is here to guard the cave. So let's get our feet moving."

"Agreed," Ryan said. He stooped as he followed the dwarf and the others out of the cave. "Hey, Sloane, where are the wolves? We need their noses."

Sloane pointed ahead. "Already ahead of us. They continued down the path."

At that moment, a large wolf appeared on the ridge.

"This she-wolf agreed to lead us when we're ready," Sloane said.

Ryan nodded. "Let's go."

---

The wolf led them through a series of roundabouts and confusing trails, past craggy rocks and down rutted, narrow paths. The path wound higher and higher, and Ryan found himself feeling winded as the air thinned. But when he looked over his shoulder and saw Ohaobbok, Aaron, and Oda pressing on unaffected, he dug deeper to ignore his fatigue.

At last the trail leveled off, much to Ryan's relief. The lead wolf stopped to sniff at the ground. She seemed uncertain.

"What's that noise?" Aaron grumbled.

Ryan concentrated, and for a moment could only hear his own deep breathing. Then he heard what sounded like hundreds of knives scrabbling against rock.

"Everyone behind me *now*!" Ohaobbok bellowed.

# REVENGE

Ryan fell behind Ohaobbok, who wielded both his sword and shield.

"What is it, Ohaobbok?" Arabelle asked.

Oda readied his mace and shield. "That's a megapede. They're very rarely seen on the mountain passes, and never at all in the valley."

Ryan gazed up the rock face that loomed before them. And there it was: a massive creature with an elongated body and more legs than he could count. Those short, narrow legs moved with blinding quickness as the monster descended the rock in a zigzag pattern, aiming for the path directly in front of them. Its menacing pincers stuck well out in front, its eyes were inky black, and its armored hide a pale yellow.

Ryan's hands flared with energy as he prepared to help his friends fight off a terrifying enemy.

"Stay behind me," Ohaobbok said. "Megapedes are very dangerous. They can spit acid up to twenty feet."

"You fight him as he rears up," Oda said to the ogre. "I will take his legs while he is down. Everyone else, stay back. We're from the mountains. Watch and learn."

Sloane strung her bow. "The creature is close enough for me to see visions of its mind. It bears a picture of Ryan and Aaron in its head. Dominic must have sent it!"

Aaron nocked an arrow. "Great. Just one more thing I owe that lisping idiot."

The sound of hundreds of chitinous legs scrambling on the rocks echoed ever louder. The wolf whined and backed away toward the rear of the group.

On the mountain pass ahead, the rumbling mass of the megapede approached, its bone-armored legs sounding like hundreds of nails on chalkboards. There seemed no end to the creature.

"How long *is* that thing?" Aaron cried.

Oda held his shield high. "They can grow over fifty feet long, rear up to fifteen feet high, and can weigh as much as a house. The best defense is to stay out of reach of those mandibles, and make it mad."

"Make it mad? Are you crazy?"

Oda scrambled to the side of the monster, and Ohaobbok readied his shield and approached the behemoth from the front.

"Oda is correct," the ogre shouted. "This thing is most

vulnerable when it rears up and exposes its underside. It only does so when it feels threatened."

Oda smacked with his mace against two of the monster's legs, shattering their hard exoskeleton. The beast screeched in pain or anger and whipped its body toward the dwarf. Oda somersaulted over the beast and scrambled out of reach.

Ohaobbok took advantage of the distraction. He swung his massive sword at the armored body, and when it clanged off, he nimbly leapt backwards, avoiding the creature's venom-dripping pincers.

Wat and Ryan simultaneously sent two torrents of fiery energy at the beast. They merely scorched the insect's armor, but it clearly angered the monster. It let loose with a harrowing screech before rearing up over a dozen feet.

Oda yelled as he attacked the far end of the insect, crushing a few more of its legs with his mace, while Aaron sent two arrows into the beast's underbelly. But it was Ohaobbok who got in the real blow. He slashed his sword into its belly, spilling gallons of a steaming greenish liquid.

The beast lurched violently, thrashing its head in spasms of pain, and spewed a stream of thick, sticky liquid that came directly at Ryan. The young wizard intensified his shield's energy, and the steaming acid washed over him harmlessly.

"Ryan!" Arabelle shrieked.

Ryan's shield was now burning the acidic goo into billowing clouds of acrid gray smoke. "I'm all right!" he yelled.

When Ryan could see again, the beast had reared back for

another attack, but not raising up as high this time. Ohaobbok plunged his sword deep into the soft underside of the head, and Sloane and Aaron buried two more arrows deep in the monster's mouth. Ryan was gathering energy for another assault when two daggers flew into the beast's black eyes, and the megapede convulsed uncontrollably.

Oda had to run from the scene. The creature coiled and stretched in violent spasms, flinging droplets of its ichor in every direction. And then it collapsed and lay still, dead.

Oda came back to rejoin the others. "See? Wasn't dat entertaining?"

Ryan shook his head. "Your idea of fun maybe. That thing was a horror."

"Dat's what made it fun."

Ryan saw Arabelle walking toward the head of the beast. "Be careful, my love. It might be leaking that acid everywhere."

She didn't pause. "If you think I'm leaving my daggers buried in this monster's head, you are sadly mistaken."

"Sorry," Ryan said with a laugh. "Let me help you."

---

The she-wolf howled when she reached a stream. A responding howl came from downstream, and she trotted toward the sound, the group following after. Sloane tried to listen to the wolf's thoughts, but after what had happened with the megapede, she found herself too busy scanning for threats.

As they moved down the stream, the ground on either side of them grew rapidly steeper until it was effectively a V-shaped ravine. It made Sloane uneasy; they were putting themselves in a position to be ambushed from above. She was just about to communicate her concern to Aaron when they came across the rest of the wolf pack, waiting patiently for them. Here, the stream led into a crevice in the side of the mountain.

Grey Wind padded up to her.

*"She-human Sloane,"* he said, *"the sour-smelling human is everywhere in this clearing. But the stench is strongest within the mountain."*

Sloane repeated this for everyone else's benefit. *"Does that crack open up into a cave?"* she asked.

The pack leader whined and yipped. *"I'm sorry. I don't like the inside of mountains. I want to help, but I cannot pass within."*

Sloane rubbed Grey Wind's head, comforting him. *"It's all right. I'll see for myself."*

"What?" Aaron said.

Sloane held her hand up for quiet as she mentally probed within the crevice. As she strained to detect anything beyond the surface of the rock, Oda erupted with a gigantic sneeze. At exactly that moment, a stick came flying from the wall of the ravine and landed next to Oda. The dwarf knelt to examine the stick. Sloane suddenly detected Dominic's thoughts within the crevice. She telepathically shared the news with the group.

Ryan waved everyone close. "Since the crevice is narrow,

we can only enter single file. And Ohaobbok can't possibly fit."

He outlined the plan. Ryan would enter first, followed by Oda and Aaron and Wat. If all went as planned, Ryan would nullify Dominic's magic, and Oda and Aaron would physically remove him from the cave. If things didn't go exactly as planned, Ryan and Wat would try to vaporize Dominic while Oda and Aaron would do what they did best: pound him. And if, by some miracle, Dominic managed to get past the four of them, it would be left to Arabelle and Sloane to lure him out of the cave so they could combine forces with the wolves and Ohaobbok.

"Assuming that Dominic is neutralized and removed," Ryan finished, "Sloane will try to tear through his memories to find out what's motivating him. Okay, everyone ready?"

---

As Ryan squeezed himself through the crack, he strengthened his shields until the threads of power hummed with energy. His concentration was so strong that he felt the very grains of the wall as his shields brushed against them.

About fifteen feet in, the crevice started to widen, and after another few feet it gave way to a chamber of impenetrable darkness.

Ryan pulled an unlit torch from his waist, but before he could light it with energy, a set of flaming eyes opened in the darkness and a spear of energy rocked Ryan's shield. The fountain of sparks from the spear pushed him backward into Oda.

Even as Ryan summoned his powers to retaliate, he focused in to find the threads of magic that circled his attacker's head. The amount of power he saw there was shocking. Ryan might not have what it took if this came down to a pure contest of strength.

He sent an invisible spear of energy, directed not at Dominic's body, but at the core of his power—the web of filaments that glowed brightly in Ryan's vision. His attack smashed against the filaments, sending them crashing into each other, giving off sparks that only he could see. Though Dominic didn't know it yet, his magic had been stunned. And Ryan now saw that it was, in fact, Dominic. To Ryan's eyes his sparking head was now a beacon of light, illuminating the entire cave.

Dominic smiled, clearly thinking that Ryan had missed. His eyes no longer flamed, but they still showed signs of the dangerous creature he'd become. He advanced and made a throwing motion at Ryan. Nothing happened. His eyes widened, and he froze, shocked. He attempted another throwing motion. Again, nothing.

It was only then that Ryan allowed himself to smile. He motioned to Oda and Aaron, who shoved past Ryan, grabbed Dominic, and dragged him out of the cavern.

Dominic grunted as Oda roughly bound his arms. Ryan looked at Sloane, who nodded her readiness. Then he stepped up in front of Dominic while Oda, Aaron, and Wat stood guard. The entire pack of wolves encircled them, emitting a constant low growl.

Dominic sneered up at Ryan. "Now what?"

Ryan stifled his desire to forcibly wipe the grin off of one of the few people he'd ever come to hate. "Why have you been trying to kill my brother and me?"

Dominic laughed. "Not just you and your brother. I wanted to kill your entire family. None of you belong in Trimoria. I loathe your foreign faces."

*"He believes what he's saying,"* Sloane communicated telepathically.

"What has my family ever done to you?"

The sparking in Dominic's eyes brightened for a moment, but he remained silent.

*"Pursue that line of questioning,"* Sloane said. *"I saw flashes of something."*

Ryan paused, considering. "When did you realize you were a wizard?"

Dominic scoffed. "Jealous?"

*"I just got a glimpse of a female elf,"* Sloane projected. *"Dominic is tightly controlling his thoughts. Try to anger him. He might lose some of that control."*

"Have you met the elf yet?" Ryan said condescendingly. "I doubt you have. She and I are close friends, but… I seriously doubt she would ever grant you that same honor."

Dominic glared, his eyes pure hatred. "What could a nobody like you know about her?" he yelled, spittle flying from his mouth as he strained at his bindings. "Ellisandrea's already promised herself to *me*. You'll never get her!"

Oda and Aaron wrestled Dominic under control.

*"That did it,"* Sloane said. *"Ellisandrea put him up to this. He obtained his power at an altar to Sammael. I now have a mental image of where it is. I think I could lead us there."*

An immense rumble sounded from the ridge above them. Ryan looked up to see an avalanche of rocks, dirt, trees, and mud tumbling down toward them. Clouds of dust billowed over the land, forcing Ryan and the rest of his companions to fall into fits of coughing. Darkness overwhelmed them.

"Is everyone all right?" Ryan yelled when at last it stopped. "Arabelle? Sloane? Ohaobbok? Wat?"

The dust cleared, and Ryan saw Ohaobbok standing knee-high in the rubble, digging at a pile of rocks.

Ryan turned to Aaron and Oda. "Hold on to the prisoner."

He raced to Ohaobbok's side, and saw Sloane and Wat's filthy forms shaking dirt and twigs from their bodies. They were disheveled, but otherwise unharmed.

*Where is Arabelle?* Ryan thought, his mind whirling. "Have you seen Arabelle?" he asked Ohaobbok, who was furiously pulling up clods of dirt.

Ohaobbok wrenched a broken log out of the ground, and beneath it, Ryan saw Arabelle's dark hair. He dived in to help dig her out.

"Find the healing potions!" he shouted. "They were on the pack animals. We'll need them all!"

The ogre lifted another log, revealing Arabelle's broken and bleeding body. Ryan felt for a pulse. He shuddered when he felt only the weakest thread of an erratic heartbeat.

"Where are the healing potions?" he screamed. "She's dying!"

Aaron was now nearby, helping Wat dig through another pile of debris. "I'm trying to get to them. Arabelle was tending the pack animals when the landslide came. They were buried along with her."

Ryan held Arabelle as her life's blood slowly seeped into the ground. He carefully wiped the dirt from her heart-shaped face. His tears fell, mixing with the blood that spilled from her nose and ears. As her breathing became more labored, he heard a gurgling sound that he could only imagine was blood pooling in her lungs.

"Ryan…" said Aaron, his voice cracking, "we found the animals, but… the potions were all crushed. We have nothing. I'm sorry."

Ryan's world came crashing down on him. He held Arabelle and waited and hoped. He buried his face in Arabelle's dirt-encrusted hair and breathed in her scent. He wanted to remember her as she'd been before the accident.

Chilling laughter floated across the clearing. Dominic, chortling with glee.

"Hey, idiot!" he yelled. "Did you know that avalanche was really meant for you? I set it up so that all I needed to do was pull one stick and the whole mountain would fall." He cackled crazily. "I pulled the stick, but nothing happened. At least at first. I guess things didn't work out as planned. The good news is that I got your girlfriend instead."

Ryan breathed methodically, ignoring the scum and his rantings. He desperately pored through his memories, trying to recall all of his anatomy lessons from Eglerion. The wise elf had taught about the body, but nothing had prepared Ryan for this moment. Arabelle's injuries were clearly internal. She was bleeding from her nose and ears. Part of her chest looked like it had been crushed, and her breathing was labored as the blood gurgled in her lungs. Ryan wished he had his mother's healing ability.

Arabelle convulsed, spewing blood from her nose and mouth. Ryan tilted her head to the side to keep her from choking on her blood.

Then suddenly, he recalled a forgotten lesson.

"Oda!" he yelled. "Bring that demon-spawn here!"

Oda dragged Dominic across the clearing and deposited him within arm's reach of Ryan.

Dominic sneered. "It happens to be my birthday today. Thank you for such a wonderful present. I love to watch a slow, painful death."

But Dominic was no longer the object of Ryan's disdain. He was the source of Arabelle's salvation.

Ryan recalled the day he watched Arabelle transfer energy from herself to the health potions, and the way her threads of power vibrated. The key lay in the synchronized use of powers in just a certain way. With his powers combined with Dominic's, he might just be able to unlock the ability to heal.

He focused on the core of the life energy that Dominic carried. He pulsed the dark wizard's threads of power in experimental ways. Only the right combination would lead to the power of healing. As he tested arrays that failed to match the correct pattern, a shower of ineffective sparks flashed around him. The rest of Ryan's companions gathered around and watched in silence as Dominic cackled with amusement.

Ryan frantically tried to duplicate the exact pattern and timings he recalled seeing Arabelle use. With each attempt, he nudged one more thread that was mistimed or misaligned into synchrony with his memory. As the pattern became a closer match, the sparking became less pronounced.

Desperately, Ryan cast the entirety of his energy web, latching onto Dominic's life force. He cried with relief as he pulled on that life force and began to see something happen. Slowly, the flows of energy left Dominic and entered Arabelle.

At first the dark wizard showed no reaction, but the moment didn't last. With a look of terror, he struggled against his bonds. Oda and Aaron held him in place. Ryan continued to drain the energy from Dominic, but his attention was on his beloved Arabelle. The life force was entering her, and the bruises on her forehead were fading. Then the crushed side of her chest began to expand, and her labored breathing cleared. The coloring of her skin turned from a deathly blue-black to pink.

The life force passing to her thinned, then faltered.

Arabelle's eyes fluttered open. She coughed, spitting up dirt and blood. "I love you, Ryan," she whispered.

Ryan gently held her in his arms. "I love you, Arabelle."

She returned his embrace. "How?"

Ryan turned to Dominic, who lay on the ground with his eyes staring into nothingness. "I traded his life for yours."

"Good trade if you ask me," Oda grunted. "Welcome back, lass. I didn't believe I was going to see your pretty eyes ever open again."

Arabelle looked sadly at Dominic. "I hope we got what we needed from him." Her eyes closed. "Can I rest? I would love to take a tiny nap."

"Of course you can rest," Ohaobbok whispered quietly. "The rest of us will prepare our camp. We aren't going anywhere until Arabelle is back to normal."

---

"Stop being a child and let me look at it, Ohaobbok," Arabelle chided.

"I'm fine," the ogre said. "It will heal without you exerting yourself."

Arabelle stomped her foot. "Enough, Ohaobbok! Show me your hands *now*!"

The ogre sheepishly knelt and held out his hands. They had been poorly wrapped in dirty bandages scavenged from the dead pack animals.

Arabelle undid the wrappings, then gasped at the torn

gobbets of flesh that remained of Ohaobbok's fingers. They dripped blood and oozed a foul-smelling greenish substance.

"Your poor hands! How could this happen?"

"I saw you buried," Ohaobbok said. "I knew I needed to find you quickly."

Arabelle's lip quivered and she took a deep breath to calm herself. "Someone get me some food. Our brave party leader nearly destroyed his hands trying to rescue me. I refuse to let him die of an infection because he's a stubborn mule."

Then she concentrated on the ogre's hands, infusing healing power and chasing away the infection growing within.

---

In the times before Trimoria, Ryan remembered his father having conference calls with people all over the world. He felt like that was what he was doing now as everyone sat around the fire and Ryan sent messages through his communication ring. They needed guidance from the king's council on what to do next.

*Yes,* he tapped. *Everyone is fine. Dominic buried in unmarked grave.*

A reply came in, and Ryan read it aloud for the sake of the dwarves. "It's Eglerion. He says, 'Was the altar to Sammael in Ellisanethra?'"

He continued to say everything aloud as the conversation continued.

*Ryan: Sloane's description matched what I remember of the elf queen's home.*

*Jared: Whatever is hidden in that altar must be dealt with.*

*Throll: Recall the seed is trapped by the First Protector. Be very careful. The elf queen attempted to unwrap the hiding spot for the seed and became trapped within.*

*Jared: Eglerion and Labri are being escorted to where Hammerthrower Clan awaits. They'll enter the elf queen's domain with you.*

*Throll: Silas wants all of you to visit Mattias Hammerthrower. Oda knows how to find him. Remind Ohaobbok to wear purple on his shoulder.*

Ryan looked up at Ohaobbok. "Purple?"

The ogre grabbed a handful of purplish berries from a hanging vine and squeezed it on his shoulder, leaving a purple splotch. "Dwarves and ogres are natural enemies. Dwarves know me as a friend by this purple stain."

"You know how to find Clan Hammerthrower?" Ryan asked Oda.

Oda laughed. "Of course! The Hammerthrowers have lived next to the Rockfists for generations."

Ryan tapped on his ring.

*Ryan: Understood. We'll meet Eglerion and Labri in Hammerthrower territory.*

*Throll: Is there anything you need? Just name it.*

Ryan looked around the group. Everyone shook their heads.

*Ryan: Nobody else wants anything, but I want permission*

to rid the world of Ellisanethra and the cursed altar behind that house.

*Throll:* Eglerion asks you to wait until they arrive before going to the elf queen's domain. However, you have my permission and your parents' blessing to wipe all hint of that evil place from Trimoria.

*Ryan:* Understood and thank you.

*Jared:* All of you, be safe. Good night. Meeting adjourned.

## THE SEED

Malphas cowered as his lord and master, Sammael, flew into a rage. The temperature soared under the demon lord's fury, and Malphas felt his skin blistering in the heat, while his lieutenants exploded, sending greasy gobbets of flesh and steaming entrails everywhere. The rocks around them began to crack from the sudden change in temperature, and Malphas worried that the Abyss would tear itself apart.

But finally, Sammael calmed and settled back on his throne. The temperature plummeted once more.

Sammael called out to Malphas telepathically.

*"Find a way through that barrier,"* the demon lord hissed. *"I am losing patience with the half-wit mortals sent to accomplish my goals."*

"My lord," Malphas said breathlessly, "I'll do everything I

can. But may I ask… what has transpired to disappoint you so?"

Sammael's bone-grating growl shook him to the core. *"The Archmage killed my minion within the barrier."* His terrifying face, which normally hid in shadows, erupted with flame. *"Find an entrance. I don't care what you have to do."*

"I'll do what I must," Malphas said, prostrating himself in front of his lord.

---

With the wolves having taken their leave to return to their hunting grounds, Oda now led the group through the winding passes of the mountains.

They were going down one particularly steep slope when Aaron began to skid out of control. He righted himself, but glared at the dwarf.

"Oda, are you trying to kill us?"

"I'm taking you through da back way. It might be a bit tougher to navigate, but we'll get there today instead of tomorrow night."

After another hour of navigating the mountain passes, Sloane held up a hand. "I sense some dwarves ahead."

"How can you tell they're dwarves?" Ryan asked.

"If you think I cannot tell the difference between a dwarf mind and some other type of mind, you're sadly mistaken."

The group came around a turn and encountered a half-dozen dwarves with long gray beards.

"Welcome, Princess Lancaster," one of them said. "And welcome to both Lord Rivertons and honored Ohaobbok. I'm sorry, but Mattias did not provide me with da rest of your names." The graybeard squinted at Oda. "You look like a Rockfist, but you," he looked at Wat, "you are unfamiliar."

Wat bowed. "My name is Wat, sir. I'm an orphan raised among the humans. I have no clan. I was called 'Crazybeard' as a child, and I have used the name since."

"As for me," Oda offered, "you were correct, sir. My name is Oda Rockfist. Mother is Edna. Father is Rock."

"Ha!" the graybeard said. "I knew it. You're a chip off dat craggy boulder, you are. Before ye leave, make sure you visit Barnaby. His leg is healing fine now dat we got a supply of healing potions from Lady Riverton."

Oda smiled. "Yessir. I want to introduce some of my companions here to my ma's mutton, anyway."

"Mattias has arranged for a feast in your honor. It will include mutton." The graybeard looked up at the ogre. "However, for honored Ohaobbok, Mattias asked me to assure you dat he remembers yer taste for carrots and potatoes. We are preparing more than even *you* could possibly eat."

---

The group had made camp outside a dank tunnel. Ohaobbok reclined beside the fire, munching on carrots, and Aaron lounged comfortably at Sloane's side. The fire flickered into the night, alighting everyone's faces with warm hope.

Moving away from the happy scene, Ryan followed Mattias into the tunnel. Mattias held a lantern to light their way.

"Young Lord Riverton," he said, his voice gravelly and soft-spoken, "what I'm about to share with ye are the archives we hold dearest. Most of our population is not even aware they exist. Only da leaders from da original twelve clans are allowed access."

"I understand. Thank you for your kindness."

"Don't thank me," Mattias said with a chuckle. "It was not I alone who entrusted ye wid our knowledge. Dis morning, da leaders of each clan met and unanimously voted to extend access to you."

They entered a wide chamber lined with rows of shelves containing a sprawling collection of books and scrolls. Along the edges of the room, were large containers of what looked like sand and rocks.

"What's the sand for?" Ryan asked.

"Oh, dat isn't sand," Mattias said with a laugh. "Dat's salt. It keeps dis room dry."

A dwarf with a stooped back and a very long white beard hobbled over from across the room. "If not for da salt," he said, "these records would have long ago crumbled away."

"Ryan Riverton," said Mattias, "meet Donlas Harbinger, da keeper of da dwarven histories. Donlas, dis here is young Lord Riverton, wizard and son of Lord Jared Riverton."

Donlas's thick lips parted to reveal craggy teeth. "And slayer of Azazel, if rumors are to be believed."

"I did have a hand in it," Ryan said with a slight bow. "Yes, sir."

Donlas reached out with his gnarled old hand and patted Ryan on his shoulder. "Dispense with formalities. You call me Donlas, and I will call you whatever you prefer. Mattias, you can leave now. Thank you."

Mattias laughed. "I know when I'm not wanted. Young Lord Riverton, yer in good hands. If ye need me, just yell. Someone will fetch me."

As Mattias left, Donlas shakily grabbed Ryan's elbow and led him to a table. "Mattias warned me about what you're looking for. I've dug up some of our oldest records to help in the search. This might take a while."

Indeed, the table was already stacked with a giant assortment of books, scrolls, and loose sheets of parchment.

Ryan groaned. *It's going to take days to sort through all this.*

---

With much help from Donlas, Ryan spent the next two days poring through the records, looking for any clues about the Seed, the sinister orb that seemed to corrupt and manipulate all who came into contact with it. They also looked for information about Ellisandrea, the elf queen, and Ellisanethra, her home.

Ryan was pleased when he and the old dwarf were joined by a newcomer.

"I'm really glad you're here, Eglerion," he said at the sight of the wise old elf. "I have lots of questions for you."

Eglerion smiled. "That's why I'm here."

Ryan pointed out a passage in one of the books. "Look at this. I've read the same passage before, in a book in Azazel's library."

*While the wealth they promised was considerable, the passages at the thirty-fourth level of the mine were deemed too deep and too hot for dwarves to traverse. Several reliable sources also cited the presence of odd creatures, including imps. This was viewed as proof that the miners had dug too close to the forbidden deep, and that wisdom called for them to withdraw.*

*Yet before the operation was called to a halt, several among their number uncovered a large spherical seed that glowed like a crystal and emanated heat. The miners brought the seed before a conclave of wizards, who determined that the seed was a flawed element of Trimoria that should, they said, never have been brought into this world. They claimed that the seed held a dark and unstable power, and that this power influenced the seed's holder in a dark fashion. The longer the seed was held, the greater the influence.*

*Ultimately, the conclave's advice was to return the seed to the location where it was found. The dwarves concurred.*

*Following this decree, it was declared by the clan elders that the thirty-fourth level was to be sealed off from the world above. The seed was returned to the mine, and the foreman blasted the entrance. Passage into the deep has been barred ever after.*

"In addition, in the First Protector's own journal," Ryan said. "he wrote about enduring a great deal of trouble hiding this thing he called the Seed. So, what *is* this crystal, really? I mean, this isn't just some random rock if it affects everyone, even including the queen of the elves."

Eglerion took a seat beside Ryan. "The records you have here are altered or incomplete. The Seed is actually an unusually large diamond. It was originally found nearly a thousand years ago, but it wasn't mined as the dwarven records here indicate. This occurred before I was born, but I've heard this account directly from those who were there, and have subsequently verified the accounts from written records we keep at Eluanethra. It seems the Seed was originally found in a chamber constructed by the Ta'ah."

"Ta'ah?" Ryan asked.

"They are among our lost brothers," Donlas said, joining them. "We dwarves are sensitive about our clan histories. Few today know that we originally comprised thirteen clans. One of those clans was called away for reasons unknown—they are known as the Ta'ah in the ancient tongue. We can only hope that somewhere, despite the demons that likely rule across the barrier, our brethren still wander to wherever their destinies have led them."

Eglerion bowed his head. "May Seder protect them."

"You mentioned a chamber?" Ryan said.

"Yes," said Eglerion. "The Conclave of Wizards was called to a sealed vault. The dwarves had discovered the door, but were unable to open it with picks and shovels, because it was sealed with magic. So they asked for help. The Conclave arrived, and studied the doors, which were not only sealed with deep magics, but covered with dwarven runes."

"What did the runes say?" Donlas asked. "I have no record of this."

"I'm not surprised. There were no dwarves serving as members of the Conclave of Wizards, and the records of the Conclave are typically sealed. The runes were a warning: *'Fie to thee who bursts asunder this chamber. For within lies power beyond imagining and the greatest evil known to Trimoria. Pray to Seder that it never walks the earth, or we are all doomed.'*"

"And they opened it anyway?" Donlas sputtered. "Whatever passed for intelligence must have fled those wizards."

"Could the Seed have influenced them even through the door of the chamber?" Ryan asked.

Eglerion shrugged. "I don't know. Perhaps. Nonetheless, the Conclave combined their powers and broke the seal. At the center of the chamber was a chest that contained many small diamonds. These were once precious, but after the decimation of the wizard ranks, their practical use was eliminated, and so was the demand. Behind the chest were two pedestals carved from the blackest of stone. On one sat the Seed, and on the other sat its twin. At first, these crystal orbs appeared to be perfect, but upon closer examination, the Conclave detected a flaw in one of them. Anyway, the dwarven account is accurate on one point: the wizards decided to seal the chamber again, abandoning that level of the mine forevermore."

"Evidently not forevermore," Ryan said, "or we wouldn't be facing that evil nugget of rock now."

Eglerion nodded. "Exactly right."

"All right," said Ryan, "now that I know what it is and where it came from, are we ready to destroy it?"

The elf shook his head. "You don't understand the significance of the crystal yet." He pulled from his robe a glowing crystal the size of a fingernail and held it up. "This diamond was used as a power lodestone by Zenethar Thariginian, the First Protector."

"A power lodestone?"

"Yes. Most wizards don't have the ability to store their energy in objects, like you have done with weapons and armor. Even the greatest of war wizards lacked the skill. Except healers—they're unusual in their ability to create potions. But Archmages are war wizards who can do something similar—they can store their energy for later. In effect, you put your energy in an object, then withdraw the energy when you need it. As a result, Archmages of ages past could command tremendous amounts of power, by tapping their private reserves."

"And that's what you were referring to you when you said

wizards created a demand for diamonds? This is what they used as a lodestone?"

Eglerion nodded. "You've worked with damantite before, and you've seen how much energy it can hold. That's because it's composed of minute crystalline structures that are highly ordered, making the metal very dense and able to efficiently store the energy you're able to infuse. Diamonds are even better. These little stones are the most efficient storage target of magical energy in all of Trimoria. One small diamond like this can hold more energy than one hundred sets of damantite armor."

Ryan gulped. "In the visions… that's how the First Protector destroyed the demons and raised the barrier, isn't it?"

"Yes. A tremendous amount of energy was brought to bear on the demons in one fell swoop. I'll admit to not fully understanding the extent of such power, but it gives you a clue of the danger we face. That seed is a giant diamond that can proportionally store more energy than we can even imagine, also, it's believed that the energy infused within it comes from the greatest demon lord of them all. It's hard to image the extent of the danger the Seed's use poses. The dwarven runes gave us a hint of just how afraid our ancestors were of this evil thing."

"What about Sammael?" Ryan asked. "Evidently the altar in Ellisanethra is dedicated to him. Could he be the evil about which the dwarven runes warned?"

"Don't mention that monster's name aloud," Donlas said. "Nothing good can come of it."

"It's possible," said Eglerion, "but there is so much we don't understand about the Seed. How it originally came into the possession of Ellisandrea, for instance. Why she later gave it to Zenethar. And why it wields such an influence on people. All we can do is arm you as best we can." He handed the diamond to Ryan. "You will need to learn how to store and retrieve energy. Unfortunately, this is something I cannot teach. No elf has ever possessed the capability."

Ryan closed his hands around the diamond. "I have some ideas on how to approach the problem."

"Good," Eglerion said. "If you're ready tomorrow, we'll visit Ellisanethra and unlock secrets that have been hidden for a long time."

---

Ryan entered the smithy to which Mattias had referred him. The heavily muscled proprietor hollered at the soot-covered dwarves hard at work in the unbearably hot room.

"Pound those impurities out of the metal or I'll pound it out of your hides! We can't have the Hammerthrower smiths known as producers of shoddy items."

He noticed Ryan and waved dismissively. "I don't want any. Come back in a century or two."

Ryan grinned and strode toward the anvil the smith was

pounding. "I'm not selling anything, and Mattias said you would be stubborn. But I'm to convince you to help me."

The smith grimaced at Mattias's name. "Just 'cause he's clan chief doesn't give him the right to tell me what to do in my own smith, I tell's ya!"

"How about we trade?" Ryan said. "I know it's hard for you to generate enough heat to melt damantite for casting. What if I offered to do it for you? Then you could help me with one small service in exchange."

The smith took in Ryan from head to foot. "How, pray tell, do you plan on melting damantite?"

"Don't you worry about how," Ryan said with a wink. "Point me to a crucible with the ore. I'll take care of the rest."

"Hey!" the proprietor bellowed to his workers. "Spiggit, Tracor, Grough! Go fill our largest crucible with damantite ore. The human here has something to prove."

The three dwarves scrambled to fill a crucible that was nearly the size of a bathtub. Ryan pulled out the diamond with which he'd been practicing, along with a bag of food. He drank several flasks of milk and ate some fruit, feeling the food topping off his energy reserves. When the crucible was filled, he was ready.

"All right," the smith said. "Let's see you melt the ore."

Ryan held his staff in one hand and the diamond in the other. After a moment of concentration, he poured a steady but tremendous stream of energy deep into the middle of the ore. He felt his energy draining, replaced by pangs of hunger, but the crucible was glowing orange with heat. He tapped the latent power held within the diamond and pushed it at the crucible. After only a minute, the pile of ore had been reduced to a bubbling cauldron of molten damantite with flakes of slag floating on top.

"Oy, you lazy anvil-banging ale-swillers!" the smith hollered. "Get off your hind ends and start casting the forms. This damantite won't stay hot forever. Hurry, hurry, hurry!"

With a buzz of excitement, the crucible was hooked up to a crane and lever system maneuvered by a team of dwarves, and its contents were poured into a series of casts.

The smith came over to Ryan, looking sheepish. "I'm sorry, Lord Wizard. You should have told me who you be or I'd not have been so… well… what can I do to help you?"

Ryan handed the smith his damantite staff. "I need to mount this diamond within this staff. I can't risk losing the diamond, so it needs to be done properly. Can you manage?"

The smith laughed. "Is that all? I'll have it done before the boys finish pouring your handiwork."

"Great!" Ryan said with a grin. "While you work, I need to grab more food. The diamond and I both need to get fully charged."

The smith looked confused, but shrugged. "Whatever you say, Lord Wizard. I'll have your staff ready in no time."

---

*"You will not be able to defeat the Archmage directly."*

Ellisandrea sighed. "Then how do I engage him?"

"*Try to convert him. If that fails, do not attack him directly with magic. That has already failed you. Use your mastery of the elements. Spread your power so he cannot attack you directly. Distract him. Injure him physically. Do not give him an opportunity to gain access to us.*"

"I understand. I'll do everything I can."

"*Yes, you will.*"

## DESTRUCTION

Everyone gathered outside Ellisanethra, the trees thick and the wilderness eerily silent.

Eglerion strode to the fore. "I can feel Ellisandrea's presence in these woods," the elf said. "If you feel or hear anything trying to lure you from the path, realize that it's a trap. Ellisandrea was always manipulative, and from what the dwarves have said, she's been leading unsuspecting victims into her web for reasons unknown. We can only assume that is how Dominic was created."

"I would recommend holding hands in these woods," Ryan added. "We don't want anyone getting lost. I'll lead, followed by Eglerion, Oda, Wat, Aaron, Labri, Sloane, and Arabelle." He turned to Labri. "Unless you want to stay with the troops? I'm certain it would be safer."

Labri shook her head. "No. I need to be there. My grandmother has much to answer for."

Sloane gasped. "I didn't realize she was your grandmother."

"Only in blood. Xinthian sent my parents along with other elves from Eluanethra to retrieve her, but she killed everyone who tried to remove her from her home, including my parents. I was just a baby at the time."

Sloane hugged her. "I'm sorry. I didn't know."

"Ryan, are you ready?" Eglerion asked.

Ryan held out his staff, the glowing diamond now embedded at its top. "I'm as ready as I'll ever be. The staff and I are fully charged. How about everyone else?"

Aaron stepped forward. "I'm ready, but from what I've heard, this is primarily going to be a magical fight. I may be the odd man out on this one."

"I'm sure we'll find a use for you," Ryan said with a wink.

---

Ryan's staff throbbed with energy as he led the group through the elf queen's mist-enshrouded forest.

"Ellisandrea's talent always fell within the areas of the natural elements," Eglerion explained. "Her ability to call up mist, rain, wind, or other elemental forces was astounding. I can smell her influence everywhere in this forest."

The mist became oppressively thick. Ryan found it impossible to see even inches ahead of his face.

"How can anyone see anything in this?" Wat yelled from behind. "I can't even see my own whiskers."

"The fog gets thicker the farther we go," Ryan said. "Just don't lose your grip on the person in front of you, or we may not be able to find you again. I can see the threads of power influencing the fog. We're not far from its source. I'm sure of it."

After another fifteen minutes of traveling slowly through the mist, they arrived at the center of the elf queen's domain: a clearing that was free of the mist, with a simple cabin at its center. From its warping facades to its vacant windows, it was an ancient place, and a mystical one.

"It reminds me of the home we kept in Eluanethra," Eglerion said.

"We?'" Ryan asked.

Eglerion shrugged. "In Eluanethra, I lived with Ellisandrea. This was prior to her unwholesome obsession with the Seed, of course. She was and is my wife."

"No!" Ryan gasped. "You're kidding!"

"Does that mean Labri is your granddaughter?" Arabelle asked.

"Yes," Labri answered. "I owe him everything."

A chill wind blew across the clearing, stirring the leaves. Ryan detected the smell of rotten eggs. And then, coalescing right in their midst, was the silhouette of a woman. It gradually began to solidify, and Aaron and Oda pushed to the fore, both wielding shields and weapons of damantite.

The smell strengthened as the silhouette turned solid and

Ellisandrea appeared before the group. With her lithe figure, her long blonde hair, and perfectly tanned skin, she exuded an appeal difficult to ignore.

The elf queen looked from face to face, and her eyes widened when she came to Eglerion.

"What are you doing here?" she asked. "I would think you would be home, awaiting my return."

Eglerion shook his head with obvious sadness. "This was decided long ago, when you set out on a quest for something not meant for you."

The elf queen hissed, turning venomous in an instant. "Your jealousy is pathetic. What difference does it make what I do?" She nodded toward Labri. "I can see you have replaced me, anyway. So much for the belief that elves marry for life."

"You blind fool!" Eglerion growled. "That is your granddaughter. Believe it or not, she wanted to see if she could save you—redeem you in some way."

Ellisandrea laughed hysterically. "Liar! I destroyed my daughter, so this is no blood of mine. I ensured that it would only be Sammael and me in the end." Her eyes flared with demonic power as she turned toward Labri. "I will not share Sammael, you harlot!"

As she sent a bolt of plasma at Labri, Ryan expanded his shield to encompass the elf. A shower of sparks exploded off the shield, holding against the onslaught.

Aaron and Oda yelled and attacked, but their weapons passed harmlessly through the queen. Ellisandrea threw another assault at Labri. This time, Aaron caught the bolt on his shield, the stream of energy pushing him backward, and Wat sent a bolt of his own at the apparition. It, too, passed through her without effect.

Ryan was watching carefully the threads of magic flying all over the clearing. It was unlike anything he'd ever experienced. He couldn't find a central mass from where the energy came. It was as if the elf queen had infused herself throughout the entire clearing. The attacks were coming from a hundred places at once.

Labri was now surrounded by Aaron, Oda, and Wat, each in their own way defending Labri from the elf queen's attacks. Ellisandrea winked out from one position, appeared in another, and viciously slammed Oda's shield, sending the dwarf flying. As the others reorganized to shield Labri, Oda ran back to them, smoke trailing from his cracked shield.

Wat intercepted the next bolt from the elf queen. He was blown backward into Labri, and they both tumbled to the ground.

Ryan grabbed Labri, held her tightly within his shield, and pulled energy from the diamond in his staff. He bent the light around both Labri and himself and waited.

"Ryan!" Wat yelled. "Labri! Where did they go?"

The apparition screamed with victory. "See, Sammael! No need to worry. I have scared away the fledgling wizard." She smiled sweetly at the rest of the group. "How would you like to gather more power than you have ever experienced in your lives?" She focused on Eglerion. "All those years of studying power with no ability to use it... it must be so frustrating,

Eglerion. I can give you the power you have always wanted. I can give it *all* to you. Join me."

Ryan watched, but not with his eyes. His magical sense saw Ellisandrea's web of power unraveling as it coalesced into the image that presented itself to Eglerion. He pulled deeply from the energy reserves he'd stored in the diamond and slammed the threads that controlled Ellisandrea's magic, hoping to disable her power.

The elf queen's eyes widened in horror at the bolt of power coming from the unseen pocket in the center of the clearing. But it was too late. The sparking threads that controlled her magic were severed cleanly, and the entire clearing exploded in a flash of blinding white.

As the elf queen vanished, the clearing became deathly quiet.

Ryan breathed in deeply and smelled the scent of flowers and pine for the first time in these woods. He relaxed the cloaking shield and both he and Labri reappeared.

"There they are!" Wat called. "Neat trick, that is. You need to teach me that one."

Ryan blinked warily as he scanned the clearing. "I don't think it's over yet. I don't feel Ellisandrea's presence anymore, but I sense something ominous behind that building. Time to once and for all see what's there."

"I just cannot believe how she reacted to her own flesh and blood," Eglerion said sadly.

Labri hugged her grandfather and held his hand as they all walked toward the back of the building.

Within sight of what looked like an altar, Ryan motioned at the others. "Wait here, just in case."

He studied the altar at the back of the yard. It was a simple construction of stone, incapable of hiding anything of any real size. But using his senses, he felt the presence of a malevolent object; it reminded him of the venom that tainted the elf queen. He studied the altar and saw threads of powers tied into a complex knot of energy. After analyzing the weave, he determined that it served two purposes: to anchor the object to the altar, and to bend light, similar to the trick he'd learned for his shield.

Ryan pushed a trickle of energy at the threads holding the object in place. The filaments parted with little effort. He studied the knot holding the obscuring threads, and with only the lightest of mental touches, pulled back three threads at once.

A body revealed itself and fell from the altar. The elf queen. In her hand, she clutched a blackened diamond.

Eglerion knelt at her side.

"Is she dead?" Ryan asked.

Labri held up her hands. A crackling web of power had bloomed from her fingertips. She closed her eyes and smiled rapturously as the power shimmered over her entire body.

"Eglerion, I can feel everything you'd said I'd feel... At long last, I can sense the magic." She looked down at the body. "Which means my grandmother is dead."

"So are you the elf queen now?" Arabelle asked Labri.

"In effect. My grandfather and I will return home to bury

my grandmother. We'll endure an official period of mourning. And then, yes, I'll be crowned as queen of Eluanethra."

Eglerion sobbed. "I had everything I wanted. And then you left me for this *thing*. Damn you, Elli! Damn you!" He stood and wiped his eyes. "Destroy it all. I want nothing to remind me of this." He turned to Labri. "My queen, I ask for a husband's right of choice. I want Ellisandrea to have her funeral pyre here, in the home she chose over the home of her people."

Labri hugged her grandfather and nodded. "As you wish, Grandfather. But we must do something with the Seed. I can feel its malevolence even now."

Oda stalked over to the blackened diamond and growled. "Fear not, Queen." The dwarf swung his glowing damantite mace in a vicious arc at the blackened orb. As the mace connected with the Seed, an explosion rocked the clearing. The dwarf was sent flying backward, the remains of his smoldering mace still in his hand.

The Seed was entirely unharmed.

"Oda!" Arabelle shrieked, running to the dwarf's side. His body was covered with burns. He spouted off several curses about legendary diamonds as Arabelle tended his wounds.

---

Ryan, Wat, and Labri applied their magical energies to destroying the home formerly known as Ellisanethra. Eglerion had already placed his wife's body inside. The old elf looked stoic and accepting as the heat reflected off the burning hulk of what had been his wife's home.

When the fire had reduced the home and the former queen to ashes, they all went back to look at the Seed.

"We have to get it out of here," Ryan said. "It isn't safe anywhere in Trimoria. It corrupts anyone that touches it."

"We stand near the mist barrier," Eglerion said, pointing past the altar.

Ryan had thought this mist was just more of the fog that Ellisandrea had created. "This is *the* mist?" he asked.

"Yes."

"So if we tossed the Seed into it… we shouldn't be bothered by it again. Because nobody can enter the mists and live."

"That is accurate, as best as I know," Eglerion said.

Ryan reached down for the Seed. It was no longer a charred black, but bore a myriad of white filaments, and as he lifted it, he sensed an intelligence from within. As he wound his arm back to throw the orb, he felt a distinct pang of regret. But the feeling passed as the orb left his hand and sailed into the mist.

---

Grog walked along the evil barrier. His job was difficult. He kept watch for living things. If a living thing was smaller, he was to eat it. If a living thing was bigger, he was to run. He preferred the eating. The more he ate, the bigger his wings.

As he walked, a rock flew out of the evil barrier and hit

him on the head. Grog snarled. He wanted to kick the rock, but was taken by its beauty. Suddenly a new thought grew in his head: *Grog must hide pretty rock.*

Grog took the rock and stumbled toward his best hiding spot. This was the place where he found all the leftover food that helped him grow. But when he reached his hiding spot, he found something he hadn't expected. Lurking nearby was one of the biggest demons Grog had ever seen.

*Grog must run. Grog must hide rock. Grog—*

Malphas squished Grog's head, picked up the Seed, and smiled.

## PREVIEW – LORDS OF PROPHECY

"I'm a murderer," Arabelle lamented, crouching with a dagger in each hand as her handmaiden held her at bay with an iron-tipped staff.

Miriam crept toward her left, trying to keep her mistress from lunging at her. "Princess, you have to stop torturing yourself over this."

Arabelle leaped across the gap between them, and sparks erupted from the dagger as she scored a hit on Miriam's breastplate.

Miriam's staff whistled through the air as she swung a vicious blow at Arabelle's outstretched arm. Arabelle dropped into a crouch, just barely dodging.

"It's been four years, and the act still haunts me. It was my choice, and my choice alone to take their lives." Arabelle crept after her handmaiden, looking for another opening as she worried over the past. "They hadn't even attacked me! I've kept this secret from everyone but you. How can I allow Ryan to accept me as his bride, having kept such news from him?"

Miriam blinked the sweat from her eyes and snarled as she attacked, sweeping her staff at Arabelle's knees. The princess leaped backward, and Miriam continued her attack with a nonstop flurry of jabs, kicks, and sweeps.

"I won't have this from you again, Arabelle. Your father may be sheikh and you may be my best friend and princess of our people, but I have to say it: you're acting like a little girl!"

Miriam advanced with determination, increasing the speed and power behind her attacks. Arabelle dodged and deflected the blows.

"You've told me many times what happened," the maid continued. "You slew those men in self-defense, or in defense of others. You're being too harsh on yourself, and I won't hear self-loathing coming from the princess of the Imazighen!"

Arabelle ducked underneath one of Miriam's attacks and knocked her off her feet with a tremendous kick to the chest. Then she signaled the end of the sparring session.

"I suppose you're right," she said with a sigh. "Our people deserve better than this from their princess."

Miriam sat up with a groan. "No, they don't deserve *better*. They deserve you. Your acts were always for the greater good, and that's all any Imazighen could hope for." When Arabelle frowned, the maid added, "But Princess, if you feel guilt over the act, then yes, you should share it with Ryan

—er, the Archmage. Do it before your wedding, if you feel you must. I'm sure he'll be understanding."

As Miriam began to strip out of her armor, Arabelle noticed a bruise forming on her handmaiden's collarbone. She applied a gentle touch to the spot, and the swelling and discoloration faded.

"I think I'll tell him," she said. "I only wish I could tell him *now*. He's not scheduled to arrive from Eluanethra until the day before the ceremony, and that's almost two weeks from now."

She pictured Ryan as she'd last seen him. She'd been drawn to his kind blue eyes even when he was but a dream of what would be, and over the years, that blue-eyed boy had grown into handsome adulthood. She closed her eyes and felt for his presence. He was many miles away, yet she knew that if she followed her senses to the northeast, her vision would lead her directly to him.

"Why don't you use your ring?" Miriam asked.

Arabelle's eyes popped open, and she saw Miriam pointing to her private ring, the one she could use to communicate with only Ryan.

"I can't confess to him through the ring! I need to *see* him." She smiled. "Actually, I have an idea."

"As long as it's safe. And remember, it's very bad luck to see your betrothed the week before the ceremony."

Arabelle fidgeted with excitement. "Then I guess I'd better tell him to hurry."

She tapped a message into her ring. Whatever Ryan was

doing, he'd immediately feel the vibrations in his own ring and translate the message.

*Ryan,* she began, *We need to talk...*

###

As soon as Ryan received the urgent but mysterious request from his soon-to-be wife, he set about rushing to quickly complete all the things he needed to do in the elven city of Eluanethra. And he wasn't the only one rushing; the scribes working with him in Eluanethra's library were fluttering back and forth among the rows of books, tracking down the titles he'd listed for them, while others were already hard at work on the painstaking process of copying each and every page of the selected tomes.

When Xinthian entered, he chuckled at the sight. "Young man, I haven't seen my scribes run around like this in years."

"They're a great help. I must apologize for cutting my visit short, but Arabelle would never have summoned me if it weren't critical."

Xinthian held out a hand. "Give me your list of needs. You shouldn't keep your bride-to-be waiting."

Ryan looked uncertainly at the town elder, then nodded and placed the list in his outstretched hand.

"Jelian," said Xinthian, passing the parchment to one of the scribes. "Make sure everything on this list gets delivered to the Riverton Castle library as soon as the copies are complete."

Xinthian then put his arm around Ryan's shoulder and escorted him from the room.

"Thank you, my friend," Ryan said when they were outside.

The town elder laughed. "And I must thank *you* for the wedding invitation! I look forward to attending. Though I can't say I reacted with quite as much excitement as did Queen Labriuteleanan. She said that these days you seem altogether too sure of yourself, and that she very much looks forward to seeing you nervous and uncertain like you were when she first met you."

Ryan gave an uneasy laugh. When he first began his training in the elf city, he and the yet-to-be crowned elf queen were the only two students of Eglerion, the elven lore master. And it was Labriuteleanan—Labri—who first made him aware of the elven custom of public bathing in mixed company. And she made him *well* aware. As soon as she realized that Ryan was embarrassed to face her when she joined him to bathe in the local stream, she made it a point to replicate the scenario as often as possible, and to insistently strike up conversations with him while less than clothed.

"You can tell Labri that I look forward to the renewed nervous uncertainty," he said.

When they arrived at the corral that held his mount, Ryan clasped arms with Xinthian. "Thanks again for all your help."

"Farewell, young Archmage, and send my greetings to your parents."

"I will."

###

After two days on horseback, Ryan spied the ramparts of

Castle Riverton rising from the surrounding grasslands. Flying high over the training grounds were the two dragons, Ruby and Pyre, that had become part of his extended family.

*And to think that less than three years ago, those two were eggs.*

In the castle's shadow stood a small city that had grown up just as quickly as the dragons. What had only recently been an empty field was now a fortified series of connected buildings occupying many acres of land. And even now there were workmen everywhere, many of them dwarves, crawling over the buildings like ants as they inspected the masonry and metalwork.

But Castle Riverton was not Ryan's destination. Instead he turned his horse toward a vast expanse of wagons and tents camped a couple miles away. The caravan where he would find his betrothed.

At the edge of the caravan, two guards came out to greet him. Both slammed their fists against their chests in salute. Ryan bowed his head in acknowledgment and dismounted.

The older of the two guards stepped forward. "Greetings, young Lord Riverton, Archmage of Trimoria, and betrothed to our princess. Welcome to the domain of Sheikh Honfrion of the Imazighen. I am Tabor, lead guard. Behind me is my second, Khalid."

Ryan handed his reins to a hostler who'd come running over from the nearest stable. "You two resemble each other. Do all of Honfrion's guards hold such a close resemblance?"

Tabor laughed. "No, Archmage. I'm proud to say that Khalid is also my son."

Khalid stepped forward. "If you don't mind, Lord Archmage, my sheikh asked that I bring you to him upon your arrival."

"I was expected?"

"Yes, my lord."

As the two guards led Ryan through the caravan's crowded merchant quarter, Ryan strengthened his shields with the slightest of mental adjustments. He knew that only he could hear the slight buzzing of the shield that clung to him like an invisible second skin.

The people of the caravan—the Imazighen, Arabelle's people—murmured, whispered, and stared openly at him as he passed.

"It's him! He's here!"

"It's the wizard of prophecy!"

"The princess is so lucky."

This last remark came from a girl with bright red hair. Ryan's eyes met with hers, and she quickly pulled a veil across her face—but boldly stared right back at him.

Three dwarves exited a merchant tent with mugs in their hands, and stopped short.

"I dinna believe it!" said one. "Is dat da Archmage? He glows like a lantern bug with his magic."

"Norgeon, shut yer yap!" said another. "He'll turn you into a mountain pony if you aren't respectful."

The third dwarf laughed. "That'll be an improvement, I

say. Ponies are handsome creatures. Norgeon's face reminds me of a ogre's hairy rear end…"

They left the merchant's quarter behind, and Tabor and Khalid led Ryan to a large tent with several serious-looking guards posted in front of it, all of whom gave Tabor a brisk salute.

Tabor turned to Ryan. "Archmage, I'm sure that when you and my sheikh are done, you'll want to visit with the princess. I will wait here to act as escort."

"And I expect you'll act as chaperone too, right?"

Tabor failed to hold back a smile. "Archmage, you know our customs. Our princess must be kept under escort whenever feasible. After the marriage ceremony, you too would be of the Imazighen, and deemed an acceptable escort."

Ryan placed his hand on Tabor's shoulder. "I'd expect nothing less. Is the sheikh ready for me?"

Tabor looked to the posted guards, who nodded. Then Tabor opened the flap and announced Ryan's arrival.

From within the tent, a deep voice boomed. "Ryan, come in, come in. Don't stand out there like a stranger, my son."

As Ryan stepped inside, Arabelle's father, Sheikh Honfrion, greeted him with a clasp of arms and a kiss on each cheek. They sat in the middle of the tent and faced each other.

Honfrion tore some flatbread in half and handed Ryan a piece. "Young Ryan, our people have long been awaiting this moment."

Ryan chewed on the freshly baked bread. "Which moment is that?"

Honfrion pushed up his sleeves, revealing heavily muscled arms. With a surprisingly light touch, he took Ryan's hands. "Ryan, my boy. Those in my family have long had visions of the future. Sometimes the events that are seen are wished-for; at other times, they are horrifying. Arabelle's mother was a particularly strong seer, and Arabelle has such abilities too."

He sat back and wiped the sweat from the top of his head with a cloth. "I, too, have visions—though for a long time I willfully blocked them, and only in recent years have they returned."

His eyes darted around, as though looking through every corner of the tent. "Ryan, I saw your arrival moments before it happened, and I sent Tabor and Khalid out to retrieve you. It was because of that vision that I knew that I must bring you to this tent, so that you could meet—"

Honfrion froze in mid-sentence, and his normally dark brown eyes glowed white. Filaments of magic—invisible, Ryan knew, to anyone but him—began swirling around the sheikh's head and sparking throughout the tent. The energy grew, expanding outward from Honfrion, who remained oblivious to the maelstrom.

And then the swirling torrent of energy coalesced into a column two feet to the right of Honfrion. A woman stepped from the column, and the sparking magic vanished.

The woman was ancient. Gray skin, tangled gray hair, growths on her chin. She wore drab gray robes, yet shimmering waves of white magical energy hovered around her.

"Child of destiny," she said, "I am here. For you, I am a messenger."

Ryan pointed at Honfrion, who was still frozen in place. "What did you do to him?"

"Do not worry, for I will give you what you need. Once I am gone, time will continue."

"Time?"

The woman stepped forward. "Enough! Listen and watch."

The woman closed her eyes, and the tent faded from Ryan's vision.

A scene materialized in his mind.

*The night is dark, the only light coming from a campfire in the distance. Four people are gathered around the campfire, all of them wearing modern clothes. Clothes from Ryan's past.*

Ryan gasped. "That's my family and me when we first arrived in Trimoria!"

*A few hundred yards away, several of Azazel's troops huddle together, studying the campfire from a distance.*

*"We already know them to be fools, drunk, or unaware of the dangers they face," said one. "Who creates a campfire so close to the swamp? Swamp cat food or slaver fodder. They deserve to be skewered."*

*"Kirag said we are to try to extract information."*

*"I don't care what Kirag said—dead is dead. It's too much trouble capturing people and interrogating them."*

Though the events of the vision had clearly happened years ago, Ryan's heart raced in his chest. "We had assassins after us even *then*? How could they know we'd be there? *We* didn't even know we'd arrived in Trimoria yet."

*Something lands in the midst of the huddled assassins, and a puff of smoke flies into their faces. As one of the men stands, a figure runs by, slashes his throat, and disappears into the night.*

*The other assassins choke, and moments later, they collapse. The mysterious figure cautiously returns.*

*A woman.*

*She glances at the distant campfire, then down at the assassins, and once again at the campfire. She moves quickly, slashing the throats of her victims, their lifeblood forming sticky pools in the grass.*

*The mysterious figure stares at her blood-soaked hands. Sobs wrack her body, and she looks up at the sky with familiar eyes...*

*"Arabelle!"*

The vision faded, and Ryan's heart pounded faster than he thought possible. He looked up at the old woman, whose face was an emotionless blank. "Arabelle saved us all?"

The woman's glow brightened. "Know that both you and your betrothed are children of destiny. She acts in Seder's interest, and thus she will always act in your interest as well, for you are Seder's champion."

Her shimmering waves of white energy flared, nearly blinding him, and then fell away, leaving the tent in darkness. Ryan tapped into some of his power and made a ball of sparkling light materialize over his head.

The old woman had not departed. But now she held something in her arms. An infant boy, wrapped in a brilliant white swaddling cloth.

She held it out to him. "Seder's champion, a gift from Seder."

Ryan took the child. It had a hint of whiskers and the proportions of a dwarf. "I... I can't take care of a baby. What am I to do with it?"

A brilliant white aura shimmered around the infant, and it grew much heavier and larger. The light dimmed, and the infant had aged into a dwarf boy. The boy wriggled out of Ryan's arms and stomped his hairy feet on the ground.

He had a full beard now, though thin, and wore billowing white robes. After checking through a series of hidden pockets, he laughed and pulled out a handful of amber dice. He looked up at Ryan.

"Do you want to play any games?" he asked.

*What in the world is going on?*

Ryan turned to the old woman, but she was already fading away, with a hint of a smile.

###

As the caravan guards escorted the young dwarf toward Castle Riverton, the child whistled merrily while juggling some wooden balls he'd discovered in one of his many pockets. Ryan was still so stunned, all he could do was watch the boy depart.

Honfrion placed his hand on Ryan's shoulder. "My vision told me you were going to meet someone strange within my tent, but I didn't realize he would appear before my eyes in a flash just as I was telling you about him."

Honfrion hadn't even been aware of the time that had passed within the tent. Perhaps because no time *had* passed. What were the woman's words?

*When I am gone, time will continue.*

He would have to ask Eglerion about this. Perhaps the lore master would be able to explain what had happened.

Honfrion saw his worried look. "You did the right thing sending him off to the castle nursery. Clearly he knows no more about his sudden appearance than we do. In fact, it seems all he's interested in is playing games."

A woman called out. "Ryan!"

As Ryan turned, Arabelle slammed into him in a swirl of flying hair and peals of laughter, knocking him backward. They both fell in the dirt as she placed kisses on his stunned face.

"Not a very dignified greeting, Arabelle," said her father, chuckling. "I thought I taught you better."

Arabelle's smile was infectious, and Ryan grinned like a fool as she pulled him to his feet. "Ryan! You were supposed to tell me when you got here!"

Honfrion cleared his throat. "My flower, that was my fault.

I asked the guards to bring him to me so the two of us could speak."

Arabelle pulled Ryan away from the crowd that was forming. As always, a handful of guards trailed behind them, including Tabor. She glanced at him and squeezed his hand, the slightest tinge of red coloring her cheeks. And she looked stunning. Her white, form-fitting dress accentuated her athletic build and curves, and it was a brilliant contrast to her dark hair and eyes.

She pulled him all the way to her tent, but before they could enter, Tabor cleared his throat. "Princess, it wouldn't be proper for the two of you to be alone."

Arabelle huffed. "But I want to speak to Ryan in private. Don't make me leave the caravan to force the issue, Tabor."

The guard scratched at his beard. "I have an idea. Follow me."

Moments later, Ryan found himself in an empty corral sitting cross-legged in front of Arabelle. The corral allowed them to talk face-to-face in private, while the guards were still able to watch them from a distance.

"Well, I suppose this will have to do," Arabelle said.

"It's fine." Ryan gave her hands a squeeze. "I respect your people's customs. I'm just happy to see you. I don't care where we are."

Arabelle's eyes glistened with unshed tears. "Ryan, I have something to confess…"

###

As Arabelle's tale unfolded, Ryan soon realized that

Trimoria's prophecies didn't involve only the Riverton brothers. Apparently Seder, the same spirit that had taken his family from a summer vacation in the state of Arizona, and led him to become the Archmage of a land called Trimoria, had also set events in motion to ensure that Arabelle received training in the use of weapons and poisons by none other than Castien, the elf sword master.

Finally Ryan understood how she'd shown such miraculous abilities in the knife-throwing competition a few years back.

But it was the last part of her tale that was truly difficult for her to reveal. As she related her view of the very same circumstances that Ryan had just now witnessed himself in a vision, her tears flowed freely, and the guilt and shame was plain on her face.

Ryan barely let her finish before blurting out what he'd just seen in her father's tent—and explained that the actions she was confessing to had saved his family's lives. And when he made it clear to her that he felt all of her actions were justified, and that there was no reason why she should feel ashamed, a torrent of emotions erupted from her as she threw her arms around him and wept, years of pent-up guilt and uncertainty draining from her.

The sun had set during her tale, and even as they held each other, Arabelle's handmaiden came walking toward them, torch in hand. No doubt that signaled it was time for Arabelle to go.

Before Ryan could lose his opportunity, he leaned in to Arabelle's ear and whispered, "I love you."

She hooked him by the back of the neck and pulled him in for a kiss.

Miriam cleared her throat. "Princess, it's nightfall. I'm here to remind you that it is *now* seven days before your wedding, and you know that it's bad luck to see your betrothed the week before your wedding."

Ryan stood and pulled Arabelle to her feet. "I'll see you in a week, Mrs. Riverton."

Arabelle stood on the tips of her toes and whispered into his ear, "I can't wait."

# AUTHOR'S NOTE

Well, that's the end of *Tools of Prophecy*, and I sincerely hope you enjoyed it.

That's book three of a four-part epic tale.

I should note that even though this story will end at the culmination of *Lords of Prophecy*, this saga doesn't end there. There is much more. Circles within circles, my friends.

By the end of this year, it is my intent to have published three books that go beyond the end of this series. It will be a new beginning, but with some familiar faces and ancient enemies. I'll tease more in the author's note for the next book.

For those of you who aren't familiar with where this tale originated, I'll note that when I wrote this story, years ago, I never intended for it to really be published. You see, I'm a stuffy science researcher type and I don't go around talking

# AUTHOR'S NOTE

about dwarves, elves, dragons, magic, and such. I just don't. The origins of this story really began because as a relatively younger father of two boys, I would come up with bedtime stories for them.

After a while, the details of the story began getting jumbled in my head, so I began writing things down. And the stories grew in complexity. It became a saga to entertain what at the time were seven and eight-year-old boys. And when I was done, those stories remained in my desk drawer for a long time.

But along the way, something had happened to me. I'd gotten the writing bug.

I learned that I enjoyed the process of creating stories, and because I can't leave well enough alone, I began thinking about maybe writing something for myself.

Don't get me wrong, I enjoy epic fantasy, and grew up on Tolkien, Eddings, and various other authors who set me on the path, but I equally enjoyed Crichton, Asimov, Grisham, and many others in genres that dealt more with action and adventure.

I'd made friends with some rather well-known authors, and when I talked about maybe getting more serious about this writing thing, several of them gave me the same advice, "Write what you know."

Write what I know? I began to think about Michael Crichton. He was a non-practicing MD, and started off with a medical thriller. John Grisham was an attorney for a decade

## AUTHOR'S NOTE

before writing a series of legal thrillers. Maybe there's something to that advice.

I began to ponder, "What do I know?" And then it hit me.

I know science. It's what I do for a living and what I enjoy reading nowadays. In fact, one of my hobbies is reading formal papers spanning many scientific disciplines. My interests range from particle physics, computers, the military sciences (you know, the science behind what makes stuff go boom), and medicine. I'm admittedly a bit of a nerd in that way. I've also traveled extensively during my life, and am an informal student of foreign languages and cultures.

With the advice of some New York Times bestselling authors, I started my foray into writing novels.

And then the unexpected happened.

People began reading them!

And then I hit a national bestseller list or two.

This hobby had suddenly become something a bit more than I'd expected.

And even though I'm not, strictly-speaking, a full-time author, by the end of this year, I should have over twenty books out in a relatively short period of time.

Those bedtime stories had turned into something much more than I'd ever imagined.

And then I opened that drawer where everything started.

The musty and yellowed sheets of printed paper I'd set aside long ago, I began reading those stories and cringing.

I am so much better than I was back then. Somehow or

## AUTHOR'S NOTE

another, I'd picked up some skills and instincts that hadn't been there a decade earlier.

I thought to myself, "Maybe it's time for me to see if I can make something of those old stories?"

After reading the work I'd done long ago, I realized the stories were still quite solid. It was the prose I was uncomfortable with, and the ages of the main characters needing to be tweaked, but it probably wouldn't be too bad to revamp the old stories and bring them to the public.

Decent book covers, proper editing, audio books, the whole shebang.

And here we are, dear reader.

I'm assuming if you're reading these words, that you hopefully enjoyed the story. If this is the first book of mine you've read, then let me explain a few things about what you'll always see in my books.

There is always an author's note to the reader. That's the section you're currently reading, and this is where I talk to you directly about what I do, who I am, and why I do it.

I did want to talk a bit about my contract with you, the reader.

I write to entertain.

That truly is my first and primary goal. Because, for most people, that's what readers typically want out of a novel.

That's certainly what I always wanted. Story first, always.

In this particular story, I dive deeply into a fantasy world that doesn't necessarily have a strong correlation to the science of our world, but this is a four-book series, and trust

## AUTHOR'S NOTE

me, there is some science coming in the upcoming books that is real and does apply.

You'll find that in this series I do what everyone says I shouldn't: I cross the streams between science fiction and fantasy.

Some have called my past writing choices eclectic, unexpected, but the vast majority of feedback I've received to date has thankfully been positive. So, thank you to those who have been readers of my other books. Posting reviews is, of course, the easiest way to let me and others know what you thought of this novel or any of my work. Word of mouth is precious to us poor authors.

However, even though I enjoy writing about events, history, science, and now dipping my toe into fantasy, my primary goal always circles back to entertaining.

As always, at the end of this book, I have an addendum where I cover certain details regarding the creation of this novel, the research that went into it, and of course, I go into the science and technology—mostly because I can't help myself.

I do hope you enjoyed this story, and I hope you'll continue to join me in the future stories yet to come.

Mike Rothman<br>
August 1, 2020

If you enjoyed this story, I should let you know there is more where this came from. Book four, *Lords of Prophecy*, picks up

## AUTHOR'S NOTE

where this story leaves off. Eventually the barrier does crumble, familiar faces from long ago will be reunited with the Riverton, and the penultimate clash between good and evil will most certainly occur.

I hope reading this saga will be as much a treat for you as it was for me to have written it.

## ABOUT THE AUTHOR

I am an Army brat, a polyglot, and the first person in my family born in the United States. This heavily influenced my youth by instilling in me a love of reading and a burning curiosity about the world and all of the things within it. As an adult, my love of travel and adventure has driven me to explore many exotic locations, and these places sometimes creep into the stories I write.

I hope you've found this story entertaining.

- Mike Rothman

You can find my blog at: www.michaelarothman.com
Facebook at: www.facebook.com/MichaelARothman
And on Twitter: @MichaelARothman